MYSTERY WOMAN

Jack Dillon Dublin Tale 11

Second Edition

MYSTERY WOMAN

Jack Dillon Dublin Tale 11

Second Edition

Mike Faricy

Mystery Woman: Jack Dillon Dublin Tale 11: Second Edition
© Copyright Mike Faricy 2024

All rights reserved. No part of this publication may be reproduced, stored in a retrieval system, or transmitted, in any form or by any means, electronic, mechanical, photocopying, recording or otherwise, without the prior and express permission of the copyright owner.

This is a work of fiction. All of the characters, organizations, and events portrayed in this novel are either products of the author's imagination or are used fictitiously.

Library of Congress Control Number: 2023920391
paperback ISBN: 978-1-962080-81-1
e-Book ISBN: 978-1-962080-82-8

MJF Publishing books may be purchased for education, Business, or promotional use. For information on bulk purchases, please contact the author directly at mikefaricyauthor@gmail.com

Published by

MJF Publishing
https://www.mikefaricybooks.com

ACKNOWLEDGMENTS

I would like to thank the following people for their help & support: Special thanks to Nick, Roy, Julie, Mittie, and Toui for their hard work, cheerful patience and positive feedback. I would like to thank family and friends for their encouragement and unqualified support. Special thanks to Maggie, Jed, Schatz, Pat, Av, Emily and Pat, for not rolling their eyes, at least when I was there. Most of all, to my wife, Teresa, whose belief, support and inspiration has, from day one, never waned.

To Teresa
"An absolute bollox…"

PROLOGUE

The two-story house was white and nestled on the side of a hill in West County Cork. Dennis Sheehan followed the winding road up through the open gate and parked next to the house. "We made it, Maureen," he said, glancing over at his wife in the passenger seat.

"Oh, thank God! Yesterday's flight from the US to Amsterdam, spend the night in the airport, fly to Ireland this morning, and a four-hour drive today from Dublin. I'm ready—"

"You're ready to take it easy and relax. We've got two weeks to do whatever we want. Let's check the place out," Dennis said, and they climbed out of their rented car.

A brick path led to the front door. He pulled the rental agreement from his coat pocket and focused on the security code. He input the code on the keypad. A half-second later, the front door unlocked, and they stepped into a paneled entry. Off to the right was a sitting room with two black leather couches arranged on either side of a fireplace. A coffee table rested between the couches.

A bottle of white wine with a ribbon around it and two wineglasses were on the coffee table.

"Oh, isn't that nice," Maureen said, nodding at the wine bottle.

"Perfect, just what the doctor ordered. How about I pour us each a glass, we toast our tenth anniversary, and check this place out?"

"I thought you'd never ask," she said and kissed him on the cheek.

Thankfully it was a twist-off cap on the wine bottle. He opened the bottle, filled both glasses, and handed one to Maureen. "To another fifteen years," he said and raised his glass.

"Only fifteen?" she said and clinked glasses with him.

They wandered from room to room. Everything looked to be just as promised. A lovely bedroom, bathroom with a jacuzzi, steaks on a platter in the refrigerator, brie and crackers on the kitchen counter, and more wine in the wine rack.

Dennis carried their suitcases up to the bedroom while Maureen arranged the brie and crackers on a small cutting board. She opened the curtain on the back window in the sitting room and took in the view of a gorgeous hillside.

He cooked the steaks on the grill in the back garden. They kissed a number of times, began to relax, and started in on a second bottle of wine. The next two weeks promised to be everything they'd hoped for and more.

It was almost 10:00, and they were in the sitting room focused on the moon rising above the hillside. It wasn't quite full, but by the end of the week, it would be. Dennis was considering a third bottle of wine. Maureen was thinking wouldn't it be fun to make love on the leather couch with the Irish moon shining through the window.

The knock on the door snapped them back to reality.

"I'll get it. Probably the owners just checking to see if we need anything."

"Hurry back, darling," Maureen said as she pulled her top over her head and tossed it on the coffee table.

"A half-minute, don't start without me," Dennis replied and hurried to the door. He pulled the door open and looked at the couple standing on the front stoop. He'd only seen a photo of the owners. Neither one of these people seemed to resemble what he recalled.

The young man smiled and said, "Well, Punchy, welcome to Ireland."

"Excuse me?" Dennis said.

"You're Dennis Sheehan?" the woman asked in an Irish accent.

"Yes, and you are?"

"Judge and jury," the young man said, pointing a pistol at Dennis's head and firing. With the silencer, the shot almost sounded like someone spitting.

Maureen heard it, thought about pulling her slacks back on, and called, "Dennis?" After a few seconds, she sat up and stared over the back of the leather couch just as the couple stepped into the sitting room. "Where's Dennis?" she asked and then focused on the pistol the man pointed in her direction. "No," was the only word she got off before he began to fire.

The young man strolled over to the couch, gazed down at Maureen, and shook his head. "Too bad, she could have been fun. I never thought of Sheehan and his wife being this young. What do you think, maybe forty, forty-five?"

"Well, they're Americans, so it's gotta be them. You heard her call his name. Well done. Accomplish the task and leave the scene, two basic rules. Oh, and don't touch anything." She glanced at the naked woman on the couch, shook her head, and thought, *Sorry, dear, I know the feeling.*

ONE

Not for the first time, Dillon gave Suel an elbow in an effort to stop his snoring. They were on the third night of a stakeout. Thus far, absolutely nothing had happened. They were parked on the street waiting for the suspected arrival of Boston gangster Dennis Punchy Sheehan. From where they were parked, they could see the entrance to the Westbury Hotel on Balfe Street. Sheehan was supposed to have arrived two nights earlier.

Dillon got on the radio and called McCarthy. He was positioned inside the hotel near the reception desk. Two clicks on the handheld radio and then one word, "Anything?"

"No. No one claimed the room. I'm thinking this reservation might have been a diversion."

Suel snorted a couple of times and readjusted his position in the passenger seat.

"What the hell was that?" McCarthy asked.

"Who do you think? Snoring his ass off."

"Serves you right," McCarthy said and disconnected.

Two hours later, 5:30 in the morning. The sun was rising as Dillon watched the car pull around the corner and park behind them. Two figures were seated in the front. He heard the clicks on the radio and then, "Good morning," a voice said.

"Glad to see you. Another night of absolutely nothing," Dillon said.

"We're thinking it's a bust."

"I wish I could disagree, but I'm thinking the same thing," Dillon said.

Suel groaned, then opened his eyes and stretched.

"Well, good morning, DI Suel. Care for a full Irish breakfast, or maybe a tea and some scones?"

Suel smacked his lips, glanced around, and said, "Another waste of a night. For feck's sake."

"Good luck," Dillon said into the handset. He turned on the car and pulled away from the curb. As he drove past the Westbury Hotel, Suel glanced out the window, shook his head, and said, "I'm thinking we should put this down as bad information and come up with something else."

"Three days late, if he's coming at all. I'm afraid we've wasted enough time, and we're back to square one."

"Ahh, the bastard," Suel focused for a moment on a blonde woman just getting off a bus. He shook his head and said, "I honestly don't know how someone can work that overnight shift, day in and day out. We've been at it for three days, and my sleep schedule is so screwed up it's going to take me a week to get back to whatever normal is or was."

"Preaching to the choir," Dillon said. "O'Brien's is the only place open at this hour. You up for it?"

Suel yawned and said, "Breakfast there three mornings in a row. You almost make it sound like a dare."

"Not far from the truth," Dillon said. He drove another block, turned at the light, and then took a left. They drove along the Liffey for a bit and took the Heuston bridge across the river. O'Brien's was on the corner, on the far side of the bridge. The building was a good hundred years old. The food would never be described as special, but there was plenty of it. At this hour, Dillon parked on the street almost in front of the diner, and they went inside.

They weren't the first ones in this early. Maybe a half-mile from the An Garda Síochána headquarters, they recognized two individuals as they entered. Dillon gave a nod and headed for a table on the opposite side of the room. The place smelled of strong coffee and fried bacon.

"Hi, ya's," the waitress said as they sat down. She held a couple of menus, but instead of placing them on the table, she asked, "The usual?"

"Yeah," Dillon said and followed up with a yawn.

"Same, and coffee, black, no tea," Suel said.

She left as Dillon gave another yawn and said, "I think we're past the point where we might be wasting time. We're definitely wasting time. I'm thinking we talk to McCabe and suggest we call it off and refocus. If

Punchy Sheehan flew into Dublin three days ago, we've missed him."

"Be best to see McCabe on a full stomach. What do you say to a leisurely breakfast, and we catch him first thing? He's usually in by 7:30."

Dillon nodded and said, "Yeah, I don't see anything happening. You think Sheehan might have come in on a ferry from the UK or France? Maybe even a private jet?"

Suel shook his head. "Maybe a ferry, but that would be a surprise. We can check with the airlines again. A private jet? The guy is notoriously cheap. I can't see him spending that kind of money."

"He's gotta be somewhere. The one thing we know is that he isn't in the Westbury hotel."

"Ain't that the truth," Suel said just as the waitress arrived with two full Irish breakfast platters and two mugs of coffee.

She set the platters down in front of them and then the mugs. When the coffee spilled over the sides of the mugs, she didn't so much as blink. "Anything else?" she said as she set a handwritten bill on the table.

Both Dillon and Suel shook their heads and shoveled in forkfuls of fried egg.

She was back four more times over the next half-hour, topping up their coffee mugs. Each time she dribbled coffee onto the table.

"She's the reason they don't have tablecloths in this place. The laundry bill would put them out of business," Suel said.

Suel's platter was clean, and Dillon had eaten everything except the baked beans. "You going to finish those?" Suel asked.

"No, help yourself," Dillon said and handed his platter across the table.

Suel scraped the beans onto his platter and handed the empty one back to Dillon. Ten minutes later, they were in the car on their way to headquarters. They were early, and DCI McCabe had yet to arrive. Dillon grabbed a razor and shaving cream from his desk and headed for the restroom. Suel set about making a tea.

They spent the next half-hour discussing how Dennis Punchy Sheehan might arrive in Ireland and came up with the same answer they'd always come up with. He'd fly and make someone else pay for the flight.

DCI McCabe arrived just before 7:30. Dillon gave him a couple of minutes to get situated before he and Suel approached his office and knocked on the doorframe.

McCabe motioned them in and continued his phone conversation. "No, six officers a day, Brennan. They're out there waiting for something, anything to happen, and the only thing that's happening is they're exhausted. I'm going to pull it today, and we'll think of something else. Clearly, this isn't working. Yes. I will. Okay, thanks for listening. Yes. As soon as I know. Thank you," McCabe said and hung up.

"Good morning, sir," Dillon said.

McCabe shook his head. "Nothing good about it. I'm going to pull the Sheehan stakeout. It's been three days, and all we've got to show for it is a wasted budget, three wasted days, and six people who already have more than enough to deal with. I'll contact the team in a moment and call them in. In the meantime, put your heads together and come up with what we're going to do next. He has to show up here sooner or later or risk losing control of his entire operation."

"So you're saying we're not on tonight?" Suel asked.

"No, I'll pull the day team off now. You two head home, get some rest and be back here tomorrow morning. Any questions?"

Dillon shook his head. "No, sir. Sorry it didn't work out. We've discussed it, and we can't see Sheehan taking an alternative way into the country."

"He's such a cheap bast…err, individual," Suel said. "We can't see him arriving by ferry and certainly not by a private jet."

"Home to get some sleep, gentlemen. Anything changes, I'll be the first to call."

Dillon and Suel both rose and headed out the door. Suel gave Dillon the thumbs-up and hurried to his desk. They walked out together ten minutes later and drove home.

TWO

illon was met at the front door by his aptly named dog, Lucifer. As he opened the door, Lucifer jumped off the front stoop and assumed the position next to Dillon's car. I know the feeling, Dillon thought and stepped into the house. Amazingly, there didn't seem to be a mess anywhere. He thought about making some coffee and decided sleep was the better option.

He grabbed a biscuit from the cookie jar and used it to coax Lucifer back into the house. He filled the food and water dishes and made his way upstairs to the bedroom. He set his alarm for noon, thinking four hours of sleep would probably get him through the day. After the four hours, if he could stay awake until 10:00 tonight, he'd be back on schedule tomorrow morning.

Five minutes later, he was in bed and vaguely aware of Lucifer settling in next to him. His cellphone ringing interrupted his dream. At first, a distant ring, but then each time it rang, it seemed to be slightly louder until he opened his eyes and pulled the phone from the bedside table.

"Hell—" He cleared his throat twice and tried again, "Hello."

"Hope I woke you, you lousy knacker," Suel said. "Just off the phone with McCabe. Apparently, they've found Punchy Sheehan down in County Cork."

"County Cork? How in the hell did he get down there?"

"I presume he drove. They're in a little village called Desertserges."

"How many are with him?"

"Just one. A woman. Oh, and they're both dead."

"Dead?"

"Our man Punchy was apparently shot in the head. The woman was shot mutiple times. Desertserges is barely a village. It's outside of Enniskeane. We're to go down there and head up the investigation."

"What?"

"There's no local Garda. Enniskeane is the nearest, but they're stretched—"

"Oh, and we're not?" Dillon asked.

"I'm just repeating what I've been told. Besides, you as an American, it's only natural you'd be involved in the investigation of the death of a brother."

Dillon took a deep breath and exhaled. "Why do I get the feeling we're not to wait until tomorrow to head down there?"

"It's that marvelous intuition you have. Pick me up in an hour. It's going to take three hours to get to the place."

"Gee, I can hardly wait. Okay, see you in an hour."

"I could go for a coffee when you arrive," Suel said.

"Goodbye," Dillon said and disconnected. He remained in bed, staring at the ceiling. He thought maybe fifteen more minutes might help and closed his eyes. After five minutes, he climbed out of bed and headed toward the bathroom. He showered, dressed, and packed an overnight bag. He let Lucifer out into the front garden and tossed him a biscuit for added encouragement. He refilled the food and water dishes and then wrote a note to Tara, his neighbor across the street, asking her to check in on Lucifer.

He walked across the lane and rang Tara's doorbell. Her car was gone and, at no surprise, she didn't answer the door. He slipped the note through her mail slot and walked back to his house. Lucifer was investigating a corner of the front garden. Dillon went inside and then encouraged Lucifer back in with another biscuit. He grabbed two slices of cold pizza from the refrigerator, wolfed them down, then tossed his overnight bag in the car and headed to Suel's.

Suel answered the door with a cup of coffee from the shop up the street and handed it to Dillon. He grabbed his suitcase and another coffee, locked the door behind him, and headed for Dillon's car.

"Since when did you become so organized? Oh, thanks for the coffee, much appreciated."

"Yeah, well, thanks for driving. I figured, for the price of a coffee, I can be guaranteed a safe drive down to Cork."

"You find out anything else?"

Suel shook his head. "I put a call into my pal, Jamie McCormick down in Bandon but haven't heard back. Hopefully, he'll call when we're on the road. All I know is there are two bodies, and one of them is Dennis Punchy Sheehan. They've got the site locked down, and we'll be leading the investigation."

Dillon shook his head as he backed out of the driveway and headed for the M50.

"Take the M50 to the N7 and head south. I'll give you directions as we—"

"How about I just listen to the GPS on my cellphone," Dillon said.

As if in reply, the GPS voice suddenly said, "In five hundred meters, take a right turn."

"Perfect, you finally have a relationship with a woman. That means I can nap and—"

Dillon took a sip of his coffee and said, "I think the safer thing might be for you to make sure I don't fall asleep."

"Don't fall asleep? That's why I got you that coffee, for lord's sake."

"That will keep me going for at least a half-hour. Remember, Paddy, you were the one snoring in the car last night while I kept watch."

"Well, all right, if you insist. I think we could stop for a late lunch and—"

"Let's just get there. It's going to be close to 4:00 before we get to Enniskeane, and who knows how long it will take to find the place after that."

"I've got the address in Desertserges. We can reset your GPS once we get to Bandon. Enniskeane is on the far side of the murder scene, and we need to check in with Jamie McCormick and the Bandon Gardaí anyway. They're the local force."

Dillon reached for his coffee. It was warm, and he took a couple of large swallows. It was shaping up to be a long journey, and they were still on the Dublin city streets.

"Turn right at the next corner and remain in the righthand lane," the GPS instructed.

It was almost three hours before they pulled in front of the main Garda Station in Bandon. The building was a two-story white stucco structure with blue trim on the windows. Two lamp posts with the Garda logo stood on either side of the entrance. A ramp for handicapped individuals leading up to the front door was on the righthand side, and a flowerbed filled with white flowers was off to the left.

They pulled the lanyards with the IDs from their pockets, slipped them on, and walked up the four steps to the front entrance. The word 'GARDA' in large blue letters along with the Garda logo was centered on the front of the building. Dillon held the door open for Suel and followed him inside.

A reception counter with a uniformed officer seated behind it was fifteen feet in front of them. As they approached, Suel did the introduction. "DI Paddy Suel and US Marshal Jack Dillon from Dublin Special Branch. We're here to see DI McCormick in relation to a double murder last night in Desertserges."

"He mentioned you'd be coming down. Didn't expect to see you for another hour."

"Dillon was driving," Suel said, pleading innocence.

That brought a smile to the officer's face. "McCormick is out at the site. He left directions for you," he said as he reached behind for a sheet of paper with handwritten directions.

"We've got GPS on the phone," Suel said.

This time the officer chuckled. "Good luck getting it to work out that way. With all the hills and whatnot, the connection comes and goes."

"Wonderful," Suel said. He took the sheet and handed it to Dillon.

"It's about a thirty-minute drive," the officer said as he looked over at Dillon and smiled. "That's if you stay at the speed limit."

"We'll be sure to do that," Dillon said.

"Oh, American?" the officer said, picking up on Dillon's accent.

"Yeah, the powers that be brought me in to mind DI Suel."

The officer nodded. "Good luck with that."

"Full-time job," Suel said.

Back in the car, as Dillon pulled away from the curb, Suel read from the directions. "Take Castledon Court to the intersection and take a right. We pretty much drive parallel to the Bandon River."

"I suppose it would be too much to ask to have the roads identified," Dillon said.

"We've got directions. We don't need that."

Dillon took a right at the intersection, and Suel directed him onto the first left a few minutes later. The road became substantially more narrow, barely wide enough for one vehicle if it wasn't too large. Dillon reduced his speed to little more than a crawl.

Maybe five miles later, he slowed to a crawl as they met an oncoming car. Both vehicles pulled to the side, essentially driving on the shoulder, except there was no shoulder, just rocky fields and weeds on either side. As they passed the other vehicle, the driver, a woman, raised her index finger in a country wave.

Dillon did the same in response.

Twenty minutes later, Suel said, "I believe that's the Kilcolman Fishery." He nodded at a gorgeous brick home as they drove past.

"A fishery? It looks like someone's house."

"Yeah, it is, but it's an AirBnB place, and you fish on the Bandon River. Quite popular, I hear. Shouldn't be too much further." A minute later, Suel said, "That must be it up on the left with the Garda car parked in the entrance."

They pulled into a stone-lined entrance covered with a leafy vine. Dillon drove down onto an asphalt parking area where two cars were parked. The house itself was an elegant two-story stone structure with a slate roof and what appeared to be a lovely glass porch attached to the rear.

As they climbed out of the car, a man stepped out of the house. He was solidly built, not fat, with ginger-colored hair. He was dressed in casual clothes, in need of a shave, and wore latex gloves on his hands. Dillon guessed he had probably been called out in the middle of the night. "It's about damn time. How you doing, Paddy?" he said as Suel opened the car door.

"Jesus, Jamie, we would have been here sooner, but we got stuck behind horses and a wagon on your major county roads down here. This is my chauffeur, US Marshal Jack Dillon. Jamie McCormick, the lead inspector for the Bandon Gardai and crossing guard for the Bandon Nursery School."

McCormick stepped around to the side and shook hands with Dillon. "Don't believe a word this knacker tells you. Pleased to meet you. I've heard about you."

"Ignore whatever you were told. I'm actually a nice guy," Dillon said.

"So, your man Punchy Sheehan is still inside?" Suel asked.

"Yeah, come on in and see for yourself. I thought you might be the medical examiner. We've been waiting on them. They should have been here hours ago, but they're hauling two bodies from a car-truck crash. It must be pretty bad if it's taking them this long. Anyway, come on in, and you can see your man Punchy and his wife."

"His wife?" Dillon said and smiled. "He's not married. I think he's had two or three wives over the years and finally got the message. Women don't like him. He usually has some escort within reach. That's probably who the woman is."

"No, we checked out the passports. Same surname, wedding rings on the both of them."

"Really? Huh, I wonder if that just happened. Let's see what you got. Any idea who did this?" Dillon asked as they headed toward the front door.

McCormick shook his head. "If I had to guess, I'd say it was professional, no shell casings. We've dusted for fingerprints but haven't found much. Apparently, Sheehan arrived here last night. We talked to the owners, Thomas and Aisling Barry. They live in Bandon and were the ones who called us. They drove past a little after 11:00 last night and noticed the front door was open. Sheehan had rented the place for the next two weeks, paid in advance. If I had to guess, I'd say whoever did this was probably here for about thirty seconds. Did what he came to do and left."

"Watch yourself now," McCormick said as he opened the front door. "Your man is just inside. There's a box of gloves on the table next to the door as you step inside. Best to slip those on so you don't contaminate the scene. We've photographed everything, and I'll email that file to you, Paddy, as soon as I get back to the station and download the images."

THREE

Dillon and Suel followed McCormick into the entryway. Suel pulled two latex gloves from the box, handed them to Dillon, and pulled out two more for himself.

"There's your man, Punchy Sheehan," McCormick said and nodded at the body lying against the front wall behind the door. A hole was centered on the eyebrow above the victim's right eye. A trail of dried blood ran down the side of his head to his ear. "The wife is on the couch in the sitting room. Looks like whoever did this may have interrupted a bit of hanky-panky."

Dillon stared at the body on the floor for a long moment and shook his head. "That's not Punchy Sheehan," he said.

"Not Punchy?" McCormick said. "Sorry, lad, but we've checked their passports. Sean, bring those passports in here, will you? We'll have us a look," McCormick called to the man standing behind a black leather couch in the sitting room. "We checked their IDs and both of their passports and driver's licenses are from the

US. The passports and driver's licenses match one another and the individuals. Your man Punchy is named Dennis Sheehan, isn't he?"

Dillon nodded and said, "Yeah, Dennis Eoghan Sheehan. But he's sixty-five years old and weighs somewhere north of three hundred pounds. By the way, he's from Boston, Massachusetts, lived there his entire life. I don't know who that is on the floor, but it sure as hell isn't Punchy Sheehan."

"Are you sure?" McCormick asked just as the guy from the sitting room handed him two evidence bags. Each held a US passport.

McCormick handed the bags to Dillon. Dillon opened one of the bags and took out the passport. "Maureen Sheehan, born 10 October 1980. That makes her forty-one. She lives in Minnesota." He opened the other evidence bag and pulled out the passport. "Oh shit, Dennis Sheehan, born 11 May 1978. He's forty-three, twenty-two years younger, and at least a hundred and fifty pounds lighter than that bastard Punchy. I'm afraid we're looking at a case of mistaken identity."

"Oh, for the love of God! Are you serious?" McCormick said, shaking his head.

"You sure, Jack? I mean, if they were this quick making the hit, wouldn't they know who they were sent to kill?" Suel asked.

"Apparently not. Unfortunately, that's why we didn't have any knowledge of him coming into the country. He isn't Punchy. It's as simple as that. Christ, let's take a look at the woman."

"On the couch by the fireplace," the other Bandon cop said. He looked at McCormick and shook his head as if to say, 'What the hell?'

Dillon stepped into the sitting room and walked over to the black leather couch. As he approached, he noticed what had to be bullet holes, two of them, in the back of the couch. He stood behind the couch and looked down at the body. The woman was dark haired and naked except for the thong pulled down almost to her knees. She was hanging halfway off the couch with a wound through her right elbow, another in her right shoulder, and one in her right temple. An empty bottle of wine rested on the floor next to the coffee table. An almost empty wineglass sat on the far side of the coffee table. A broken wineglass with lipstick was on its side on the coffee table, close to the woman's body. Dillon guessed she probably knocked it over when the three rounds slammed into her, moving her off the couch.

Her left arm hung down to the floor, and Dillon walked around the couch to look. Sure enough, there was a diamond ring and a wedding band.

"It looks like whoever did this interrupted a bit of a private celebration," Suel said and shook his head. "Fecking idjits. Sheehan is a common Cork surname. What the hell? They were too lazy to check it out?"

"Well, it proves one thing. Apparently, there are some folks around who aren't going to be all that happy to see Punchy whenever he decides to arrive."

"Yeah, if he ever shows up. This could be a game-changer for Punchy. He may just decide not to come and walk away from the business here," Suel said.

"I suspect there's a fairly large amount of money he's already invested, and let's not forget, it's the doorway to the rest of Europe. We need to find out how we got the information on Punchy coming over. Was it a setup? Did someone pay for this couple's trip, knowing they'd be taken out? And what about Punchy? Just where in the hell is that worthless piece of shit right now?"

They heard a car door slam outside, and McCormick said, "It's about damn time. Hopefully, the medical examiner is finally here."

Dillon and Suel followed McCormick and his partner out the front door. The medical examiner's van was backed into the parking place next to Dillon's car. The rear doors were open, and two men were in the process of rolling a gurney out of the van. Two black body bags were resting on top of the gurney.

"Hi lads," a gray-haired man said. "Sorry it took so long to get out here, but we had a hell of a mess to deal with down south of town. A car accident, one of the vehicles caught fire. A sad state of affairs. I hear you got some big-name mobster inside."

As he spoke, his partner walked around to the side of the van and opened a small door. He pulled out two blue hazmat suits and walked back, setting one on the gurney. The other he unfolded and began to step into it.

"Mick, Devlin, this is DI Paddy Suel from Dublin and Jack Dillon, an American attached to An Garda Síochána," McCormick said. "They're down here to help with the investigation into our murder of the American gangster, only everything just went to hell."

"What do you mean, 'went to hell'? Is he still alive?" Mick, the older of the two, asked.

"No, unfortunately. But Dillon just told us that's not the gangster inside. It's just some poor knacker with the same name."

"What?" Both men stopped halfway into pulling on their hazmat suits and looked at Dillon. "Are you sure it's not your man? I thought there were passports and IDs identifying both individuals."

"There are," Dillon said. "Same name, but unfortunately, it's not the Dennis Sheehan we were all hoping for."

"You're sure?"

"Very. I met the bastard once. It's not him. The victim here is some twenty years younger and at least half the weight."

"Well, we'll still have to take them to the lab and do the examination. They're American?"

"Yeah, we got that part right," McCormick said and shook his head.

They examined the bodies for about forty minutes and then set them in the body bags, zipped them closed, and wheeled them one at a time out to the van. After a brief conversation, they climbed in the van and drove back to Bandon.

McCormick watched the van turn onto the road and disappear. Still staring at the now empty lane, he said, "We've got the two of yous staying in the Munster Arms Hotel. There's not much more we can do tonight. I'm not sure about the likes of ya's, but I could use some dinner and a pint. How's about we head back to town? You can check in. The room is reserved under the department name." He glanced at his watch. "We'll meet for dinner in the hotel. They serve a good meal. The Guinness is good, and we can go over what our plan is for tomorrow. We've still got two Americans murdered and no suspects."

"That sounds like a plan," Dillon said. "Paddy?"

"Fine by me. It'll be an early night, lads. We were on stakeout the last three nights. As a matter of fact, waiting for Punchy Sheehan to check into the Westbury Hotel. Needless to say, we came up empty-handed."

"Lot of that going around," McCormick said. "We'll lock up here and meet you in the dining room at 7:00. Sound like a plan?"

Dillon and Suel nodded and headed for the car. As he drove off, Dillon waved and pulled back onto the road. Suel gave a loud exhale and said, "I'm thinking the way our luck has been running, this wouldn't be the best time to buy a lottery ticket."

"Yeah, you can say that again. I'd say the Bandon department had high hopes they were going to be dealing with Punchy Sheehan's murder."

"Amazing," Suel said and shook his head. "Can you believe it? The same name and they're Americans. Punchy is supposed to be arriving, and it all blows up in our face. Talk about a cluster feck."

"We'll have to get to McCabe early tomorrow morning. I want us to be the ones to tell him. We're still going to be here for a day or two dealing with this investigation."

"Humf, we'll be lucky if it's only a day or two. Could be a week or longer," Suel said and shook his head.

"Jamie McCormick seems to have his act together. It will be interesting to see what he comes up with tonight."

"I'm thinking whoever did the shooting last night probably isn't local," Suel said.

"Why not?"

"It's a major hit, professional, or at least it looked that way. I want to ask McCormick tonight if they found cash on site. If so, that would suggest that whoever pulled the trigger did the job and got out of here. What did he say? It might have been thirty seconds start to finish. Looked like he and the wife were just getting started and there's a knock on the door or maybe they see a car pull in. Either way, your man opens the door and is shot. Whoever it is steps into the sitting room, fires from probably five or ten feet, and puts three rounds into the wife.

"Maureen," Dillon said. "Yeah, no shell casings. You see any sign of an exit wound?"

Suel shook his head. "Not on the wife. Couldn't have been more than a few inches from your man when he fired. Small caliber, maybe a hollow point that raises hell inside the skull, but nothing large enough to exit."

"We'll see what those examiners come up with, hopefully, tomorrow," Dillon said.

FOUR

The Munster Arms Hotel, a three-story, cream-colored structure on Oliver Plunkett Street, was located in the center of Bandon. Dillon parked just down the street. They walked into the hotel lobby and headed for the front desk, actually a white-tiled counter.

"Good evening, gentleman. Do you have a reservation?" the woman behind the front desk asked and followed up with a smile. She was dark haired and blue eyed. She wore a long-sleeve black top. Dillon guessed her age to be late twenties or early thirties.

"I believe we've rooms reserved by Bandon Gardai," Suel said.

"Oh yes, they phoned us this morning. We've actually a two-bed suite reserved for you," she said, running her fingers across a keyboard. "I'll need to see some ID. It says here DI Paddy Suel and Marshal Jack Dillon?"

Suel took out his wallet and pulled out his An Garda Síochána card. Dillon pulled the lanyard from around his neck and placed his ID next to Suel's.

The woman leaned over and glanced at them, then flashed a quick smile. The printer behind her suddenly started up and printed off two sheets of paper.

"We offer a complimentary breakfast in our dining room. You're in room one-twelve, just up the stairs to the next floor and then take a right. Your reservation is for the next two nights. Should your stay be longer, just let us know. Any questions?" she asked as she took the two pieces of paper from the printer and placed them next to their IDs. She typed on the keyboard again and then reached down and set two keycards on top of the printed pages along with a hotel brochure.

"I think we're good for the moment. What time do you serve breakfast?" Suel asked.

"Our complimentary breakfast is available from 7:30 until 10:00 seven days a week," she said, following up with another quick smile.

Suel handed a keycard to Dillon, grabbed the brochure and the printed pages, and said, "Do you need us to sign anything?"

"No, you're all set. Enjoy your stay, gentlemen."

"Thank you," Dillon said, and they headed for the staircase.

Room 112 was on the second floor. The room was six doors down the hall. Suel inserted his keycard into the reader. It flashed green, and they heard the door unlock. Suel pushed it open, and they entered the room.

The room had two twin beds with a bedside table next to each bed. White pillows were leaning against the headboards, and a smaller, purple pillow rested against the white pillows. A small chest of drawers and a credenza affair were against the wall opposite the foot of the beds. A flatscreen TV was mounted on the wall above the chest of drawers.

"Home, sweet home," Suel said and tossed his suitcase on the first bed. Dillon set his overnight bag on the credenza, then walked over to the curtains and pulled them back. The window overlooked the main street below.

"You notice there isn't an elevator in this hotel?" Dillon said.

"Part of its charm," Suel replied. "To be honest, after working the last three nights and our interrupted sleep this morning, this bed is looking awfully comfortable. I'm going to sleep like a baby tonight."

"Promise?"

"What do you say to heading down to the bar for a pint? Jamie McCormick will be here in a half-hour. I don't feel like twiddling my thumbs up here for the next thirty minutes."

"Sounds good to me. I'll buy a round."

"I have a better idea. We'll just charge it to the room, and the Bandon Gardai can have the honor of buying us a pint."

"Then let's go," Dillon said and headed for the door.

The barroom was part of the dining room and was approximately half-full. They grabbed a table for four in the corner and ordered two pints of Guinness. Jamie

McCormick and his partner arrived about two minutes after the pints were placed on the table.

"Oh, at no surprise, I see you couldn't bear to wait, Paddy," McCormick said and pulled out a chair.

"Say, before I respond, we were never introduced. I'm Paddy Suel," Suel said and held out his hand to McCormick's dark-haired, green-eyed partner.

"Sean Lynch, nice to meet you," he said as they shook hands.

"Sean, I'm Jack Dillon. Nice to meet you," Dillon said and extended his hand.

McCormick waved the waitress over and said, "Teresa, two pints, please. Oh, and we'll be needing some menus as well."

"Back in a bit, Jamie," she replied and hurried off toward the bar.

"You a regular here?" Suel asked.

McCormick shook his head, "No, I've known her since primary school. She grew up a couple of doors down from our place. Her brothers and I were on the same hurling team. Nice girl, a nice family, actually. Say, I sent off the file with the scene images to you. Also sent a copy to DCI McCabe. We've been instructed to keep him in the loop."

"We'll be calling him first thing tomorrow morning to let him know this Dennis Sheehan isn't the knacker we were hoping," Suel said.

"Have you mentioned that to the owners? That it wasn't Punchy Sheehan?" Dillon asked.

McCormick shook his head. "No, we didn't mention anything regarding Punchy to them. As far as they know, it was some random act of violence. Some nutcase knocking on the door and murdering whoever answered."

"What about news outlets?" Suel asked.

"I believe at this stage they're unaware. That'll no doubt change by tomorrow morning."

The waitress set a pint of Guinness down in front of McCormick and another in front of Lynch.

Lynch raised his glass and said, "Here's to you, lads. Thank you for coming down. Sorry we didn't have your man."

"Amen," Suel said, and everyone clinked glasses.

"Is your department working on a press release?" Dillon asked once they'd finished the toast.

"Umm, so the press release," McCormick said and set his glass down. "Yeah, we've a lad working on that. Soon as it's approved, it will be released. I would guess that will be early tomorrow morning. There's bound to be a storm of media activity. A double murder is big news down here, so God only knows how the press will end up twisting it."

"Were you able to go through the place and check the luggage? I'm hoping maybe they brought laptops. Did they have any cash?"

"I think what you're suggesting, Dillon, is, were they robbed after being shot? From what we can determine so far, no, they were not robbed. Clothing was contained in two suitcases. Wait, let me rephrase that. Your man's clothing was still in his suitcase. His wife's clothing—"

"Maureen," Suel said.

"Yes, her clothing had apparently been in a suitcase and a garment bag. A number of items were hanging in the bedroom closet, three dresses, a couple pairs of slacks, two sweaters. What am I forgetting?" McCormick said to Lynch.

"Your woman had three pairs of shoes in the closet and undergarments in the chest of drawers. As far as a laptop goes, we didn't find one, and there was nothing like cords to charge a computer or even a travel adapter for electrical outlets. Oh, and your man's wallet was on top of the chest of drawers, umm two hundred and fifty euros in the wallet."

"Yeah, I'd guess our shooter didn't venture any further than the sitting room, shot the woman, and left," McCormick said. "Your man's suitcase had their return flight details, flying from Dublin to Amsterdam, Amsterdam to Atlanta, Atlanta to Minneapolis. I can't recall the airline at the moment. The flight was scheduled twelve days from yesterday, business class seats."

"Sounds like it was probably Delta," Dillon said. "How long did they book that AirBnB unit for?"

"Ten days. They had a reservation at the Maldron Hotel in Dublin the day before their departure."

Dillon thought for a moment and said, "I think that's the hotel right at the airport."

"Yeah, it overlooks terminal two," Suel said.

"So they journey down here and plan to stay for the better part of two weeks. Any idea why?" Dillon asked.

McCormick shook his head. "Not really. All I can guess is, they had a great bargain on the price, fifty euros a day. It's a lovely place, private. They could journey around the south of the country on day trips. I know they booked the place almost two months ago. The Barry's were thrilled to have renters for a two-week stretch. If they're lucky, it's usually a weekend couple, check in on Friday night or Saturday and leave Sunday."

"You looked at their passports, the travel?"

"Yes, both passports were issued two years ago. There was a three-day trip to Paris eighteen months ago and then the Dublin airport stamp three days ago. Other than that, apparently no travel outside the US."

"Sounds like they had planned this as their big trip," Suel said.

Lynch nodded and said, "We've someone set to check that. The Sheehan surname is fairly common down here, maybe family history, you know, famine people who made it to the States. Or maybe they just always wanted to come, and this was their big opportunity."

Suel shook his head and said, "Pity."

"Have you had a chance to look at the menus?" Teresa, the waitress, asked.

"Give us just another minute. Is there a special tonight?" McCormick asked.

"Every night is special with me, darling," she said and smiled. "Tonight, we're also serving Beef and Guinness stew."

"I'd better have that," McCormick said.

"Make it two," Lynch added.

Dillon and Suel nodded.

"So all four of ya's?" Teresa asked.

Everyone nodded, and McCormick said, "Better bring another round of pints as well."

"Coming right up." She gathered the untouched menus and headed toward the bar.

"Have you any idea where the real Punchy Sheehan is or when he might be arriving?" Lynch asked.

Dillon and Suel shook their heads. "At the moment, it's a blank page," Suel said. "I doubt he's in the country, but he could be, and we've no way of knowing. Obviously, whoever killed this couple last night was just as much in the dark as we are."

FIVE

The fresh pints of Guinness arrived, and shortly after that, bowls of Beef and Guinness stew. They were all quiet for the next few minutes as they started in on the stew. McCormick was the first to set his fork down. He grabbed a dinner roll from the plate and said, "We haven't talked much about whoever pulled the trigger. How did he know about the Sheehan couple in the first place? How did he even know where they were?"

"Yeah, and who in the hell paid him?" Suel added.

Dillon reached for a roll and dipped it in the remnants of his stew. "My first thought is that the owners probably mentioned the booking to someone. Casually mentioning the name Sheehan and the fact it was a couple of Americans for two weeks. They probably told a number of people if it was as great a deal as you said. Someone mentioned it to someone who talked to someone else, and the word was spread around. If they booked two months in advance, that's a lot of time for gossip to spread. The wrong person hears the Sheehan name, Dennis Sheehan as a matter of fact, and unfortunately, this is the result." He took a bite from his roll.

"I think you should talk to them tomorrow morning," Lynch said. "You never know, a name might come up, although it seems like a hell of a long shot at this stage."

"At this stage, it's about all we've got," McCormick said.

"Autopsies will be performed tomorrow?" Suel asked.

McCormick had just tossed the rest of his dinner roll into his mouth and nodded as he chewed. "Mmm, yeah," he said and swallowed. "Based on what we saw, I'm guessing small-caliber rounds, fired from a fairly close range. Certainly inches from your man, and the wife on the couch was no more than five or six feet."

"Can you think of anyone local who might have done this?" Dillon asked.

Both McCormick and Lynch shook their heads.

"I have a tough time thinking this is some local knacker," McCormick said. "The bodies were discovered by the Barry's at approximately 11:00 last night. So they were shot sometime before then. That may have been dusk at this time of year, but it would not have been dark. That suggests to me that the shooter was experienced. He kills Sheehan with one shot, and then possibly he's surprised there's a woman in the sitting room? Did she hear the shot and scream? She's shot three times on the couch, so it would appear she didn't try to flee. I can't help but think if it was a local burglary, your man would have wandered upstairs and taken the two hundred and fifty euros from Sheehan's wallet. Maybe he would have tried to get the woman's diamond rings. At this stage, it appears once the shots were fired, the individual left, which suggests to me it was professional."

Lynch nodded. "I have to agree. Maybe someone from Dublin, Cork, or even Belfast. Hell, it could have been someone who came into the country, did the job, and flew out this morning to Paris or Amsterdam. Who were the Costa Del Sol lads you put away last year?"

"You mean the Linnehan's?" Dillon asked.

"Yeah, that's the bunch. It's not too far a leap to think they might have wanted to eliminate Punchy Sheehan. Someone flies in from Spain, pulls the trigger, and takes a ferry back to France the next morning."

"Don't forget the Doyle's up in Limerick. They certainly wouldn't be sad to see something happen to Punchy. It would be even easier for them. Someone just drives down from Limerick, shoots, and heads back. They'd be home for last call at their favorite pub," Suel added.

Dillon closed his eyes for a moment.

"You still with us, Marshal?" McCormick quipped and smiled.

"Yeah, I just think the list of potential people would increase by the power of ten with every new name. Would you mind if I join you tomorrow when you chat with the Barry's?"

"No, not at all," McCormick said. "I don't think all four of us should go." He turned toward Suel. "Would you be up for going back to the AirBnB with Sean tomorrow morning and doing another sweep of the place? A fresh set of eyes could only help."

"Works for me," Suel said. "I'm guessing I'll need a ride."

"I can give you a lift. Let's meet here in the dining room at 9:00. We all need a decent night's sleep after the last twenty-four hours," Lynch said.

"I'll pick you up, Dillon. Why don't we all meet here at 9:00? Grab a breakfast and see if anyone has come up with an award-winning idea overnight," McCormick said.

"Sounds like a plan," Dillon said. "Let me sign the dinner tab, and then I think those two pints of Guinness are just about to put me to sleep."

They chatted for a few more minutes, but nothing was said that would help in the investigation. Dillon signed the bill, said good night, and he and Suel headed up to their room.

Once in the room, Suel called the front desk and asked for a wake-up call at 7:00.

"Why so early?" Dillon asked.

"There's a workout room I want to try," Suel said, then laughed. "I'm kidding, but with any luck, DCI McCabe will be in around 7:30 tomorrow morning. I want to be on my best behavior, sounding awake and giving him an update as to what we're doing. No point in him getting second-hand information from some high and mighty at the Bandon station."

Dillon nodded and said, "Good call. God, talk about a can of worms. Hey, just a thought, I'll mention this to McCormick and if you could mention it to Lynch. Let's say someone drove here from Dublin or Cork. They're going to get the hell out of here once their mission is accomplished. Let's see if they can think of any petrol stations with security cameras. Maybe we see someone refueling, between, say, 10:30 and 11:30, who might be just the person we're looking for."

"Good idea. The more I think about this and the fact that nothing appears to have been stolen, I can't see some random local pulling it off. I'm ninety percent convinced it had to be a pro. Be interesting what you learn from the couple that owns the place. What's their name?"

"Barry, I can't remember the guy's first name."

Suel seemed to think for a moment. "You know this will work, maybe. At least it will give McCabe the idea we've got the semblance of a plan. Let's sleep on it and see if we come up with anything in the morning. I have to tell you, man. That bed is looking pretty good to me right now."

Dillon tossed his trousers on a chair in the corner then pulled off his shirt and laid it on top of the trousers. "All I ask is that you don't snore tonight," he said as he climbed into the bed.

"Well, if I do, it's not going to bother me, and that's all I care about," Suel said.

They left the bathroom light on in case someone had to get up in the middle of the night. Both were sound asleep in about sixty seconds. Suel did snore for most of the night, but Dillon was so tired he never heard it. The phone ringing at 7:00 the following morning woke both of them.

Dillon picked up the receiver just in case it was a live call. "Hello."

"Good morning, sir. This is the front desk. The time is 7:00."

"Thank you," Dillon said and hung up the phone. He debated closing his eyes for a few more minutes but decided he had better hit the shower. He grabbed his shaving kit and headed for the bathroom. He shaved and showered, and when he stepped out of the bathroom, the TV was on a news station. Suel was sitting up in bed.

"Well, it's about time. You finally finished in there."

"I'm as good-looking as I'm going to get," Dillon joked.

"How unfortunate, but it answers a lot of questions. You can call DCI McCabe while I hit the shower," Suel said and headed for the bathroom.

SIX

Dillon watched the news for a few minutes before calling DCI McCabe up in Dublin. There was no mention on the morning news of the double murder in Desertserges. At 7:40, he placed the call. McCabe answered on the second ring.

"McCabe."

"Good morning, sir, Marshal Dillon."

"What's the word, Dillon?"

"Not good, sir. Dennis and Maureen Sheehan, husband and wife, and both Americans, were murdered. Not the Dennis "Punchy" Sheehan we were hoping. We'll begin to delve into their background today, but at least for now, it appears to be one big cluster…umm…mistake."

"And you're sure it's not your man?"

"Yes, sir, without a doubt. Based on his passport, the victim is twenty-two years younger. I met Punchy Sheehan some years back. He was fat, obese actually, and this young man was an average weight. Our guess is, somehow, someone got wind of the name and the fact they were American and made an assumption. We'll be interviewing the owners of the AirBnB this morning. I don't know this for sure , but it's not far-fetched that they may have mentioned the name of their guests, and someone picked up on the gossip. Initial thoughts are that this was a professional hit. Nothing appears to be stolen. The victim's wallet contained two hundred and fifty euros. His wife still wore a diamond ring and wedding band."

McCabe was quiet for a long moment before he said, "Damn it. See if you can wrap this up and get back here in the next forty-eight hours."

"Yes, sir. Any news on Sheehan possibly arriving in Dublin?"

"No, nothing, and my fear is, if he was hesitant before, this incident is liable to cancel any plans he may have made."

"That would seem to be the smart move. I've had the news on for a bit. No mention yet, but it can't be too long. Bandon police were preparing a statement last night. My guess is it will only be an hour or two before the official word is out there. If Sheehan somehow made his way into the country, he'll flee before the day is over."

"Unfortunately, I have to agree," McCabe said just as Suel stepped out of the bathroom with a towel draped around his waist. He smiled and gave Dillon the finger. "Anything else?"

"No, sir, anything changes, we'll be in touch."

"Very well, back here as soon as you can. Thank you for the call," McCabe said and disconnected.

"What'd he say?" Suel asked as he pulled on a pair of red checked boxers.

"Just that he'd like us up in Dublin as soon as possible and no word on Punchy coming into the country."

Suel sat down on the bed, shook his head, and began to pull on his socks from yesterday. "I've been thinking. I said last night that Sheehan is a common Cork surname. Let's say, for the moment, this was a professional hit. That seems to suggest that whoever is behind this had information that Punchy Sheehan was due to arrive in Ireland. It's the same reason we wasted three long nights sitting outside the Westbury hotel. It's not all that far-fetched that, if they had information that Dennis Sheehan was arriving in Desertserges, the automatic assumption was that it was Punchy. An isolated area, quiet, private, it makes sense. Your man opens the door, and the shooter immediately knows it's not Punchy, but he fires anyway just to eliminate the possibility of being identified later on."

"Yeah, that makes sense. But then so does the idea that the shooter left thinking that he did, in fact, kill Punchy Sheehan. That still leaves us with two murdered individuals, Americans, and we've no idea who did it."

Suel shook his head and pulled on his other sock. They were back down in the dining room at 8:30, a half-hour before McCormick and Lynch were due to arrive. The television behind the bar was on, and they had just sat down at a table and ordered coffee when the news-woman announced a local double murder coming up right after the commercial break. The station immediately switched to an ad for Bord Gáis Energy.

"God save us," Suel said. "So much for keeping things quiet."

"They had to issue a statement sooner or later," Dillon said.

"I can only hope they've someone stationed at the scene to keep the media at bay, or they'll find a way to get into the house and contaminate everything."

"Do you want to head out to the scene?"

"No, if there's no one out there, it's already too late. They've known for at least an hour, probably longer, if they've already got the Gardai statement. Let's see what they have to say."

It was another four and half minutes before the news report was back on. Dillon and Suel left their table and settled onto stools at the bar. "Earlier this morning, Bandon police released a statement regarding a double murder in Desertserges, County Cork. For more on this, we go to Padraig James. Padraig."

"Yes, thank you, Roisin. Two Americans were found murdered in the half-parish of Desertserges just a little before 11:00 Sunday evening. At this stage, their names are being withheld pending notification of family. Here is detective Eamon Roche with the Bandon Gardai at the briefing this morning." The image switched to the front of the Bandon police station. Three serious-looking uniformed officers stood just outside the front door. In front of them was a small crowd of a half-dozen reporters, three women, and three men. Two individuals, both men, were holding cameras and filming the briefing.

"Good morning. Thank you all for being here. It is my unfortunate duty to inform you that the bodies of two individuals were found in a home in Desertserges. The victims, a male and a female, are both American. Names are being withheld until families and American authorities can be notified. At this time, we are pursuing a number of leads and will release information as it becomes available. I can take a question or two, but let me caution again, this is very early in our investigation, and we are exploring a number of avenues."

"Any idea who may have done this or why?" someone shouted.

"At this time, we're pursuing a number of leads and following up on tips that are coming in."

"The victims? A man and woman. Were they a couple?" a woman asked.

Detective Roche looked to one of the uniformed men next to him. The man nodded, and Roche said, "I can state that they were husband and wife. Their passports indicate that they were from the state of Minnesota in the United States."

"Were they staying with relatives?" someone called out.

"They were not staying with relatives. It's early on in the investigation, and we are in the process of exploring any connections they may have had to family, friends, or business here."

"In other words, they're completely in the dark," Suel said and shook his head.

One of the uniformed men leaned forward and said something to Roche. He gave a slight nod and said, "I want to thank you for your time. As we obtain more information, we will keep you informed." All three turned as one and hurried back into the station. The members of the press called out questions as the men disappeared from view.

"How were they killed?"

"Were they shot?"

"Was there any evidence of sexual assault?"

There was a long pause, focused on the front of the Bandon police station, and then it was back to the news team in the studio. "Well, more to come, I'm sure. In other news, the GAA has announced that…"

"Not much in the way of information," Suel said.

"I'd like to say they're keeping everything close to the vest, but in all honesty, other than the victims' names and their flight schedule, I don't think they have anything else."

"Well, look who's all lined up at the bar. Guinness for breakfast, is it?" Jamie McCormick called as he entered the room and headed toward Dillon and Suel.

"Oh, Jamie, you just missed the press conference, such as it was," Suel said.

"Not a bother. I caught it on the telly out in the lobby. God, but I'm glad I don't have Roche's job. He'll be hounded for days to come."

"Interesting, no one asked when this happened. It was more than thirty-six hours ago, and the information is just coming out now," Dillon said.

"Things move a bit slower down here," McCormick said. "Were you finally able to get some sleep last night?"

"Both out like a light until our wake-up call this morning. What about yourself?"

"The same. I think I was asleep before my head hit the pillow."

"Is there anyone managing the crime scene?" Dillon asked.

McCormick nodded. "We've had a lad out there since six this morning. He replaced the lad who was there through the night. There's been someone on scene since we first learned of the incident if that's your question."

"We have that table over by the window. Let's grab it and order some breakfast before I waste away," Suel said.

DI Lynch stepped into the dining room as they headed to the table.

"Did you catch the press briefing?" McCormick asked.

"Yeah, listened to it out in the parking lot. Not that they had much to say. I imagine we'll have to make our way through a crowd once we head out there this morning," Lynch said to Suel.

"Breakfast first, and then we'll head out," Suel said.

"You're meeting with the Barry's?" Lynch asked McCormick.

"Yeah, just after 10:00. They wanted to go to Mass this morning, not that I can blame them. Whatever the number of bookings they had scheduled, I would guess that's all but done for. I can't imagine anyone wanting to rent where two people were murdered."

They ordered breakfast and cleaned their plates in about fifteen minutes. Lynch and Suel headed out to the scene of the crime. McCormick and Dillon chatted over another coffee until 10:00 rolled around, and then drove to the Barry home.

SEVEN

Aisling and Thomas Barry lived in a two-story brick home with a large front garden and a paved driveway leading to a three-stall garage in the rear of the lot. Based on the architecture, both structures appeared to be at least a hundred years old. McCormick parked out on the street, pulling halfway onto the sidewalk like all the other vehicles nearby.

A four foot high brick wall ran across the front of the lot. McCormick opened the elaborate wrought-iron gate, black with gold painted accents, and they followed the winding path up to the front door.

A brass door knocker hung in the middle of the door. McCormick ignored it and rang the doorbell. They immediately heard the chimes inside. "Thomas and Aisling Barry. He was a barrister, retired now for the last two or three years. She taught primary school, I believe," McCormick said.

The door suddenly opened, and a blonde woman Dillon pegged at early to mid-sixties flashed a smile. "DI McCormick, please come in. We're just home from Mass and about to have some tea in the library. Can I possibly talk you into a scone and a cup of tea?"

"Say no more, yes to both," McCormick said. "Oh, let me introduce Marshal Jack Dillon. He's with An Garda Síochána in Dublin and here to help with this dreadful affair. Marshal, this is Aisling Barry."

"Very nice to meet you, ma'am. I'm sorry it happens to be under these circumstances."

"Nice to meet you, Marshal. Let me take you to Thomas. He's in the library, and then I'll be back in just a moment with some tea and scones. This way," she said, and they followed her across a large entryway to the second door in the hallway. She knocked on the door as she opened it and called, "Thomas, I've DI McCormick and Marshal Dillon. Gentlemen."

The furniture in the room was antique and looked like it might be original to the house. The loveseat and chairs had mahogany legs and trim and were upholstered in tufted red velvet. A coffee table was positioned between the loveseat and chairs with what looked like a manila file folder resting at the far end.

Three of the walls were lined with bookcases five feet high. The books on the shelves were leather bound with gilt decorated bindings and at least as old as the house. Three large gilt-framed landscape paintings were centered on the walls above the bookcases.

Thomas Barry stood staring out a window. He was slightly stooped with bent shoulders and looked like he might be original to the house as well. Clearly older than his wife, he had ginger-colored hair around the side of his head that was brushed behind his ears and a long and very thin comb-over across the top of his head. Both ears held hearing aids.

"We met the other night," McCormick said. "Good to see you again, sir. This is Marshal Jack Dillon. He's down from Dublin to assist in the investigation."

Barry shook hands with McCormick but gave Dillon the once over before he held his hand out. "A pleasure to meet you, Marshal, is it?"

"Yes, the last name is Dillon."

"Oh, you're an American. Of course, the victims were American. Sad, oh so very sad. Please take a seat, gentlemen," Barry said and motioned toward the loveseat and two chairs.

McCormick headed for one of the chairs, and Dillon settled into the other one. In Dillon's mind, the chairs gave them the sense of just a bit more authority and hopefully the ability to control any discussion. No sooner had they settled into the chairs, then Aisling entered the room carrying a large silver tray. A stack of plates, scones, cups, saucers, cream, sugar, jam, spoons and a teapot filled the tray.

She set the tray on the table and settled into the corner of the loveseat. Once she was seated, Thomas Barry carefully lowered himself into the opposite corner of the loveseat.

"Tea, gentlemen?" Aisling asked.

"Yes, please, milk and two sugars," McCormick said.

"Tea, no milk or sugar," Dillon replied.

She quickly served the tea as if she did so every day, which was probably the case. She mixed the third tea for her husband, adding just a drop of milk and a half spoon of sugar.

As she handed the tea to him, he laughed and said, "She watches me like a hawk."

"Left to his own devices, he'd take all the sugar," she replied then quickly set a scone on a plate and passed one to McCormick, another to Dillon, and finally one to her husband.

Once they were served, Barry took a sip of his tea, smiled at McCormick, and said, "How may we be of assistance?"

EIGHT

McCormick said, "I'd like to review our discussion from the other night. You mentioned that the Sheehans had reserved the BnB a few months prior to their arrival."

Barry nodded, picked up the manila file folder in front of him, and handed it to McCormick. "All the information should be in there. They contacted us through the email service. Payment was made in advance, I might add. Aisling deals with all of that. It's all on the computer, and I'm the last person in the world to be dealing with a computer."

Aisling smiled. "We have the unit listed on a number of sites. They contacted us, filled out our registration form, and paid in advance, just as Thomas stated."

"And did they send you a check, or do you accept credit cards?"

"We do accept credit cards, as well as checks drawn on local, Irish banks. The Sheehans paid us via a site called PayPal. They weren't the first to pay in that manner. It's really quite easy for us. Our account is set up regardless of where the payment is initiated, and the funds are deposited into our account in euros. All I have to do is turn on the computer and see that the deposit has been made."

"And I'm from a place and time when we counted the pounds and passed them across the counter to the bank teller," Thomas said and laughed.

"You'll find all our contact information with the Sheehans in that file. We never spoke on the phone or in person. We double-checked the home the morning they were to arrive. We always have a bottle of wine waiting for our guests, cheese and crackers, oh, and for the Sheehan's two steaks in the refrigerator. They were going to be our longest-staying customers ever. Usually, we've just a weekend stay, maybe three days at the most. They'd booked it for almost two weeks."

"Any reason why they booked for that length of time?" Dillon asked.

Aisling shook her head. "I think in one of their emails, Mr. Sheehan mentioned that it was their anniversary, and they wanted a quiet getaway. He said something about taking day trips, but he never said where. Maybe he had family from Cork originally or something along those lines, but he never mentioned anything. We were just glad to have almost two weeks booked."

"And you stated you never met them in person."

Both Barry's shook their head. "We were returning from a family get-together. Our daughter and her husband celebrating their wedding anniversary," Thomas said. "I'd conveniently dozed off, and Aisling was gracious enough to help clean up. We left their home around

10:30 and decided to drive past Desertserges. No reason, really, just curious, I guess."

"Thomas noticed the front door open. I pulled over and waited for a moment."

"More like three or four minutes," Thomas said.

Aisling nodded and said, "I pulled into the garden, we waited another minute or two and then Thomas went to check on them."

"I saw your man's feet just inside the door. My first thought was a heart attack, but one look at the lad and the blood…"

"Thomas wouldn't let me see them. He had me phone the Gardai, and we waited for them to arrive."

Thomas shook his head. "Tragic, absolutely tragic. Who would do such a thing? Have you made an arrest?"

McCormick shook his head. "Not yet. We're still in the process of gathering facts."

"You've someone watching the property, don't you?"

"Yes, we've three officers there at the moment. We'll most likely be finished by the end of the week."

Thomas shook his head. "Unbelievable. Who in God's name would have thought this could have happened here? Absolutely tragic. You've notified family back in the States?"

"We're in the process of doing that," McCormick said.

"I'm sorry we didn't have more information. We've no idea who you could contact," Aisling said.

"We were able to get that information from the airline. The American embassy is contacting the emergency number they listed. As soon as we have an update, we'll let you know."

"You had mentioned this was one of the longer bookings you'd had for the BnB," Dillon said.

"Actually, it was the longest, by far. Usually, it's Irish people from Dublin or maybe Wexford just having a getaway weekend. This was unusual, and we'd secretly hoped that it might lead to a number of international visitors. People wanting to stay for longer than just a night or two. Maybe looking up family histories or just enjoying the getaway. Now, well, I'm afraid this may well bring an end to anyone wanting to stay," Aisling said.

"Damn," Thomas said and shook his head.

"Did you mention the booking or the Sheehan's to family or friends?" Dillon asked.

"After this, lord no," Thomas said.

"What about before? Say over the course of the last two months, once they'd booked. From what you said, it sounds as though this could have been a very profitable shift in your rentals," Dillon asked.

"We're not the sort to count our chickens before they hatch," Thomas said and gave Dillon a look.

"Thomas, we did mention the fact that we had acquired a lengthy booking to some people. Dermot Collins, the O'Mahaneys, Kevin Byrne, Teresa Foley, the Reilly's, to name a few."

"They wouldn't have mentioned it to anyone. It's of a private nature."

"Would you be able to provide me a list of people? We'd like to check with them, just as a matter of covering all aspects," McCormick said.

"Yes, surely," Aisling said.

Thomas set his teacup on the tray and crossed his arms.

"Let me just draw up that list for you. It's only a few names," Aisling said and set her teacup on the tray. She stood and began to reach for the tray.

Dillon was on his feet and said, "Please, allow me. Thank you for the tea and scones, very good. If you'll lead the way, I'll follow with the tray."

Thomas shot a look at Dillon as he followed Aisling out of the room. They walked down the hall, and Aisling pushed open a swinging door that led into a pantry of sorts. "I'm sorry, you'll have to forgive my husband. He's mortified that we're associated with something like this."

"Oh, believe me, I completely understand. You may find that your real friends will be there, watching over the two of you. Then, there'll be the usual cast of characters who are only interested in the gossip. People are funny. You and your husband are innocent victims, and your help is much appreciated. We'll pursue this to the best of our ability, and we're still in the early stages of our investigation. When they booked, did the name Dennis Sheehan ring any bells?"

Aisling shook her head. "To the best of our knowledge, we'd never heard of the man. A gangster? Had we known, I can assure you Thomas would have never allowed them to rent from us. We just had no idea and then, coming from the United States, no knowledge at all. We sent our emails back and forth. They were just another nice couple. Exactly the sort of people we want to rent to. Now, well, I'm afraid that's all gone down the drain. Any idea who may have done this?" she asked.

"Not at this point, but that could change any second. Someone makes a comment, maybe a phone call. We never really know. We just keep our nose to the grind-stone and continue following the facts."

"Oh, if you wouldn't mind setting the tray over there," Aisling said, pointing to an open space on the counter.

The cabinets in the kitchen were painted white, and the countertops appeared to be linoleum with a stainless steel counter edge trim. It reminded Dillon of his great grandmother's kitchen, that and the kitchen apron sink with the drainboard. Nothing appeared to have been up-dated since the 1940s.

"How long have you been here? I mean living here," Dillon asked.

Aisling opened a drawer and smiled as she pulled out a note tablet and a pen. "I've been married to Thomas for twenty-three years. He grew up in this house, which ac-counts for a number of things not being updated. He's comfortable with them, and I find them umm…somewhat charming, I guess."

She began writing a list of names on the tablet. When she was finished, there were at least twice the names she had originally mentioned. She handed the list to Dillon.

"And this after the name? Is that the street they live on?"

"Yes, exactly. I don't know the address, but I'm sure Detective McCormick will recognize them. Dermot Collins worked for years in the mayor's office. I taught with Teresa Foley. She's still at Presentation Primary School. I've added our phone number at the bottom. Feel free to call any time with a question."

"Thank you, this will help," Dillon said, folding the sheet of paper and placing it in his pocket.

"Please don't be upset with Thomas. We're not like Dublin. A murder, let alone two murders, is not an everyday occurrence down here. Add to that his embarrassment at having had it happen at a property he owns. Well, if that wasn't bad enough, he invested a lot of money updating that house, and he's of a mind now just to sell it, but who would want to buy it after the murders? This has been very difficult for him."

"Believe me, I understand. Thank you for the names. As we said before, if anything comes up, we'll keep you posted. Hopefully, we'll be out of there in the next day or two."

She smiled and said, "No rush. I expect the one reservation we have will probably cancel."

They heard McCormick and Thomas Barry moving down the hallway toward the front door. Aisling raised her eyebrows, nodded toward a swinging door on the far wall, and headed toward it. They left the kitchen and stepped into a formal dining room with a fireplace and dark wood paneling on the walls. They walked through the dining room, into a sitting room, and then into the entry. McCormick was talking to Barry at the front door. As Dillon stepped into the entry, Barry glanced at him, then took hold of the brass doorknob, and held the door open.

"Thank you very much for your time," McCormick said and nodded at both of them.

"A pleasure to meet you both. We'll keep you posted. Thank you," Dillon said as Barry closed the door on him before he could finish.

"Well, Marshal, you apparently made quite the impression," McCormick said and grinned.

NINE

As they headed out the front gate to the car McCormick asked, "Did you get the list of names?"

"Yeah, maybe twice as many names as she mentioned, but my guess is she was just being on guard with that crabby old husband of hers in the room."

McCormick handed Dillon the file with the email transcripts and said, "Look through this while we head out to Desertserges. We can check on that list of people later this afternoon. I'd like to return to the scene and see how Lynch and your man Suel are doing. We've an officer at the gate so, hopefully, the media will be kept at bay."

"Yeah, that sounds like a good idea. God forbid they found a business card or discovered a CCTV file with images of a car and a license plate." Once they climbed in the car, Dillon opened the file and looked at the two and a half pages of emails. "Did you have a chance to look at these, or did Barry tell you they were for the chief's eyes only?"

McCormick chuckled as he drove down the street. "He's just part of the privileged sort who view this whole unfortunate incident as tarnishing his otherwise sterling reputation. I guess the bad news is, he's probably correct, at least as far as his contemporaries are concerned. They come from a much different generation, and I'm sure they'll be whispering things like, 'Renting a house. What did he expect?'"

"Yeah, to tell the truth, I've got friends who would probably feel much the same way. It's too bad and just when Aisling seemed to think they might be on track to really do some business."

"Yeah, well, I would guess that's finished after this event."

Dillon paged through the emails. There were nine in all, including one that listed the payment having been sent via PayPal. All the emails were between Aisling and Dennis Sheehan. Most of the emails were no more than a couple of sentences. The questions and replies were just what you'd expect, general sorts of questions from Sheehan about the area and Aisling asking about dates and any special needs. There were plenty of thank yous back and forth from both parties, and in the end, nothing stood out as unusual. Dillon placed the list of names from Aisling in the file and reached into the back to set the file on the seat. "More of the same, nothing, unfortunately."

"Unless something changes, I'm of the opinion that this was probably due to someone telling someone over the course of two months, and in short order, if at all, we won't be able to track it. This appears to have been a professional hit with Sheehan's wife essentially playing the part of the innocent bystander," McCormick said.

"Both of them are innocent bystanders. The only thing Sheehan did wrong was to have the same name as Punchy Sheehan, and that's his parent's fault."

They both chuckled at that and drove on for the next twenty minutes, occasionally commenting on the case. "Will you look at this?" McCormick said.

Dillon looked down the empty lane but didn't see anything out of the ordinary. "What? I'm not seeing anything. What is it?"

"Just that, I half-expected a line of onlookers and news vans. There's nothing. No one standing around."

"I'd call that a blessing," Dillon said.

McCormick slowed and lowered his window as he turned into the entrance and stopped. "How's it going, Aiden?" he said to the officer leaning against the hood of the squad car.

"Hi ya's, Jamie. Not a bother. Maybe four or five cars slowing down as they drove past, but that's over the course of the last five hours. No one stopped. No news vans. I thought two people were going to try and walk in, but it turned out to be a couple jogging. They just gave me a nod and kept going."

"They didn't mention the address in the press release this morning," Dillon said.

"Those reporters would have probably had it before the conference even began. No doubt some knacker probably opened his mouth in the hopes of a free dinner or tickets to Croke Park," McCormick said.

"Maybe they know there's absolutely nothing to see," the officer said.

"Yeah, maybe." McCormick turned to Dillon and asked, "What do you think?"

"I think we should count our blessings."

"Yeah, you got that right. Okay, well, keep up the good work, Aiden," McCormick said and pulled into the parking area next to Lynch's car.

As they climbed out, Dillon said, "I'm going to leave that file in the car so lock the doors just to play it safe."

McCormick pressed his key fob, the doors locked, and the horn beeped in response. They walked up to the front door and stepped inside. Dillon glanced at the floor where Sheehan's body had lain yesterday. There was nothing to suggest anything had happened.

"Lynch?" McCormick called.

"Back in the kitchen, Jamie," Lynch said in response.

The kitchen was in the rear of the house, and they walked through a small dining room to get to it. Lynch and Suel were seated at the kitchen table, sipping mugs of tea. "We just turned off the kettle a minute ago. More mugs in the cabinet next to the sink," Lynch said as Dillon and McCormick stepped into the kitchen.

"Care for a mug?" McCormick asked as he moved to the kitchen counter and opened the cabinet.

"Yeah, sure," Dillon replied as he pulled back an antique wooden chair and sat down next to Suel. "Find anything of interest?" he asked.

Both men shook their heads.

"The bed hadn't even been used. A pity, really. How did your meeting go with the Barry's?" Suel asked.

"About what you'd expect. Nothing out of the ordinary. They seemed to hope this two-week rental might be the beginning of a lot more rentals. Instead, this sad situation is probably going to kill what little business they were getting," McCormick said as he refilled the kettle. He set the kettle on the stove and turned on the burner.

Lynch shook his head. "Too bad. It would be a lovely spot if you were looking for a quiet getaway. Unfortunately, word travels fast. They'll probably have all sorts of online trolls posting comments."

"I predict this will end up being a quiet purchase by someone who wants a holiday home and finds the idea of a couple of murders exciting," Suel said. "So nothing from the Barry's?"

"Nice enough couple, I guess. Your man could have fathered the wife. I'd place his age at close to twenty years her senior," McCormick said as he leaned against the kitchen counter, waiting for the kettle to boil. "We've copies of the emails back and forth between them and the Sheehans."

"Two and a half pages, nine emails, nothing out of the ordinary. The wife, Aisling, gave us a list of names they mentioned the Sheehan rental to. Most, if not all of it, I'm guessing, was due to the length of the rental rather than anything to do with the name Dennis Sheehan. We obviously know Punchy Sheehan, but they run in different circles and had no idea who we were talking about, well until this incident," Dillon said.

Lynch took a sip of tea and said, "We're more or less finished here. No signs of a break-in. Based on what we didn't find, it would seem to confirm the idea that whoever did this was here for all of about thirty seconds. Did what he came to do and left."

"Which reminds me," McCormick said and pulled out his phone. He tapped his screen a moment later and placed the phone to his ear. "Yes, Deidre, Jamie McCormick. Fine, thank you. Say, we'll need to request CCTV footage from any petrol stations on the way to Cork, Cobh, Limerick, and Dublin. No, I'd say a fifty-mile radius between maybe 10:00 p.m. and midnight. Yeah, I know it's a long shot, but it's about all we've got at the moment. Yeah, maybe an hour or so. You too. Thanks in advance," he said and disconnected.

"With any luck, the CCTV footage will be waiting for us by the time we get back. If not, we can start in on contacting the names Aisling Barry gave us. The more I think about it, the less that list of names is liable to work. She told us they had no knowledge of Dennis "Punchy" Sheehan. Said the name didn't ring a bell with either of them, and if it had, her husband wouldn't have rented to them."

The kettle began to boil. McCormick turned off the burner, filled the mugs, and brought them over to the table. As he sat down, the wooden chair gave a loud cracking sound, and McCormick froze for a moment.

"Is that thing going to stay in one piece?" Suel asked.

"That would be the icing on the cake for the Barry's. I could sue them for faulty furnishings and retire on the million euro award I'd get."

Everyone laughed at that. They chatted over tea, came up with nothing other than heading back to the office and phoning Mick Kelly, the medical examiner.

TEN

On the drive back to Bandon, it rained for fifteen minutes while Dillon went over the emails and, once again, came up empty-handed. "Damn it, nothing out of the ordinary. I'm afraid we're going to get the same result when we contact those friends on Aisling Barry's list."

"If they didn't cop on to the name Dennis Sheehan, and they apparently didn't, why would they even mention it? I'm thinking Barry, being a barrister of some renown locally, would naturally avoid mentioning the client's name," McCormick said. "It's almost as if some knacker just chose the house at random and shot whoever answered the door."

"Oh man, don't even go there," Dillon said.

They pulled into the parking area behind the Bandon station. Dillon made a mental note that although there were security cameras mounted on the back of the building, they didn't have to drive through a gate and flash an I.D. to a guard.

Once he turned the car off, McCormick hung his lanyard around his neck. Dillon did the same and followed McCormick into the building. They took the stairs up to the second floor and down a hall. McCormick opened a door with a frosted glass panel. The words 'Criminal Investigations' were painted in black letters on the glass. As they stepped inside, the room was similar to the Special Branch office in Dublin, only smaller. There were four desks, wooden, and all empty at the moment. The desks were at least fifty years old and pushed together, two desks facing one another alongside the other two desks. Not exactly a layout that would allow for a private conversation.

McCormick tossed his car keys on a desk and said, "Just running to the jacks. I'll be back in a minute. Grab a seat," he said and nodded at the desk opposite his.

Dillon settled into the desk across from McCormick's and glanced around the room. One wall was lined with file cabinets. A large, round clock hung in the center of the wall and immediately reminded Dillon of a school classroom.

"Can I help you?" a voice behind Dillon suddenly said.

He turned to look at a man, probably about fifty, wearing a Garda uniform. Dillon recognized him as one of the individuals from the morning press conference yesterday. He immediately stood and extended a hand. "Hi, I'm Jack Dillon with An Garda Síochána Special Branch in Dublin. I'm here with DI McCormick. He just ran to the restroom."

The man smiled as he shook hands with Dillon. "DCI Neely. You're down here with another lad, aren't you?"

"Yes, DI Suel. He should be along shortly. He's with DI Lynch."

"And you're the American?"

"Yes. I'm with the US Marshals. I've been assigned to An Garda Síochána in Dublin for the last few years."

Neely smiled. "A pleasure to meet you. How are things going on the double murder?"

"Slow but sure. We're in the process of eliminating a variety of options."

"In other words, the investigation is completely banjaxed."

"That might be a little harsh. It seems pretty clear whoever did this was in and out in no more than a minute. Your man's wallet still had cash—"

"Two hundred and fifty euros if I recall."

"Yes, nothing appeared out of sorts in the BnB. The Sheehan couple had only been there for a few hours. We spoke to the owners." Dillon nodded at the thin file on McCormick's desk. "They gave us a copy of all the emails back and forth, a total of nine. All routine, nothing out of the ordinary."

"You're the one who initially said the victim wasn't Punchy Sheehan?"

"That's right. I met him a few years back. Punchy is twenty-some years older and at least twice the size of the man murdered, and he doesn't have a wife."

"God save us," he said and shook his head. "Well, don't let me hold you up. A pleasure to meet you. Best get on with it."

"We're on it," Dillon said and watched as Neely headed into the corner office and closed the door. As if on cue, McCormick stepped back into the room a moment later.

"Dillon. For God's sake, take a seat."

"I was just talking to a big fan of yours, DCI Neely."

"Neely?" McCormick said and glanced over his shoulder toward the closed office door. "He's okay, gives us plenty of room, as long as we come up with results."

"Then we better get started," Dillon said.

Over the next half-hour, they made eleven phone calls to the names on the list Aisling Barry had provided. At no surprise, they came up empty-handed. Only four individuals could recall mentioning the rental to anyone, and none of them had been aware of the name Dennis Sheehan.

Just as they finished up, McCormick's cellphone rang. He jotted down information on a notepad and disconnected. "That was Deidre. I've got a link to CCTV tapes at the petrol stations. There are more coming in, but we can get started. I'm wondering where in the hell Lynch and Suel are. They should have been back by now."

"You want to give Lynch a call?"

"No, I'd rather give them both a hard time once they return. Let me bring up those images. Wheel around here, and we can watch them together. Two heads are better than one."

Dillon rolled his chair around to McCormick's desk as McCormick pushed his computer screen back. All the tapes would be black and white. This first one was a continual image, no three or five-second jumps. The tape began at exactly 10:00 p.m. and continued for the next ninety minutes. McCormick was able to speed through long sections where no vehicle or customer was filmed. They 'viewed' ninety minutes worth of tape in sixteen minutes.

They were on their fifth or sixth tape when Lynch and Suel wandered into the office. "It's about time. Everything all right?" McCormick asked.

Lynch reached into the paper grocery bag he was carrying and proceeded to place white Styrofoam take-out trays in front of Dillon and McCormick. "Sorry it took so long," he said, placing two more trays on the desks next to McCormick's. "Had to get petrol. Then we waited in line to order the lunches. I should have called. You've already got CCTV tapes?"

"Yeah, we've been through a few, more coming in." He handed the notepaper with the URL to Lynch. "Log on, and we can all watch as we go through. So far, nothing heading up Limerick way."

Dillon opened his take-out tray and unwrapped the paper napkin with the plastic knife and fork. "What is this? It smells good."

"Cashew Chicken. It's from a Thai restaurant down the street. We're on a first-name basis with them, and they give us a discount."

"I like McDonalds," Suel said ane all three gave him the look. "Just kidding."

ELEVEN

They'd finished their Thai chicken over an hour ago and were still coming up empty-handed on the tapes. McCormick and Suel were on their third tea. Just now, they were viewing the tape from an Esso on the Run station on the M8 highway located on the outskirts of a village called Silver Springs.

"Hey, wait a minute. Back up a bit. Can you enlarge the image of your man?" Suel said and suddenly sat up.

Lynch turned the computer screen toward Suel as McCormick ran his fingers across the keyboard. The computer was focused on a man climbing out of a black four-door with a Volkswagen logo centered on the front of the vehicle. He was lean, with a dark, scruffy beard and a shaved head. As he climbed out from behind the wheel, he glanced around, displaying a tattoo on the back of his skull.

"That car is a Volkswagen Jetta," Lynch said.

"Yeah, and the shaved head with the tattoo, that has to be your man Keegan Donnelly. What the hell is he doing on the M8 in Silver Springs at 11:00 at night?"

"How do you know him?" McCormick asked and paused the tape.

"A real knacker. He's been trying to make it into the big time for the last couple of years. Did time on an assault, was arrested for carrying a firearm. That was at least two years ago, maybe three. He's slowly but surely getting connected. I could see him doing this. We had a bit of a disagreement some years back."

"And he drives a Volkswagen Jetta?" Dillon asked.

"Well, apparently, he was driving one that night. Is it his? It might be. Could just as easily be stolen or borrowed."

"He could have rented the thing for all we know. Can you run a check on him?" Lynch asked.

"Doing it now," Suel said and pulled his phone out. A moment later, he said, "Yeah, Eamon, DI Suel, Special Branch. Say, I'm down in Bandon working a case with Marshal Dillon. Yes, that's the one. We're going over security footage, and we've come across a knacker from the Liberties, name of Keegan Donnelly. Yeah, one and the same. Can you see if there's anything recent on him? I'd like his current address, and can you check to see if he owns a car, specifically a black or dark-blue Volkswagen Jetta? Once you get it, call me or send me an email. You've got my address? Good, thanks in advance. I owe you a pint. What? Okay, I owe you a number of pints. Yeah, you too. Thanks," he said and disconnected.

"Let's see if we can't get a license number on that car," McCormick said. He ran the tape forward and backward three different times and still came up empty-handed.

"This Donnelly, could you see him doing this?" Dillon asked.

"No doubt. It would be a step up for him, but yeah, he's good for it."

"Put him on the list and let's see who else we can find," McCormick said. They went through tapes for the next forty-five minutes and never found anything else. The phone on McCormick's desk rang, and he picked it up.

"DI McCormick. Oh yeah, Mick. Thanks for calling. What did you find out? Mmm-hmm. Same weapon? Okay, no, thank you, much appreciated," McCormick said and hung up. "That was Mick Flanagan. They finished the autopsies on the victims. Same weapon was used on both. A small-caliber weapon, .380 auto. Oh, and a 1.2 alcohol level on your man and 1.6 on the wife."

Dillon shook his head. "Wouldn't you know. A couple is finally able to kick back, and some ass head arrives at the door. .380 auto, that's a relatively limited line. Small, pocket carry pistols. Glock .42s come to mind, but there are a number of others. Would something like that fit with your man, Donnelly?"

Suel nodded and gave a shrug. "It could. Knowing him, someone either gave it to him or he stole it from somewhere. Don't get me wrong, I think he's an idiot, but only because he's bright enough to be successfully employed, and instead, he wants to be a professional criminal. If he pulled the trigger, it's almost a sure bet that weapon is no longer in his possession. That said, he's more than capable."

"Let's look at more tapes, but I'm thinking unless we find anyone else, we might pay Mr. Donnelly a visit tomorrow," Dillon said.

"With any luck, Eamon will be back to me with a current address," Suel replied.

The afternoon grew even longer and, if possible, even more boring. Dillon lost count of the number of tapes they reviewed. Nothing of value appeared on any of them. They were left with the one weak link, Keegan Donnelly refueling in Silver Springs. They were in the midst of a much-needed ten-minute break when Suel's cellphone rang.

Suel glanced at the screen and answered with, "Yeah, Eamon, thanks for calling back. What did you find out?"

Everyone went silent as Suel gave off one-word answers. "Yeah. No. Okay. Yes. Hang on." He reached for a pen and a pad of paper.

"Okay. Good. When? Grand. Feck. Thanks," he finally said and disconnected.

"Interesting conversation. My sympathies to poor Eamon. What'd you find out?" Dillon asked.

"I've got his address in the Liberties. He's not registered as the owner of a Volkswagen Jetta or any other vehicle for that matter. But that's not the best part. It turns out our man Keegan Donnelly failed to make an appearance on his scheduled court date. Now there's a warrant out for his arrest. We can act on that. We can arrest the dozy bastard and in the process search his house."

"Fantastic," Dillon said and turned toward McCormick. "I think we'll head up tonight unless there's something you need our help on, Jamie."

McCormick shook his head. "I'd say the case, at least for the moment, has moved to Dublin. Could it be that simple that we spotted your man on the CCTV footage, and you're able to haul him in on an outstanding warrant? I suggest you check out of the hotel and get back to Dub as fast as you can."

Suel looked at Dillon.

Dillon nodded and said, "Yeah, can we scam a ride with one of you?"

"Bus stop is right out in front," Lynch said, and everyone laughed.

Once back in their room, it took Dillon and Suel all of ten minutes to pack up and clear out of the room. Five of those minutes amounted to Dillon on the phone with DCI McCabe, telling him they would be back in Dublin late that evening and providing him with the information for an arrest early the following morning. McCabe promised to have a team ready to go at 7:00 a.m.

TWELVE

It was almost 8:00 when Dillon dropped Suel off at his place. From there, he drove to the headquarters building. There were only two people in the Special Branch office at this time of night. Both were on the phone, so Dillon was able to make it to his desk with just a wave and a smile. The lights were off in DCI McCabe's office, and the door was closed.

Dillon logged onto his computer and read the message from McCabe. Four other officers would meet Dillon and Suel in Special Branch at 6:00 a.m. tomorrow morning. The six of them were to drive to Keegan Donnelly's address on Reginald Square in the Liberties section of Dublin. They would arrest Donnelly on his outstanding warrant and hold him in a waiting cell at headquarters. A copy of the outstanding warrant and the arrest paperwork were locked in the service vault.

Dillon walked over to the service vault just off to the side of McCabe's office. There were eight separate units, four across and two high. Each unit was 14 by 14 inches with its own door and keypad. The warrant and documents were in unit eight. Dillon input the code on the brass keypad. He waited a moment for the beep, then pulled the lever down and opened the door. A file rested inside. He pulled it out, closed the door, and returned to his desk. He opened the file and began to read.

Keegan Donnelly had been arrested on an assault charge and was supposed to appear in court three months ago. A warrant had been issued for his arrest two weeks after that. Garda had made an attempt to serve the warrant the following week, but no one answered the door at Donnelly's residence.

Dillon figured Donnelly had probably glanced out the window, saw it was two uniformed officers, knew exactly why they were there, and kept quiet till they left. He made a mental note to take along a battering ram. This time, they were going to enter whether Donnelly opened the door or not. He returned the file to the wall safe and drove home.

As he pulled into his front garden, he counted three deposits left by Lucifer. The good news was that meant Tara, across the lane, had received his note and let Lucifer out of the house and probably refilled his food and water dishes. He'd deal with cleaning up sometime tomorrow.

Lucifer met him at the front door and dashed out of the house as Dillon stepped in. The dog assumed the position next to the driver's door of the car and proceeded to add one more deposit. Dillon tossed his overnight bag on the staircase. He took a biscuit out of the cookie jar and tossed it to Lucifer in the garden.

He stepped into the kitchen and looked around. Things seemed to be in decent order. He pulled the wastebasket off the kitchen counter, refilled Lucifer's water dish, and opened the freezer. Fortunately, there was one more frozen pizza. He set the pizza on the counter, turned on the oven, and coaxed Lucifer back in the house with another biscuit.

Dillon ate the pizza in the den while watching the evening news. Once the news was finished, he headed upstairs and set his alarm for 4:15 a.m. He fell into a deep, dreamless sleep almost immediately and woke to the alarm. He showered, shaved, and had a breakfast of coffee and toast. He carried Lucifer outside just after 5:00 a.m. and was back in the office twenty minutes later.

Suel arrived ten minutes after Dillon, and they reviewed their morning procedure with four uniformed officers in the conference room. A Google maps image of Keegan Donnelly's residence was on the large screen monitor. At ten minutes before 7:00, the three vehicles pulled into Reginald Square.

The units were all attached single-story structures, approximately a hundred and seventy years old, and painted various shades of white with black slate roofs. Donnelly's place, number 8, was the corner unit. It was twelve feet wide with a worn wooden door and a large crack in the stucco, two feet off the ground running the width of the unit.

A wooden bench sat in front of the place with three empty beer bottles beneath it.

At this early hour, no one was on the street. Dillon and Suel stood on either side of the front door. Two officers stood in the alley, just behind Suel, and two stood four feet behind Dillon on the far side of the unit's narrow front window.

Dillon looked at both pairs of officers and got a nod indicating they were ready. He pushed the doorbell hard three separate times but never heard anything. He pounded on the door and shouted, "An Garda Síochána, Keegan Donnelly. Open the door."

He pounded a second time, even harder, and felt the door shake as he did so. "Keegan Donnelly, we've a warrant for your arrest. Open the door, or we'll be forced to knock it down."

He waited a long minute, then gave the two officers a nod and pulled the pistol from his shoulder holster. The officers stepped in front of the door with the steel battering ram. One officer stood on either side.

"Okay. Go for it," Dillon said.

They swung the battering ram back and then forward, slamming into the door just next to the doorknob. The door burst open and bounced off the interior wall.

Dillon and Suel rushed past the men with the battering ram, shouting, "An Garda Síochána. An Garda Síochána. Keegan Donnelly, An Garda Síochána."

There were four rooms in the place. A small front room with a narrow fireplace, a worn couch that had seen better days, and a folding lawn chair. Just behind the front room was a small kitchen with a single cabinet, a small sink, and a two-burner stove. Behind the kitchen was a four-foot-wide bathroom. The bedroom was at the rear of the unit. Keegan Donnelly was still in bed, which seemed surprising.

"Keegan, don't—" Dillon started to yell and then stopped and stared.

Donnelly was sitting in bed wearing black boxer shorts. Based on the glassy eyes, the bullet hole about where the heart would be, and the large blood splatter across the wall, he hadn't been able to answer the door.

"Ah, damn it, for the love of…We got up early for this?" Suel said. "Will you look at him? He's not about to go anywhere."

"Damn it," Dillon said. "Place a call. We're going to need forensics and the medical examiners. Everyone out. No one touch anything."

THIRTEEN

DCI McCabe shook his head. "So we now have three bodies. The American couple down in Bandon."

"Actually, Desertserges, the half-parish just outside of Bandon, sir," Suel said to DCI McCabe.

"Thank you," McCabe said, meaning anything but. "We've no idea where this Punchy Sheehan is. And we find ourselves at the proverbial dead end. Any thoughts, gentlemen?"

Dillon waited a long moment for Suel to say something. When that didn't happen, he said, "My sense is we don't know who is ultimately behind the murder of the Americans, but it would seem to be a strong possibility that Keegan Donnelly's murder confirms the fact that he was at least involved. Even if he didn't pull the trigger, he helped kill the Americans. Whoever thought they were eliminating Punchy Sheehan decided having Donnelly alive wasn't the best idea, so they had him killed. Who is high enough up the ladder to want Punchy Sheehan dead? Who has the ability to get the information somehow that an individual named Dennis Sheehan, an American no less, will be staying in a remote BnB down in Cork? Who can murder the Americans three or four hours after they arrive in the BnB, and is that the same person that murdered Keegan Donnelly 48 hours later?"

"We need to go back to Donnelly's place," Suel said. "He had to be paid to kill the Americans. The car he was driving—"

"The Volkswagen Jetta," Dillon said.

"Yeah. It wasn't anywhere around his place, so either he rented it, or someone lent it to him."

"Or it was stolen," Dillon said.

"What about payment to kill the Americans? Was he paid? And if so, where's that money?" Suel said.

"A number of questions in need of an answer. Don't let me delay you," McCabe said.

Dillon and Suel nodded, stood, and hurried out of McCabe's office. "I don't know about you, but I could sure go for something to eat," Suel said. "Let me make a call, and we can pick something up on the way."

"Sounds like a plan. Might I suggest we both drive in the event we come up with something we could actually follow up on?" Dillon said.

"Sounds more like wishful thinking, but it's probably a good idea. Head back to the Liberties. I'll meet you there with a late breakfast."

As Dillon arrived back at Donnelly's, the forensic team was just finishing up. Actually, they had finished, but the two officers were in the process of drinking plastic cups of tea from a thermos, and they were both eating a chocolate-covered tea biscuit.

"Oh, Marshal, hello. Brendan Davis. You're just in time. Can we interest you in a tea? Sorry, but we're finishing with the last of the tea biscuits," he said and held up half a biscuit.

"No thanks. Please tell me you found something of interest."

"I only wish. Nothing, actually. Some beer bottles beneath the bench in front. We'll dust them for prints, but they're liable to belong to the victim, Donnelly."

"Nothing like a wad of cash or a computer with emails?"

"I'm afraid not, sorry."

"Is it all right to go in and look around?"

"Yes, we're finished. We'll be heading back to the lab in just a few minutes."

"Any thoughts?" Dillon asked.

Davis shook his head. "Unfortunately not. The shots were fired at close range, only a foot from the victim. The medical examiners said there was residue on the skull and the man's chest. They'll have a more definitive result once they do an autopsy. Nothing to base this on but just the way your man was positioned on the bed and in his underwear. I'm thinking there could have been a woman on the scene."

Dillon thought about that for a moment and nodded. He hadn't considered that option.

"Another supposition. In a manner of speaking, the place is more or less spotless. You've got worn furniture, the couch has a tear, the bedsheets are soiled and probably haven't been changed for months and yet there's no debris. No wastebaskets full or overflowing. No dirty dishes in the sink. Not so much as an empty liquor or wine bottle in the place. No clothes on the bedroom floor. No soiled clothes waiting to be washed. It doesn't seem to fit with my limited impression of the victim."

"But you did get the beer bottles from beneath the bench in front?"

"Yes, but those were outside the house and under the bench. If someone made an effort to whisk the place clean, they could have easily missed them."

"Be interesting to see what turns up when you run them."

"We should have something later this afternoon."

"At this stage, anything would help," Dillon said. He pulled out a business card and handed it to Davis.

"Thanks, I've got the info on my computer, but I'll hang onto this. I don't have a card with me but let me give you my cell. Call if you come across anything." He gave Dillon the number and Dillon input it on his cellphone. "Good luck with this one. My sense is, whoever did this has experience."

"Yeah, unfortunately. Guess I'll take a look around."

"Be my guest. We're out of here in just a moment," Davis said.

The front door was closed, but there was a hole and a pretty serious gash running from the top to the bottom of the door after it was hit with the battering ram. Dillon pulled on a pair of latex gloves, stepped inside, and carefully closed the door. He was standing in the front room, such as it was. The worn couch faced the fireplace, and Dillon noticed the torn cushion Davis had mentioned. Soiled yellowed plastic foam was hanging out of the cushion, suggesting it had been that way for quite a while. The stains on the seat cushions possibly suggested some extra-curricular activity. The folding lawn chair next to the couch appeared old, and he thought it could well have been stolen from someone's garden.

Behind the couch was a board on two small sawhorses that apparently served as a small dining table. An ancient wooden chair, battered and with black electrical tape around one of the legs, was pushed partially beneath the board. The bathroom in Dillon's house was almost larger than this front room. The kitchen was barely large enough to turn around in. He opened the upper cabinet. There were three plates and a mug with the words 'Kennedy's Coffee' written on it. Two Guinness glasses that had most likely been stolen from a pub stood behind the mug. The drawer in the lower cabinet held a few pieces of silverware, none of them matched, and they had probably been stolen one at a time from diners and restaurants. A small cast-iron frying pan rested on the two-burner stove. He opened the small refrigerator. It contained two bottles of beer, a bottle of cider, and three slices of pizza.

What Davis had said about the place being 'more or less spotless' was making sense. A guy steals glasses and

silverware from pubs and diners, and there's nothing lying around—no clothes on the floor, no unopened mail,
no computer, and no TV, which struck Dillon as strange.

Donnelly's body was no longer in the bedroom, but
the blood and bits of brain matter were still splattered
across the wall. The double bed was pushed against the
far wall. There was a twelve inch open space between
the foot of the bed and the grimy wall. The sheets on the
bed were soiled, not so much from the shooting as from
being used for months on end. How was it that the bed
was filthy, yet there weren't dirty clothes on the floor or
shoes scattered about?

A small white armoire leaned against the wall next
to the bedroom door. The little wooden doorknob was
soiled and grimy from untold decades of being opened
and closed. A pair of jeans hung on a hook in the armoire. As Dillon lifted them off the hook, they made a
thumping sound. He felt the front pocket and looked inside. A cellphone rested inside the pocket. He laid the
jeans on the bed.

"Hello, anyone home?" Suel called from the front
room.

"Back here in the bedroom, Paddy."

Suel appeared at the door a few seconds later.
"Thinking of renting the place?"

"Is the forensics team still out front?" Dillon asked,
ignoring Suel's joke.

"No, I didn't see them."

"I found what I think is your man's cellphone in a pair of jeans. Let me give them a call," Dillon said and pulled out his phone. He pressed the number he'd entered less than thirty minutes ago.

It rang three times, and Davis answered. "Marshal Dillon, don't tell me you found someone under the bed."

"No, not quite, but I did find a cellphone."

"A cellphone? Where? For God's sake, how'd we miss that?"

"In a pair of jeans hanging in the white armoire in the bedroom."

"Dillon found a cellphone in the armoire, that one in the bedroom," Davis said. Dillon guessed he was speaking to his partner.

"You want to turn around and get it, or I can drop it off, probably in the next hour, unless we find something else."

"If you would be so kind as to place it in an evidence bag and drop it off at the tech lab, that would be just fine. Take some cellphone pictures of where you found it. I'll let them know you're going to drop it off."

"Will do. We'll have it to you later today," Dillon said and disconnected. "Did you bring breakfast?" Dillon asked Suel.

"I did. I'd like to suggest it's a lovely morning, and we could dine outside rather than in this rathole."

"Sounds like a plan. Let me take some pictures, and I'll be out in a couple of minutes."

"I'll be waiting, my love," Suel said and left.

Dillon took a photo of the armoire and another of the inside of the armoire. He photographed the jeans lying on the bed, took a closeup of the cellphone in the front pocket, then headed out to join Suel for breakfast.

FOURTEEN

Suel had arranged their breakfast, such as it was, on the hood of his car. Two cups of coffee, two chocolate doughnuts, and a half-dozen slices of streaky bacon, all arranged on a length of white butcher's paper.

"Thanks for picking this up," Dillon said.

"Yeah, well, you always seem to need some sweetening. You said you found Donnelly's cellphone?"

"I think it's his. It was in the front pocket of a pair of jeans hanging in the armoire."

"That grimy white thing in the bedroom?"

"That's the one," Dillon said. He pulled off his latex gloves and grabbed a chocolate doughnut. "Davis in forensics said to bag it and bring it to him."

"Did you look at it?" Suel asked.

Dillon shook his head, took a large bite of his doughnut, and savored the chocolate. Once he swallowed, he said, "Davis did make an interesting comment. Donnelly lived here. By the way, your comment regarding the 'grimy white thing' is spot on. We've got a guy who was basically a slob—"

"Like most of us," Suel said and reached for a piece of bacon.

"Yeah, okay. Except that this place is relatively clean. Not the door on the armoire in the bedroom, but all the rooms, the kitchen, the front room, even the bedroom. There are no clothes or shoes on the floor. No beer or whiskey bottles next to the filthy couch. No stacks of unopened mail or porn magazines. Did you notice there's no TV and no computer?"

Suel nodded. "Maybe he just has someone come in and clean the place."

"Yeah, okay, but what about the TV or computer? Wouldn't you think someone like Donnelly would like to watch movies, catch a rugby match, or check out some porn flick? When was the last time you saw someone that age who wasn't posting on Twitter, Instagram, or the hundreds of other sites out there?"

"Maybe he rented a storage area, and the stuff is in there," Suel said.

"What? He goes there to watch TV? Davis thought, and I have to agree with him, that someone has been through the place. Quite possibly the person who killed him. His bed sheets are filthy and look like they haven't been changed for the better part of a year. But there are no clothes scattered across the floor. No clothes piled up waiting to be washed. The guy was in bed wearing a pair of boxer shorts, probably waiting for a woman to join him, and no clothes on the floor? No beer bottles or wrappers from takeout food? There isn't even dust under the bed."

"Okay, so someone goes through the place and straightens it up. They take his computer and TV, but then they miss his cellphone? That doesn't seem to make any sense," Suel said.

Dillon shook his head. "I wish I could disagree with you." He crammed the last of the chocolate doughnut in his mouth and slowly chewed, savoring the taste and trying to come up with a logical reason there was no TV or computer in the place and yet Donnelly's cellphone was still in his jeans.

They chatted for a few more minutes, and then Dillon grabbed a large evidence bag from the trunk of his car. He bagged the pair of jeans, leaving the cellphone in the front pocket. He sealed the bag, wrote the date, time and address, and locked it in his trunk.

Going through a place would normally take hours, sometimes even days. Keegan Donnelly's place was so small they'd been through everything twice within an hour, and other than the cellphone, they came up empty-handed. Dillon walked back into the bedroom. Suel was on his hands and knees looking under the bed. "Anything there?" Dillon asked.

"I wish. Nothing here, including no dust. You were right. This place has definitely been cleaned recently. You wouldn't really notice unless someone said something."

"Yeah," Dillon said. "If it weren't for Davis saying something I'm not sure it would have registered with me. There's just enough grime, the wall with the blood, the bedsheets, the door on the armoire, but someone cleaned this place very recently."

"So why?" Suel asked.

Dillon shook his head. "You got me. Maybe fingerprints. Get rid of anything suggesting contacts, try to eliminate DNA traces. You notice the place is clean, even under the bed, but there isn't a vacuum, a mop, or a broom on the premises. I don't know, maybe Donnelly was running some other scam, and he did it. So he cleans up all the dirty clothes and tosses them in a laundry bag. But where's the laundry bag? There isn't a clothes washer in this place. Where are your man's dirty clothes?"

"You think he might have a girlfriend or maybe a mother who does that?"

"Damn it," Dillon said. One more thing in the investigation that wasn't adding up. "We need to check to see who owns this place. Was it Donnelly, or was he renting? If it turns out he's been renting, we need to contact the landlord. Can you check on that? I want to get that cellphone to the tech lab and see if anything turns up."

Suel groaned as he stood. He glanced at the grimy bed sheets and shook his head. "Your man Donnelly would have to keep the lights off if he wanted to entice some lady into that bed. "I'll check to see if there's a landlord. You go on back. Maybe all our answers are on that cellphone."

"One can only hope," Dillon said and drove back to headquarters. He walked down the hall to the tech lab before going up to Special Branch. He pushed the button on the intercom next to the door.

A moment later, a woman's voice answered, "Yes?"

"Emily?" Dillon asked.

"Dillon, is that you? Davis called and said you might be stopping by."

"Yeah, I've got a pair of jeans with a cellphone in them from the Keegan Donnelly site."

"Be right there," Emily said, and thirty seconds later, she opened the door. She was dressed in navy blue slacks and wearing a white lab coat over her blouse. A light blue face mask and white latex gloves completed her ensemble. "Good to see you, Dillon."

He handed her the bag with the jeans and cellphone. "Thanks for doing this, Emily. We think this phone belonged to Keegan Donnelly. Hopefully, there's something on there that will get us moving in the right direction. At this point, we're running on empty as far as any clues go."

"You have a minute? I could hook this up to the computer and see if we can gain access."

"Yeah, that would be great. I'll be the guy with all his fingers crossed standing right behind you."

"Let's get started. Shouldn't take but a minute," she said and held the door as Dillon stepped into the tech lab.

He followed her past a number of counters loaded with all sorts of equipment and bottles. She set the bag on a table, pulled a blank form from a drawer, and quickly filled in some basic information on the form. She opened the evidence bag, pulled out the pair of jeans, and arranged them on the table.

"The phone is in the front righthand pocket," Dillon said. "I took photos of the jeans hanging up and the phone in the pocket."

"Text those to me when you have a minute. Did you touch anything?"

"You mean like the phone? No. I had latex gloves on but never touched the cellphone."

"Okay, let's hook this up and see what we find." Using a six-inch pair of tweezers, she pulled the cellphone from the front pocket and placed it in a metal pan. She set the pan on the counter behind her and turned on the computer. "Hmm, a Motorola razr," she said, glancing at the phone. "Standard cost is about thirty euros a month. Call it a mid-range phone," she said as she lifted the phone with the tweezers and examined the bottom of it.

"I think this is the cord that fits," she said, pulling a black cord from the half-dozen hanging from the computer. "Yeah, that works." She inserted the cord into the bottom of the cellphone. "Okay, let's see what we find." She ran her fingers across the computer keyboard, and the screen suddenly came to life. She clicked a number of different options, and a moment later, a long list of cellphone messages appeared.

"I'll start with the most recent one and move back from there," Emily said.

The first message was just two words, 'half-hour.' Unfortunately, where the sender's contact information would normally appear, the words 'Information unavailable at this time' appeared.

Dillon noted the time the message had been sent and did the math using his fingers to add the final five hours. "So this came through forty-three hours ago."

"Yes, that would have been, umm, the other evening, two days ago."

"And we find the body this morning around 7:00. Yeah, he could have been dead thirty-six hours or so by then. Any way you can tell me who sent that?"

Emily shook her head. "I can give you an educated guess. The information unavailable line suggests it was someone who knew what they were doing. This wasn't their first time in the race. I would say it's probably a pretty safe bet that, right now, that phone is either at the bottom of the Liffey or somewhere along the Royal Canal."

"Of course," Dillon said. "Well, let me know what you find. I'd better get upstairs and report this."

"I'll print out what we have. With any luck, I'll be able to go back at least thirty days."

"Okay, Emily. Call me when you have something, and I'll run down. Thanks again." Dillon headed out of the tech lab and up to Special Branch. Suel's desk was empty, and he could only hope he'd learned something from a landlord. Dillon gathered a bowl with remnants of cereal, along with the three tea mugs scattered on his desk and carried them into the break room. He settled in and phoned Brendan Davis in Forensics.

Davis answered on the second ring. "Davis."

"Hi Brendan, Jack Dillon. Say I dropped off that cellphone at the tech lab. Emily is going over it as we speak. Hopefully, she'll be able to get a list of text messages and phone calls from the last thirty days. The most recent text message came in about 8:00, two nights ago. Just two words, 'Half hour,' that's all the message said. Don't know if Donnelly was supposed to meet someone, if they were going to arrive at his place, or hell it could have been a pizza delivery for all we know at this point."

"She'll turn that over to Quinn O'Neal for fingerprints after?"

"I presume that, but she didn't mention it."

"She probably will. I'll give her a call, just to make sure."

"Thanks, Brendan. The more we looked around Donnelly's unit, the more we like your thought that someone went through and cleaned the place. The bed linens and the cabinets were a mess, but no dirty clothes on the floor, no clothes waiting to be washed, no computer, no TV. It doesn't make any sense."

"Yeah, it's strange. When you figure it out, you can let me know."

Dillon chuckled and said, "I'll be sure to do that."

He hung up and brought up the most recent arrest record on Keegan Donnelly. Thirty-three months ago, he was arrested for carrying a firearm. His court date for that crime was the one he never showed up for, which led to the warrant that allowed them to enter his residence this morning. The arresting officer had been Sergeant Devin Bell, working out of the Crumlin Garda station. Dillon phoned the station, was transferred to Bell's phone, and got dropped into voice mail. "This is Sergeant Bell. Please leave your message at the beep, and I'll return your call as soon as possible." Beep.

"Yes, Sergeant Bell, my name is Marshal Jack Dillon with Special Branch. I'm calling for information on an individual you arrested over two and a half years ago. The man's name is Keegan Donnelly. He was arrested for carrying a firearm. He had a prior record and never showed up for his court date. You can reach me at…" Dillon left his number and hung up.

FIFTEEN

S uel entered Special Branch a half-hour later. He grabbed the mug from his desk and headed for the break room. As he passed, he signaled with a nod of his head that Dillon should join him.

Dillon grabbed his mug and followed. "You find anything out?" he asked as Suel set a tea bag in his mug and filled it with boiling water.

"Yeah, according to the landlord, a gentleman by the name of Conor Buckley, your friend, Donnelly, was a royal pain in the ass. Buckley owns a number of properties in the Liberties, and he was getting ready to evict Donnelly."

"Was he causing problems? Maybe threatening Buckley?"

"No, but he was routinely late on the rent, virtually every month. He was two months in arrears. Buckley received complaints about Donnelly from a couple of neighbors. There'd been damage done to the place from time to time, a broken window, the front door was kicked in a year ago Easter. He had regular arguments with the neighbors. In short, Donnelly was the classic bad customer. When I told Buckley that Donnelly had been killed, his one-word response was, 'Good.' Oh, and then he asked how bad the mess was."

"What'd you tell him?"

"I told him the bedroom could maybe use a paint job but didn't go into any detail."

"Was Donnelly aware he was going to be evicted?"

Suel shook his head. "Buckley was in the process of getting everything lined up. He had a solicitor actually drafting the eviction notice. They were going to erase the two months' rent owed provided he just left and didn't damage the place. I think it's a fair comment that Buckley was overly cautious when it came to Keegan Donnelly. I asked him if he knew any of Donnelly's friends and he said he tried to stay as far away as possible from the man and anyone associated with him. Did you learn anything on the cellphone?"

"Yeah, it looks like Emily will be able to access the text messages. She's hopefully going to be printing them off. The most recent one was just two words, 'Half hour,' and that came through two nights ago. There's a good chance it came from whoever saw him last."

"Namely the killer," Suel said.

"Yeah, the bad news is, Emily's initial take was that message probably came from a burner phone, and no name or number was available."

"Jesus Christ," Suel said as he dipped his tea bag up and down in the mug. "We sure as hell aren't catching any breaks."

"Would you happen to know a Sergeant by the name of Devin Bell working out of the Crumlin station?" Dillon asked.

Suel thought for a moment, then shook his head. "No, that name isn't ringing a bell. What's he done?"

"He arrested Donnelly a couple of years back for possession of a firearm. No information in the arrest report, so I put a call into him. Ended up leaving a message."

"It would be nice to track down Donnelly's acquaintances, give them the information, and see if that doesn't yank their chain."

"Yeah, all we have to do is find out who they are," Dillon said, and they both laughed. They chatted for another ten minutes but never came up with anything and wandered back to their desks.

Dillon's desk phone had a blinking light signaling a message. He pushed the button to listen to the message.

"Yes. Dillon, Devin Bell, returning your call. I'm just off duty and heading to the Halfway House for a pint. Happy to meet up with you if it serves, or feel free to call me on my cell," Bell said and then left his number.

Dillon checked his phone. The call had come through just six minutes earlier. He called Bell's cellphone. Bell answered on the third ring. "This is Devin."

"Hi, Devin, Jack Dillon returning your call."

"Oh, yeah. I'm just about to head out to my car and go over to the Halfway House for a pint. Happy to chat on the phone, or feel free to meet me at the pub. You're at headquarters in Phoenix Park?"

"Yes, I am."

"You're no more than fifteen minutes from the pub."

Dillon took that to mean Bell would prefer to meet at the pub. "I'll meet you there."

"I'll stake out a corner booth. I remember your picture in the Irish Times. I'll keep an eye out for you. A pint of Guinness to your liking?"

"That would be perfect, much appreciated. See you shortly," Dillon said and hung up. He walked over to Suel's desk. "I'm off to meet Devin Bell. He arrested Donnelly two and a half years ago. Meeting him at a pub called the Halfway House. You care to join us?"

Suel shook his head. "Thanks, but I'll be making some phone calls. Trying to shake out some information on Donnelly, see if I can get a handle on who his mates were. Enjoy, I've been in that Pub a couple of times. It's a nice place."

"Touch base later," Dillon said and headed out to his car.

Bell had been correct. Not quite fifteen minutes later and Dillon was pulling into the parking area alongside the Halfway House pub. The lot was two-thirds full, but it was still early, just a bit after 4:00. He locked the car and headed inside.

The pub was a two-story stucco building with a double-door in the middle of the structure leading into what looked like a fairly large restaurant area. At the far corner of the building was a door labeled 'Lounge,' and that was where Dillon entered. He stepped inside and blinked a couple of times to adjust his eyes to the darker light. A guy in a corner booth with close-cropped salt and pepper hair gave a wave, and Dillon headed toward him.

"Marshal Dillon? Devin Bell, a pleasure to meet you," Bell said. He extended his hand and gave Dillon a rock-solid grip. Two pints of Guinness were on the table, both untouched, and once Dillon slid into the opposite side of the booth, Bell raised his glass. Dillon did the same, clinked glasses, and took a sip. It was good.

"So," Bell said, "you've had a run-in with that scum Keegan Donnelly. The lad needed a good hard kick up the backside when I brought him in. It sounds like nothing's changed. Too bad, he had the brains, a bright enough lad, but definitely on a path toward destruction. What's he done this time?"

"Unfortunately, those brains you mentioned were blown out the other night."

"What?"

"Yeah, based on him never showing for his court appearance after the arrest you made, we were able to obtain a warrant. We entered his place over in the Liberties this morning and found him in bed. He'd been dead about thirty-six hours."

"What was the charge?"

"You hear about the double murder down in Cork?"

"Outside of Bandon? Yeah, but I forget the name of the place."

"Desertserges, a half-parish. Two Americans, husband and wife. Your man's name was Dennis Sheehan, and from what we can determine, he was mistaken for Dennis Punchy Sheehan, even though he was twenty-some years younger. It looked like no more than a thirty-second event, start to finish. Your man takes one from maybe six inches, and his wife takes three rounds from no more than ten feet. They weren't searched. Cash was still in your man's wallet and his wife's purse. We caught CCTV footage of Donnelly refueling just outside of Cobh in a village called Silver Springs. It was 11:30 at night, and he was at an Esso on the Run station. We watched the tape not twenty-four hours later. Entered his residence the following morning and found him in bed, dead."

"Good lord," Bell said.

"A couple things are interesting, first off, the idea that Donnelly was even involved. I should add, we haven't confirmed that. We're basing our supposition on the fact that he was in the general area at 11:30 at night and that he was murdered twenty-four hours later. Interestingly, his place is basically spotless. His bed sheets were beyond filthy. There's grime on cabinet doors. The shower stall hadn't been cleaned in years. But there were no clothes on the floor. No dust under the bed or dirty dishes in the sink. No empty beer or whiskey bottles in the place, but there were three empty beer bottles outside underneath a bench. Our thought is whoever killed him took the time to clean the place afterward. We found his cellphone in a pair of blue jeans hanging in an armoire."

"You get anything off the cellphone?"

"It's in the tech lab as we speak. I know the most recent text message was sent to him at 8:30 the night he was murdered and was just two words, 'half-hour.' Tech said it came from a burner phone, so there's no number available. There's just about a hundred percent chance the burner phone is at the bottom of the Liffey."

Bell nodded and took a sip of his Guinness. "Well, I interviewed him. I can send you a copy of the transcripts. It's basically me asking questions and your man Donnelly not replying. After about fifteen minutes, I packed it up. He was released later that day, and well, you know the rest. He was a no-show."

"Did you get a sense of him?"

Bell chuckled as he shook his head. "Oh yeah, he was smarter than you and me put together. Just ask him. Very high opinion of himself, although looking at his lifestyle and his history, you'd never be able to understand why. He'd a juvenile record, doing the usual nonsense. He just never grew out of it. I did have the sense that he wasn't stupid. He just, I don't know. You run into these idiots from time to time. They've got the brains, but somehow the wires seemed to be crossed, and they make one bad decision after another. From the friends they keep to the life decisions they make, it's never good. At the end of the day, it's only logical they end up behind bars or, in Keegan Donnelly's case, dead."

"What about friends, acquaintances?" Dillon asked.

Bell seemed to think about that for a moment then shook his head. No one really comes to mind. There is one lad you might talk with, another knacker by the name of Fintan Murphy. Although, I haven't seen hide nor hair of him for almost two years. God forbid he might have gotten the message and copped on to the straight life. Last I knew, he was in the Liberties, not far from your man Donnelly if he was still on Reginald Square."

"He was and about to be evicted I might add, but that's where we found him."

"Last time I checked, Murphy was over on Ash Street, maybe two streets away from Donnelly. They were quite the pair at one time, but like I said, I haven't heard of Murphy for a couple of years."

"Fintan Murphy, I'll look him up," Dillon said. "Buy you another pint?"

"Oh, thanks, but I'll have to take a rain check. One's the limit and then home to the wife."

"Probably wise," Dillon said.

"Makes for a much more enjoyable evening. Let me know if I can be of any help to yous."

"Much appreciated," Dillon said. They walked out together and went in different directions.

Sixteen

Dillon headed back to the office. He stopped in the tech lab to get an update from Emily on Donnelly's cellphone. He pushed the intercom button, waited a bit, and pushed it again. He was about to push it a third time when a male voice came across, "What?"

Dillon immediately recognized Quinn O'Neal's voice and attitude. "Hi Quinn, Marshal Dillon, here to see Emily. Can you buzz me in, please?"

The door suddenly unlocked, and Dillon stepped into the lab. O'Neal was nowhere to be seen, which meant that he must have answered from his lair, around the corner. Emily gave Dillon a wave from her office and indicated she was on the phone.

Dillon headed in that direction and then stood just outside while she finished her call. "Sorry to keep you waiting," she said as she hung up and stepped out from behind her desk.

"My apologies for being such a pain, Emily. I just wondered if you'd found anything in Donnelly's text messages."

"Whoever he was communicating with on that initial text, there were four earlier messages. All about as worthless as the 'half hour' text. I printed off thirty days' worth of messages. Most appear to be strictly social, but you be the judge," she said and handed Dillon a file almost a half-inch thick. "I also printed off the list of calls, incoming and outgoing. Maybe you can get something from that."

"Did you find anything specific?"

"Unfortunately, no, nothing."

"Did that burner phone show up again?"

"Yeah, like I said, four other times prior to that final message. Nothing that immediately suggested anything untoward if that's what you're asking. Whoever that is, it's not their first dance."

"You still have the phone?"

"It's now in the possession of Mr. O'Neal. He's only had it for an hour. I would guess he might have results sometime tomorrow at the earliest. I told him it was a rush."

"What did he say to that?"

"He said, 'They're all a rush, Emily. Give me some time, and maybe I'll come up with something.' That was his good side, by the way."

"There's probably a slim to none chance. If someone other than Donnelly left their prints on that phone, I think they would have taken the thing and tossed it in the Liffey."

"You never know. Go through those text messages," Emily said and nodded at the file Dillon was holding. Give a yell if there's anything I can do."

"Thanks, appreciate your help," Dillon said and headed up to Special Branch. There were five other officers at their desks, three on the phone, two on their computers. DCI McCabe's office door was open, and the lights were on. Dillon set the file on his desk. He grabbed two dirty tea mugs from his desk, walked into the break room, and set the mugs in the sink. He debated for a moment about getting a candy bar, decided against it, and settled in at his desk.

He highlighted the 'half hour' text message with a yellow marker. The previous message, 'no contact,' was just as bland and had been sent at 10:47 p.m. on the evening of the Sheehan murders, roughly twenty-four hours earlier. That would have been no more than an hour before the CCTV footage of Donnelly refueling his car.

The message prior to that was sent at 3:07 p.m. on the afternoon of the Sheehan murders and was just one word, 'gloves.' An earlier message that same day came across at 9:37 a.m. This time just two words, 'same place.' The first message of the batch came through at 8:51 p.m. the previous evening, one word, 'tomorrow.'

One thing seemed clear. Someone was giving directions to Donnelly, telling him when to meet, where to meet, reminding him to bring gloves, instructing him after the shooting not to make contact.

The final message from the burner phone, 'half-hour,' suggested to Dillon that the individual would meet Donnelly in a half-hour. Was the meeting at Donnelly's place? What were they going to do? Get in bed with Donnelly? Pay him? Congratulate him? Whoever it was, there was a very good chance they either murdered Donnelly or brought along someone to do that particular chore. Apparently, Donnelly was comfortable with whoever it was. In fact, at some point, he pretty much undressed and climbed into bed.

More questions. Did they realize a mistake had been made, and that was why Donnelly was killed? Had that been the idea all along, to kill the killer?

Dillon went through the rest of the text messages. Nothing seemed relative to the Sheehan murders. There was a back and forth of eight text messages with someone, apparently a woman, who canceled on a dinner engagement. A text regarding a Friday night meet-up at a pub that Donnelly never responded to. There were five different offers for day jobs, including moving an office of furniture and selling banners and caps at a hurling match at Croke Park in Dublin. Three different messages offered to loan a taxi car to Donnelly on an evening. The cost for that would be a hundred euros. Did that mean Donnelly was driving a taxi? Or, was there some ulterior motive? The rest of the messages were nonsensical items that didn't appear to be of any interest.

Dillon switched to the list of phone numbers and began to input them into his computer, getting names and addresses on almost all the numbers except for the burner phone. He input the name Fintan Murphy, the individual Devin Bell had mentioned as a one-time friend of Donnelly. Dillon called the number using his cellphone and ended up leaving a message.

"This message is for Fintan Murphy. My name is Marshal Jack Dillon. I'm with An Garda Síochána, Special Branch. Fintan, if you would please, give me a call. I have some unfortunate information regarding a gentleman you once knew. I'm hoping you might be able to help us out. You are in no way under investigation or in any way connected other than hopefully providing background information. I look forward to hearing from you. Thank you."

Murphy returned the call twenty minutes later. Dillon recognized the number and answered with, "Hi Fintan, Jack Dillon, thank you for returning my call."

"What's this about?"

"I'm wondering if we could meet. I'm working a case and hoping to get some general background information on a friend of yours, maybe a former friend, Keegan Donnelly."

"Keegan?" Murphy half-laughed. "What in the hell has he done now?"

"He's been murdered." Dillon waited a long moment and then said, "Hello, Fintan? Are you there?"

"Keegan's been murdered?"

"Yes, just a few days ago. Would you be able to meet with me? I'm just trying to get any information I can on the man. I'd like to find out who may have done this."

"I wouldn't know who killed him. I haven't seen Keegan for, well, almost two years."

"I'm aware of that. I'm hoping maybe you could just help me, you know, maybe provide contacts he may have had, a woman, pals, jobs."

"Jobs? Well, he never really had a job. Always looking for the quick cash, which as you might imagine led to a good deal of trouble."

"Believe me, I get it. Anything you could tell me would help at this stage. I'll meet you anywhere you'd feel comfortable."

"I could meet you in, say, an hour. Can you get to the O'Connell Street Bridge?"

"In the city center? Yes, of course."

"Good, I'll meet you on the bridge."

"I suppose I could do that. You don't want to meet in a pub or someplace? I'll buy a round and—"

"No offense, but I'd feel more comfortable in a public place. I think the nonstop traffic on the bridge should make me feel just fine."

"Okay, you said in an hour?" Dillon asked.

"I did. Tell me what you're wearing."

Dillon looked down at himself. "I'm wearing a pair of blue jeans, a light blue button-down shirt, and…" he pulled open a desk drawer just to be sure. "And I'll have a dark-blue cap with a green shamrock and the word Ireland in white letters. What are you wearing?"

"Not to worry. I'll find you. I'll see you on the bridge," he said and disconnected.

An hour, Dillon wondered if Murphy worked in the city center or maybe lived down there. Either way, he'd better get going since he wanted to be early, and he could think about that on the way. He typed in Murphy's name on his computer, brought up a disorderly conduct booking photo from five years earlier, and studied it for thirty seconds before he headed out the door.

By the time he drove into the city center, dealt with the traffic, found a parking place, and headed toward the O'Connell Street Bridge, he only had five minutes to spare. He stepped onto the bridge, walked to roughly the middle, and stopped next to a guy sitting on the sidewalk holding a cardboard sign that read 'Homeless.' Crowded foot traffic traveling in both directions swept past as he looked around, hoping to spot a guy coming toward him. He never did spot anyone who looked like the photo he'd studied. Suddenly, a voice shouted from across four lanes of traffic, "Dillon?"

He turned and looked across the bridge. A large, red-haired guy with a beard signaled with a wave of his arm that Dillon should cross. He had to wait another minute before there was a brief opening in the traffic, and he hurried across to the median and then ran across the next two lanes and jumped up onto the pedestrian walk. Some guy driving past had to slow half a moment, and he leaned on his horn.

SEVENTEEN

The large red-haired guy was a good four or five inches taller than Dillon and looked down at him as he spoke," Dillon?"

"Yeah, you're Fintan?"

"I am."

Dillon held his hand out, and they shook. Fintan glanced around, apparently checking the crowd, and then said, "Come on. We can grab a seat at Fitzgerald's and talk there."

Fitzgerald's was a small old-style pub with a sign above the door advertising whiskeys. They waited for the light to change and then hurried across Aston Quay with twenty or thirty other people. Murphy held the door as Dillon stepped into the darkened pub. There was one couple seated at the bar. They had glasses of beer in front of them and a Dublin city map spread across the bar.

"How 'bout over there?" Murphy said and pointed to a small table in the corner.

Dillon headed over and settled into a chair. Murphy pulled out a chair across from him and sat. The chair creaked as he settled in.

"Come here often?" Dillon asked just as the bartender stepped out from behind the bar and over to their table.

He tossed two cardboard coasters onto the table and said, "What'll it be, lads?"

"A pint for me," Murphy said.

"Same," Dillon said.

The bartender left without giving a reaction.

"So Keegan was murdered?" Murphy asked.

"Yeah, two nights ago. We found him in bed, shot in the heart and in the head."

"How come I haven't heard anything about it on the news?"

"We only found him this morning."

"Where did this happen?"

"At his place. When was the last time you saw him?"

"Keegan?" Murphy shook his head. "A little over two years ago."

"And you haven't seen him since?"

"Nope. My wife. I met her three years back. She gave me a choice, her or Keegan. Told me in no uncertain terms I couldn't have both. It wasn't a tough decision. I got a decent job now. The wife is pregnant. Life is good, and honestly, if I was still running with Keegan, I'd either be dead or headed to jail. I'm sorry he's dead, but I'm not really surprised. You know who did it?"

"We've got a pretty good idea," Dillon lied.

"Well, I'm sure you've got a fairly long list. Keegan could be a nice enough lad when he wanted to, but at the end of the day, it was all about him. When my wife came into my life, I'd pretty much made the decision anyway, so it wasn't a tough choice."

The bartender arrived with two pints of Guinness. "Anything else?" he asked as he set the pints on the table.

"Fintan? I'm buying."

"The pint is just fine."

"Same with me," Dillon said. He handed a twenty euro note to the bartender and said, "Keep the change."

The bartender gave a slight nod and left.

"Who did Donnelly hang with?" Dillon asked.

"A couple three lads. Noel Barrett, Tommy Thompson, and a lad by the name of Brennan O'Rourke. That's all dated information, by the way. I haven't seen any of them in over two years. I know Barrett's been locked up in the Joy for the past ten or twelve months. I think he's currently serving a five-year sentence. Thompson and O'Rourke, I got no idea what they're up to other than it's probably no good."

"You said you got a job?"

Murphy nodded. "Yeah, I'm a tinsmith."

"Union job?"

"Yeah, and it's a good union. They take care of us. We've been busy with all the construction going on around town. I start work at 6:00 and finish at 2:30. Plenty of overtime if I want it."

"And do you want it?"

"Yeah, most days, unless somethings happening with the wife."

"Donnelly have any women in his life?"

"Oh yeah. He was always riding someone. Course they never stayed around too long, and at least the ones I knew, you wouldn't want them around. They were a right pain in the hole."

"Nice looking?"

"Yeah, usually. Once in a while, he'd get desperate and lower his standards, but don't we all?"

Dillon nodded. "Can you remember any names?"

"Names? Of the women? Yeah, let's see Mary Cassidy. I think she still tends bar at the Palace. There was one who was a stripper, can't remember what…Oh, yeah, Katie Leary. She was a piece of work. Last I heard, she was stripping at the Barclay, but again, that was a couple years ago. I did hear Keegan had taken up with an older gal, don't know her name. Late thirties, maybe even forty. I'm sure she was little more than a one-night stand."

"Were you ever in his place in the Liberties?"

Murphy took a large sip of Guinness and nodded. "You mean that dump on Reginald Square? I was there a couple of times. The place was a shit show. Christ almighty, you'd want to get a shot once you got out of there. A real dive. I remember one time he must have had ten or twelve empty pizza boxes stacked next to his ratty couch. He'd lay around on that damn couch all day, drinking and watching TV. The place reeked. I wanted to burn my clothes when I got out of there."

"He ever use a computer?"

"Keegan? Hell yes, he'd watch a ton of porn. A couple of times, he'd go on there and get some slapper to come over for a ride. Give her a hundred euros. He always bragged how he had a stable of women just begging to come over, but everyone knew he had to pay them, and I'm sure they ran out of the place as soon as they could."

"Any idea who he was dating lately?"

Murphy drained his glass and then shook his head. "No, like I said, I literally haven't seen or talked to him in over two years. If I knew something, I'd tell yous. I don't owe him anything, and we didn't part on the best of grounds. He'd dissed the wife and then denied it, but I knew he was lying. Big surprise."

"You want another pint?"

"Thanks, but I should probably head home."

"You mind if I give you a call if a question comes up?"

"I guess that would be okay. Call me any time after 3:00. If I'm working overtime, I won't answer, and you can just leave a message. I'd appreciate it if you didn't mention my name to anyone. I don't know who, but there's bound to be some pissed-off lads when the word gets out he was murdered."

"Probably tonight's news," Dillon said.

"Like I told you, it's not really a surprise. Keegan's been headed toward this for ten years at least. Actually, longer, hell, his whole life."

"Thanks for filling me in. Sorry it's under these circumstances. When's the baby due?" Dillon asked as they both stood.

"Nine weeks," Murphy said.

"Healthy mom, healthy baby, that's all you want."

Murphy nodded and held out his hand. They shook. Murphy headed out the door, and Dillon headed to the restroom.

EIGHTEEN

Back at the office, Dillon logged onto his computer and looked up the addresses of the three men Murphy had mentioned, Noel Barrett, Tommy Thompson, and Brennan O'Rourke. He wrote down their addresses and then brought up the files on all three men. Murphy's assessment was basically correct, juvenile offenders who had graduated into being adult offenders. All three individuals had been arrested a number of times. They had all served time and, apparently, hadn't learned anything other than to continue to break the law and get caught. Noel Barrett, currently serving time in Mountjoy Prison, was arrested for felony assault with a firearm and sentenced to five years.

Suel entered Special Branch. He dropped three or four files on his desk and walked over to Dillon. "You coming up with anything?"

"Not really. I met with a former friend of Donnelly's. He hadn't seen Donnelly in two years, so any information was dated. He did mention that Donnelly spent a lot of time lying around on the couch, watching TV, and checking out porn on his computer. Be nice to know who took the computer and the TV and why. You learn any-thing?"

Suel shook his head. "Not really. I pulled a couple of files on people, but I'm not expecting much."

Dillon glanced at his computer screen. "Do the names Tommy Thompson or Brennan O'Rourke ring a bell?"

"Thompson is one of the files I pulled. How'd you come up with him?"

"The guy I met with mentioned those two along with another idiot currently doing time at the Joy, fella named Noel Barrett."

"Not familiar with him."

"He's served a year on a five-year sentence. Felony assault with a pistol."

"So we can cross him off the list. You got addresses on the other two?" Suel asked.

"Thompson and O'Rourke? Yeah, just wrote them down," Dillon said and handed his note tablet to Suel.

"Mmm, this O'Rourke knacker. I think that address is the Ballymun Apartments. Not too far from your place."

"Yeah, I've been past it a million times," Dillon said.

"How 'bout I follow you over? We knock on your man's door and see if he's home."

"Yeah, I can do that. I've got the feeling we're grasp-ing at straws. It would be nice to finally get something, anything."

"Give me half a minute to clear things," Suel said and hurried back to his desk. Dillon logged off his computer, locked the desk drawers, and walked over to Suel's desk just as he was locking up. They took the elevator down to the first floor and headed out to the parking lot.

"I'll follow you. Wait for me by the entrance," Suel said as Dillon climbed into his car.

With people heading home from work, the drive took the better part of thirty minutes. After stopping at literally every traffic light, Dillon eventually made it to Ballymun Road and headed up toward the apartments. He passed the Eurospar at the corner of Ballymun and St Papin's Road that led to his place. He pulled into a parking place a mile further up the road. Suel pulled in a half-dozen spots past Dillon. They waited for a break in the traffic and hurried across Ballymun Road.

Ballymun had gone through a major renovation in the early 2000s. It had been populated by thirty-six separate housing blocks between four and fifteen stories tall all built in the 1960s. At no surprise, the area suffered from a combination of drugs and crime, and the last of the housing blocks were torn down in 2015. A perfect example of well-meaning thoughts that never really worked. The housing blocks were replaced with four and five-story modern-looking structures that would hopefully serve a better purpose. The jury was still out. Right next door to the Ballymun apartments was the Ballymun Garda Station.

"You think we should pay a visit to the station?" Dillon asked.

"First, let's see if your man is even home," Suel said. They walked across the paved plaza and into the apartment building. The entry was a small room with a digital phone attached to the wall and directions on how to contact an apartment unit. Just as they approached, three young girls, seventeen or eighteen, hurried out the security door.

Each girl was texting on her cellphone and too busy to glance over at Dillon or Suel. Dillon grabbed hold of the door before it closed and watched as the girls exited the building.

"So much for security," Suel said as they stepped in through the security door. They took the elevator up to the third floor and then walked down the hall to apartment 317.

Dillon knocked on the door and then placed his finger over the peephole. The door opened about five seconds later.

"It's about fecking time. Where in the hell have you—Who the hell are you lot?"

O'Rourke stood a couple of inches shorter than Dillon. His hair was dark, curly, and hung an inch or two above his shoulders. He had a full beard and deep blue eyes.

"DI Suel and Marshal Dillon. We're with An Garda Síochána, and you're just the lad we're looking for, Brennan O'Rourke."

"I ain't done nothing wrong."

"I sincerely doubt that, Mr. O'Rourke. Thank you for inviting us in," Suel said as he stepped past O'Rourke and into the unit. Dillon followed.

"I'm not telling you lot anything. I want my solicitor."

"We talked with him," Suel said. "He told us he would be busy tonight, and we should just chat. That's what we intend to do. Just talk a bit."

O'Rourke got a funny look on his face and said, "Talk about what?"

"Your good friend, Mr. Keegan Donnelly."

"I don't know where Keegan is, honest. Besides, even if I did, I wouldn't be telling the likes of you two."

"Oh, not a problem. As a matter of fact, we know where Keegan is. I suppose you could pay him a visit if you wanted. He's enjoying a quiet evening over on Griffith Avenue in the Dublin City Morgue. You see, someone blew his brains out two nights ago."

"Ahh, here now, you're taking the piss, aren't you?"

Suel shook his head. "God's honest truth. As a matter of fact, give this a look," he said and pulled out his cellphone. He swiped his finger across the screen and brought up an image of Keegan Donnelly in his bed. The bullet hole in his chest was plainly visible, and there was no way you could miss the blood and bits of matter splattered across the wall.

O'Rourke stood with his mouth open and slowly began to shake his head. "What? What happened? Oh my God."

"It's pretty obvious what happened. Someone got fed up with your man and blew his brains out."

"Did you arrest the bastard?"

Suel flashed a quick smile and said, "Hard to believe, but they didn't wait around for our arrival. We'd like to find out who did this."

O'Rourke shook his head. "I honestly don't know. When did this happen? I talked to him on the weekend. We were going to meet up for a pint, but he never showed."

"This happened a couple of nights ago. We found him this morning. I asked him a couple of questions, but he refused to give me an answer," Suel said.

"You're messing with me, now."

Suel nodded. "Yeah, I am. But let me give you a warning. Whoever did this isn't fooling around. They intended to kill your man, and as you can see, they did. We'd just like to stop them before they do it again. Any assistance you could give us in getting whoever is responsible would help."

O'Rourke shook his head. "Honest now. I've no idea. I don't know what he was doing. He told me he had a job but never said anything about where or who with."

"He mention any names? Someone he'd been with recently?"

"No, honest. We only talked for a couple of minutes, and he had to go. Never mentioned where he was going, and I didn't think to ask, you know."

Suel pulled out a business card and handed it to O'Rourke. "You hear anything, I'd appreciate a call. Whoever did this, they aren't fooling around, and I'd be surprised if they're finished. You think someone is following you or asking about you, let us know before you end up like your man Donnelly."

O'Rourke took the business card and nodded. "I hear anything I'll let yous know," he said and sounded serious.

"See that you do, Brennan. For your own good," Suel said. He nodded at Dillon, and they stepped out into the hallway. They didn't speak until they were back on the elevator.

"Short and sweet," Dillon said.

"Your man was in shock," Suel said. "I doubt he knows anything. Hopefully, we put the fear of God in him, and he'll be looking over his shoulder if he goes anywhere."

"There has to be someone, somewhere, who knows who or what Donnelly was involved in."

"I can only hope you're right. We sure as hell haven't found them so far."

"Donnelly's murder will be on the evening news. Maybe that will spur someone to give us a call," Dillon said as the elevator came to a stop on the ground floor and the doors opened.

"Like you said before, grasping at straws. You up for a pint?"

"You know, thanks, but I think I'll take a pass. I need to get home and take Lucifer out for a walk and just sit and think. Something somewhere has to click."

"I'll see you in the morning then. You come up with something, give me a call."

"Don't hold your breath," Dillon said and headed for his car.

NINETEEN

Dillon pulled into the parking space in his front garden and climbed out of his car. Lucifer met him at the door. As Dillon stepped aside, Lucifer hurried out of the house and squatted next to the driver's door. He stared at Dillon as he did his business.

Dillon stepped inside but left the door open. He walked into the kitchen, surveyed the knocked-over wastebasket and the wrappers and food scraps scattered across the floor. It was as bad as he expected, but he swept up everything in a matter of minutes. He grabbed a biscuit from the cookie jar and tossed it out the front door to Lucifer. He went upstairs, slipped on a pair of running shoes, and came back downstairs. He grabbed the leash, locked the door behind him, clipped the leash onto Lucifer, and they headed out on their walk.

They took the long route along Dean Swift Road and then crossed Ballymun Road and walked into Albert Park. They were just early enough to miss the after-dinner crowd of walkers, and they walked around the park three times. Once that was accomplished, Dillon led them across one of the playing fields, and they settled onto a park bench in the evening sun. Lucifer hopped up onto the bench and settled next to Dillon with his head resting on Dillon's thigh.

Dillon scratched him behind the ears and started thinking about the Sheehan and Donnelly murders. After twenty minutes, he pulled out his notebook and wrote a couple of reminders. He wanted to compare the rounds that killed the Sheehan's with the rounds that killed Donnelly. Next, he wanted to find out where, exactly, Dennis Punchy Sheehan was. Finally, he planned to spend tomorrow morning reviewing the phone numbers Emily had found on Keegan Donnelly's phone. Somewhere on that list, there had to be a link.

When Dillon stood, Lucifer hopped off the bench, stretched, and they headed home. Dillon warmed a frozen dinner in the microwave and settled in on the couch to watch the news. The story of Keegan Donnelly's murder didn't lead the news, and once it finally ran, the report couldn't have been more than ninety seconds long. At least they mentioned him by name and that he lived in the Liberties. Hopefully, that was enough to get the news out and maybe generate someone calling in, although Dillon had been praying for more.

Apparently, he dozed off because his cellphone ringing woke him up. He glanced at it, Paddy Suel. "Please tell me someone has confessed, and they're locked up as we speak," Dillon said.

"I could tell you that, but it would be a lie," Suel said. "Did you catch the news?"

"I did. I wish it had been a little longer report. I wish they would have shown a picture of Donnelly or mentioned that his murder happened down in the Liberties, but at least the news is out there."

"I think we should pay an early morning visit to Tommy Thompson. There's a good chance O'Rourke phoned him or, God forbid, Thompson actually watched the news. It might be a good idea to roust him early. Hopefully, he'll be hungover, and we may just learn something."

"It can't hurt. I'm trying to think, was his address in Finglas?" Dillon asked.

"Cabra, actually. Not far from the Cabra Club. Do you have it?"

"Yeah, written down on my notepad. You want to meet there?"

"Yes. You up for half-past six?"

"I can do that," Dillon said.

"I'll see you there. Half-past six, don't be late," Suel said and disconnected.

Dillon let Lucifer out the front door, then set the coffee pot for two cups. He let Lucifer back in, and they headed upstairs to bed. He woke just before his alarm went off the following morning. He showered, shaved, dressed, and then woke Lucifer and coaxed him downstairs and out the front door with a biscuit. He poured a coffee, put two pieces of bread in the toaster, and thought about questioning Tommy Thompson.

He slathered the toast with blackberry jam, finished both pieces in about thirty seconds, and headed out the door. It was a sunny morning, and at the moment, there was a cloudless sky. At this hour of the early morning, it was barely a ten-minute drive to Tommy Thompson's house in the Cabra section of Dublin.

Thompson's house was a narrow, two-story attached unit on Killala Road, just around the corner from the Cabra Club. The house was a faded beige stucco, and the peeling brown paint on the front door and the windows of the unit looked original. One of the panes of glass in the front window had apparently been broken and was now covered with a piece of cardboard.

Suel's car was nowhere to be seen, so Dillon pulled to the curb at the corner and waited then waited some more. After fifteen minutes, he phoned Suel and was dumped into voicemail. Suel appeared two minutes later, speeding down the street toward him.

He pulled alongside Dillon's car and lowered his window. "Sorry I'm late. My bleedin' alarm never went off."

"And I'm the one you told not to be late. That's Thompson's place with the antique front window and the worn brown door. I checked yesterday and couldn't find a record of a car registered to him, so I'm thinking we ring the doorbell and pray that he's home."

Suel nodded and said, "Park in front of the gate. I'll turn around and park facing you. That way, if your man attempts to take off, no matter which direction he takes, one of us can run him down." With that, Suel backed up and pulled onto the sidewalk in front of Thompson's house. Dillon pulled up onto the sidewalk facing Suel's car.

They walked through the open rusted gate. The small patch of front lawn was nothing more than weeds. "This dump could use some work," Suel said as they stepped onto the front stoop.

Dillon gave Suel a quick look, then pressed his finger on the doorbell and held it for a good fifteen seconds. They could hear it buzzing inside, sounding like a power saw. Dillon removed his finger then pounded on the door a half-dozen times. He waited a brief moment and then held the doorbell for another fifteen seconds. He was about to repeat the process for the third time when the door opened, and a bleary-eyed man of average height stood in the doorway. He cleared his throat twice and said, "What do you lot want?"

He was wearing black socks, a wrinkled shirt with what looked like a wine stain down the front, and jeans with the belt undone.

"Thomas Thompson?" Suel asked in a deep voice.

Thompson nodded and attempted to focus.

"DI Suel and Marshal Dillon with An Garda Sío-chána. We'd like to talk with you for a bit."

Thompson blinked a couple of times, cleared his throat once more. "Talk to me? What about?"

"If you'd invite us in, we could explain. You aren't under any suspicion, at least at the moment," Suel said.

"We simply wanted to give you some information regarding your friend, Keegan Donnelly."

"Keegan? Oh God, I got the phone call last night. Umm, yeah, sure, come on in. You want something to drink?" Thompson asked as he staggered into the small sitting room. He settled onto a worn leather couch with a stained pillow at one end. Two empty wine bottles had rolled partway beneath the couch. There were paper napkins and two empty wine glasses on the coffee table. One of the wine glasses had lipstick on it. Thompson picked up a glass with what looked like a hint of whiskey in it and drained the glass.

"Sure I can't get yous something? Terrible fecking news," he said. He reached along the far side of the couch and pulled up a bottle of Paddy's Irish whiskey. He poured what was left in the bottle into a glass and took a hearty sip.

"Yeah, it's sad, tragic, actually. Keegan Donnelly didn't deserve that," Suel said. "Can you help us? We're trying to find out who might have been involved."

Thompson attempted to refocus on the coffee table and shook his head. "I can't think of anyone. We got along, never had any problems. I was gonna meet up with him last week but he'd a date with a woman. Said he had the feeling it was gonna lead to something good, so I can't blame him for canceling."

"Who was the woman? You remember her name?"

Thompson seemed to think about that for a very long moment.

Eventually, Suel said, "Tommy, the woman's name?"

"I'm not sure he ever told me." His eyes closed to half-mast, and Dillon nodded toward the door.

"We'll leave you to it, Tommy. You think of anything, give us a call," Suel said and tossed a business card on the table.

Thompson gave a slight nod and looked like he was about to drop his glass. Dillon reached over, took the glass, and placed it on the coffee table. Thompson remained in the same position, more or less passed out sitting on the couch.

Suel was up, heading for the door. Dillon reached over, grabbed a paper napkin, picked up the wineglass with the lipstick, and followed Suel out the door.

"You need another wineglass?" Suel asked.

"Thought I might have forensics look for fingerprints. See if a name comes up."

"It will be a woman," Suel said.

"Given the lipstick, I would hope so. I'd like to talk with her. Maybe Thompson was a little more lucid when she was there, and he said something. You heading to the office?"

Suel nodded and said, "Yeah, I've got to stop and get some petrol, but then I'll be in."

"See you back there," Dillon said. As Suel left, Dillon opened the trunk of his car and pulled out a plastic evidence bag. He placed the wineglass in the evidence bag, sealed the bag, and then laid it on the floor of the passenger seat.

TWENTY

D illon parked in the lot behind the headquarters station and headed in the rear door. He punched in the entry code on the keypad, stepped inside, and walked down the hall to the forensics lab. He pushed the intercom button next to the forensics door. A moment later, a voice said, "Can I help you?"

"Hi, Marshal Dillon with Special Branch. Is Niall Reid available?"

"Just a moment, and I'll check."

Half a minute later, Reids voice came across the intercom. "Dillon, you there?"

"Hi, Niall. Yeah, I've got a wineglass I'd like to have checked for fingerprints. Can you help me?"

"Come on in," Reid said, and there was a loud buzz, signaling the door was unlocked.

Dillon stepped inside the forensics department just as Reid stepped out of his office. "Hi, Niall," Dillon called.

"Someone run off without paying their half of the tab?" Reid asked.

"Actually, no." Dillon went on to tell him about the early morning visit to Tommy Thompson. "My guess is he commiserated with some woman last night. She didn't appear to be in his house, but we never checked the upstairs. I would guess at some point Thompson passed out, and she fled the scene. We woke him up before 7:00 this morning, and he was back to finishing off the bottle of whiskey within a minute or two. Even if we talk to him when he's finally sober, there's a good chance he won't remember much of anything."

Reid took the plastic evidence bag from Dillon and glanced at it. He pulled a pen from his lab coat and said, "This is the Keegan Donnelly murder?"

"Yeah, I got the glass this morning from the home of Tommy Thompson. Hang on just a moment," Dillon said and pulled out his pocket notebook. "His address is in Cabra on Killala Road." As he spoke, Reid wrote the information along the top of the evidence bag.

"I suppose you want the results yesterday."

"Or sooner if you can get it," Dillon said.

"I'll give you a call this afternoon. Do not, upon penalty of death, tell anyone that I'm rushing this for you."

Dillon held up a hand and said, "Scouts honor. Thanks, Niall, much appreciated."

"Thank you in advance for the dinner you're buying at the Autobahn one of these next evenings."

"It's a deal," Dillon said. He headed out of Forensics and up to Special Branch. Apparently, Suel was still out. Dillon grabbed his coffee mug, collected three plates from his desk, one of which had a half-eaten piece of toast on it. He carried them into the break room, dumped the toast in the trash, stacked the plates in the sink, and filled his coffee mug.

He didn't sip the coffee until he was back at his desk. He grimaced at the harsh taste and took another sip. He turned on his computer and brought up the file of phone numbers Emily in the Tech lab had listed from Keegan Donnelly's phone. Dillon proceeded to run the phone numbers through a site that provided both a name and an address. When he finished, he had almost fifty names, six of which were retail outlets that he immediately deleted. He placed a call to Hugh Healy in the Medical Examiner's office.

Healy answered on the third ring. "This is Healy."

"Hi, Hugh, Jack Dillon up in Special Branch."

"Dillon, let me guess. You want the update on your man Keegan Donnelly."

"Well, yeah, I guess, I mean if you have it, but that's not the reason I'm calling."

"Oh?"

"We're looking at Donnelly for the murders of an American couple down in—"

"The double homicide down in Bandon. I'm blanking on the name of the half-parish."

"Desertserges," Dillon said.

"Yes, and the couple was Dennis and Maureen Sheehan?"

"Yeah, right. What I'm hoping is you can arrange a comparison on the rounds recovered in that case to the rounds used in the murder of Keegan Donnelly."

"You're thinking there's a connection?"

"Yes, I am."

"Let me make a call down to Bandon and have them email those files up."

"That would be great, Hugh. If you can give me a couple of minutes, I'll call down there and ask the officer in charge of the Bandon investigation to get the ball rolling. Just in case someone thinks they can drag their feet."

"Let me know once you talk to them," Healy said. "Leave a message if I don't answer. I'll be cutting someone up shortly."

"Enjoy yourself," Dillon said and hung up. He phoned Jamie McCormick's cellphone.

"Dillon?" was how McCormick answered.

"Hi, Jamie. Hey, we're working Donnelly's murder up here. I'm thinking it might be tied to the Sheehan killings in Desertserges. I was hoping—"

"Your man Donnelly refueling on the CCTV footage?"

"Yeah, would you mind giving Mick Flanagan a call? Our man up here in forensics is going to call him and ask for the files to be emailed up here. We're thinking there's a chance the rounds in the Sheehan killings might match Donnelly's."

"Be happy to call. You have anything that looks like a lead in that case?"

"Unfortunately, no. We've got even less than you have in the Sheehan murders. At least on that, we have the CCTV footage on Donnelly. Whoever killed Donnelly apparently stayed around long enough to clean the site. Your man was a typical slob, yet all the clothes were picked up, no dirty laundry. Hell, they even cleaned under the bed and washed dishes. I'd like to find them and invite them over to clean my place before I arrest them."

McCormick laughed at that and said, "I'll call Flanagan as soon as I'm off the line with you. Everything else going okay?"

"Everything's fine if you ignore the brick wall we've run into as far as suspects go."

"Anything pops up, please let me know. We're facing a similar situation," McCormick said.

Dillon disconnected, then called Hugh Healy back and told him McCormick was going to phone Flanagan. "Maybe give him a few minutes to make the call. Keep me posted if you find anything."

"Will do, Dillon. My schedule is pretty open. Let me know when you can fit in dinner at the Autobahn."

As Dillon disconnected, Suel entered the office. He grabbed a mug from his desk and headed for the break room, stopping at Dillon's desk along the way.

"Anything?" Suel asked.

Dillon told him about the calls to Healy and to McCormick down in Bandon. "I've got a list of names and phone numbers from Donnelly's phone. I'm going to start calling them in a moment. You interested in contacting two dozen folks?"

"At this stage, do we have anything else to go on?"

Dillon shook his head. "Afraid not."

"Let me grab a tea, and I'll get started."

"I'll email you a list. Willing to talk to anyone who gives the slightest indication they may have a morsel of information."

Dillon began calling the twenty-four names on his portion of the list. He was dumped into voicemail on nine numbers. Two people hung up on him. Ten people spoke with him, six of whom were unaware of Donnelly's murder. One claimed to have not seen Donnelly in the last month. One said Donnelly owed him money and asked who he should call to be paid. And then there was a woman named Amelia Maher.

TWENTY-ONE

Dillon said, "I'd like to speak with Amelia Maher."

"Yes. Who's calling, please?"

"My name is Jack Dillon. I'm with An Garda Síochána." There was a long pause. Dillon blinked first and said, "Is this Amelia?"

"This is about poor Keegan, isn't it? It's so sad. He was such a smart lad who just continued to make bad choices. I've lost count of the times I told him to never contact me again, only to answer his phone call a week or two later. We'd known one another since we were children. I just could never understand why he did the things he did. Tragic. Absolutely tragic."

"I wonder if we might meet up, Miss Maher. I—"

"Please, call me Amelia. Yes, I'd love to meet with you. I'll do anything I can to help you find whoever did this dastardly act. I want to see them arrested and jailed."

"Okay, umm, Amelia. I can meet at a time and place of your choosing. Any information you would be able to provide would help in our investigation."

"Well, I'm self-employed. Would you happen to be free for lunch today?"

"Why, yes, I'd be happy to meet you for lunch. You tell me where, and I'll be there," Dillon said.

"I have an appointment with a client in the city center this afternoon. Are you familiar with the Chapter One restaurant in Parnell Square?"

"Yes, I know where that is," Dillon said, knowing where it was but never having been in the place. It was one of the top restaurants in the city and Dillon always felt it was one of those expensive high-class places that he simply wouldn't enjoy.

"Shall we say half-past twelve?" she said. "They open at that time, and I would love to provide any information I can."

"That will work. I look forward to meeting you."

"Wonderful, I'll call and reserve a table in my name."

"Are you sure? I could call and—"

"No, that's very kind of you, but I insist. It's the very least I can do to help in your investigation. I look forward to meeting you…Detective Dillon."

Dillon saw no point in correcting her and said, "Thank you. I'll see you at half-past twelve, Miss Maher."

"Please, it's Amelia. See you soon," she said and disconnected.

Dillon typed her name into his computer and came up with an ID photo. She was attractive, blonde, and he thought, if nothing else it would be a nice lunch.

"What are you grinning about?" Suel asked, suddenly standing in front of Dillon's desk.

"Oh, nothing. I've been working my way through this list of names. Voicemail, two buttheads hung up on me, no one seems to have seen Donnelly in over a month, and now I'm just off the phone with a woman who would like to tell me everything she can to help catch whoever shot him."

"Does she actually know anything?"

"I'll find out in a bit. I'm meeting her for lunch. She did say Donnelly was smart, but he continued to make bad choices."

"Where are you meeting?"

"Some cafe in the city center," Dillon lied.

"Let's hope you learn something," Suel said and headed for the break room. Dillon spent the next hour searching online for any current information on Dennis Punchy Sheehan. He wasn't finding much, so he placed a call to Eric Bergman in the American Embassy.

"American Embassy," a man's voice answered.

"Hi, this is US Marshal Jack Dillon calling for Eric Bergman."

"Please hold, sir." A moment later, he was back on the line. "I'll connect you now, sir."

"Hey, Marshal, how's it going?" was how Bergman answered his phone after one ring.

"Things seem to be heading right down the proverbial toilet," Dillon said. "We're working on a murder, actually three murders. Two down in the Bandon area and one up here."

"That wouldn't be the Donnelly killing I heard on the news last night, would it?"

"Yeah, that's the one. The two down in Bandon were a case of mistaken identity. A couple named Sheehan mistaken for Dennis Punchy Sheehan."

"Husband and wife, right?"

"Yeah, which leads me to my call to you."

"Oh?"

"Can you get me an up-to-date track on Punchy Sheehan? I'm guessing he's still back in the States, but I don't know that for sure. From the little I know of him, the killings down in Bandon would put a hold on any planned trip to the Emerald Isle he may have had. We had word he was due a few days ago, but as far as we could determine, he never arrived. Anything you could find would help. We're really grasping at straws at the moment."

"I'll check to see what I can find out. Have you con-tacted your pals back in the States?"

"That's my next call. I called you first because I know how anxious you always are to help."

Bergman laughed at that. "Let me see what I can find out. I'll try to get back to you today, but no promises."

"Thanks, Eric. Anything would help at this stage."

"Later," Bergman said and hung up.

Dillon looked at the time on his computer screen, ten minutes before noon. He turned off the computer and went down to his car. Twenty-five minutes later, he was parking on Blessington Street, three blocks from the Chapter One restaurant. With fifteen minutes to spare, he didn't feel the need to hurry and took a leisurely walk to the restaurant.

The Chapter One restaurant is one of the very top restaurants in Dublin. It's located in Dublin's city center, in an area called Parnell Square. The four-story brick building overlooks the Garden of Remembrance, but since the Chapter One restaurant was located on the lower level, it didn't really overlook anything. Dillon took the stairs down to the lower level just as the entrance door was unlocked, and three couples who had been waiting entered the restaurant. Dillon followed and waited while the couples ahead of him gave their names and were seated. Dillon eventually stepped up to the maître d' counter.

"Reservation?" the maître d' asked. He wore a gray suit with a white shirt and a dark-gray tie.

"Yes, the name is Maher, Amelia Maher."

He looked at a list of a half-dozen names, nodded, and said, "If you would follow me, please." He led Dillon into the dining room. The walls were brick, the tablecloths were white linen, the oil paintings had gilt frames, and the windows looked out onto the small patio and the set of steps Dillon had walked down just minutes before. The maître d' placed two menus on the table. He pulled out a dark-brown leather upholstered chair, and

Dillon sat down. "A waiter will be with you in just a moment."

Dillon nodded and picked up the menu. He glanced out the window just as a red-headed woman came down the steps and headed for the restaurant door. He was pretty sure it was Amelia Maher, although her hair appeared shorter than the image he'd seen online, and it was red. Two minutes later, she was escorted in by the maître d', who told her not once but three times that she looked lovely.

Amelia extended her hand to Dillon, smiled, and said, "How very nice to meet you, Detective Dillon."

Dillon took hold of her hand, and her eyes seemed to flare excitedly for just a second. "Thank you for making the time to meet me and for choosing this charming location."

The maître d' pulled the chair out for her, scowled at Dillon, and hurried out of the dining room.

TWENTY-TWO

They chatted about everything and nothing for five minutes. Maher ordered a glass of white wine with her salmon entrée, and Dillon ordered coffee and the organic black chicken. Once their order was taken, Dillon turned to business.

"You mentioned on the phone that you thought of Keegan Donnelly as smart yet making bad decisions."

"Oh, and here I was hoping we might put him aside. I must say, I'm enjoying your company, Detective."

"And I yours, but Donnelly is the reason we're here."

"At least initially," she said and smiled.

Dillon liked that.

"So, Keegan Donnelly. Where to begin," she said. "He could be quite charming, if he felt like it or wanted to share a bed. I meant what I said on the phone. He is, or rather was, very intelligent. But that said, he never seemed to put his intelligence to good use. He never seemed to work hard at the things that mattered, education, a job, even relationships. He had the reputation of being a lazy lout, and unfortunately, I would have to agree and say that he definitely earned that reputation."

"You said he made bad decisions," Dillon said just as the server returned with Amelia's wine and Dillon's coffee.

"Yes, he does, or well now I guess I should say, he did. Everyone makes a mistake from time to time, and hopefully, we learn from the mistake and move on. Keegan kept making the same basic bad decisions and never seemed to learn anything. There's no good way to put it. He wanted to run with the criminal crowd and then was amazed when the Gardaí would arrest him. In case you haven't checked, his arrests seemed to happen on a fairly regular basis."

"And yet he still continued," Dillon said.

"Not only did he continue, but he wore the arrests like some sort of badge of honor. You'd think, at some point, he'd catch on, but he never seemed to do that. I think he figured it added to his reputation as a criminal mastermind or something. I have to believe that anyone involved in that sort of lifestyle would attempt to keep him at a distance and avoid the whole guilt by association thing. If you were a career criminal, wouldn't you want to keep a low profile? You wouldn't want to be with someone the Gardaí arrested on a regular basis. You certainly wouldn't want Keegan Donnelly listing you as a friend."

"Did he ever tell you about the things he was involved in?"

She shook her head. "He did at first. This was years ago. We were adolescents, and he was literally bragging about being arrested for stealing someone's car. Can you imagine? I told him I didn't want to hear about it. I said what he should do is contact whoever owned the vehicle and apologize."

"Did he do that?"

"Heavens no. Their home was burglarized shortly after Keegan's arrest. He never admitted to doing it, but I know he did. We drifted apart for a few years. I went to university. Keegan wasted his time. Life was always up and down for him. If he had money, he'd spend it foolishly until it was gone, and he'd end up on the street again. He dated a lot of different girls. I mean, let's be honest. He was good-looking and smart, and you'd think you could maybe fix him, you know, get him on the right path. But after a few weeks, maybe a month or two, if you had any sense, you'd give up. Some friend or girlfriend would take him in until they couldn't stand it any longer, and they'd kick him out. These last two or three years, he became more isolated. Frankly, I think he'd finally just burned all his bridges, and everyone had had enough."

"But you still kept in touch."

"Occasionally. I would meet him for lunch or maybe breakfast. By the way, I'd always end up paying. I didn't like to meet him in the evening because he'd want to go to some dreadful pub that was full of the worst lot you could imagine. He'd spend the evening drinking too much and trying to show off."

"But you kept seeing him?"

"Don't make it sound like a romance. It wasn't in any way, shape, or form. I told you he kept making mistakes and bad choices. I told him more than once I didn't want to hear from him. He'd contact me two or three months later. My bad choice was staying in touch and thinking, hoping, praying, he would finally straighten out. You know how well that worked."

"Did he tell you much about his criminal friends?"

"He tried for a while, a long while, actually. But I wasn't having any of it. Eventually, even Keegan caught on and knew if he went down that road, I was not going to sit and listen to that nonsense."

"Do the names Tommy Thompson, Brennan O'Rourke, or Noel Barrett ring a bell?"

She seemed to think for a moment then shook her head and said, "No, I'm sorry, but they don't. Should they?"

"Just friends or maybe sometime acquaintances of Donnelly's."

"I made it a point some time ago not to associate with any of Keegan's so-called friends. No good could ever come from it."

"What is it that you do, Amelia?"

"Oh, I'm self-employed. I have a small marketing firm, Maher Marketing Group. Basically, just me. I do digital projects for small to medium companies."

"And is it working?" Dillon asked.

"It must be. I've been doing it for twelve years, and I'm still here," she said and laughed.

The server arrived with their meals, and the conversation switched to travel and more pleasant undertakings than Keegan Donnelly. Dillon found it interesting that Amelia Maher never asked if they were making any progress on determining who killed Keegan. Based on what she said, she apparently traveled outside Ireland quite a bit. She'd done business in Spain, Italy, France, Thailand, and Australia. She was fluent in French, Spanish, Irish, and obviously English. She casually mentioned that she wasn't seeing anyone in particular, and Dillon made a mental note of that.

The server arrived to clear the dishes and asked if they would like to look at the dessert menu. "Amelia?" Dillon asked.

"Thank you, but no. Besides, I've got a meeting in a bit and I should let you escape my ramblings."

"On the contrary, this has been most enjoyable for me. It's been very nice meeting you."

"The pleasure was all mine. Thank you so much for listening to me rant. It's just the logical end to a most unfortunate life. Keegan had such potential, and he never did a thing with it. Listen, if I can be of any help, please don't hesitate to call," she said. She reached into her handbag and pulled out a business card. "Would love to get together sometime for a social evening," she said, raising her eyebrows for a brief moment.

"Thank you. I'd find that very enjoyable. Feel free to call me anytime, and if it's social, I promise not to discuss Keegan Donnelly, well, unless you want to," Dillon said and then stood and pulled her chair back as she stood.

"Thank you again. It was very nice to meet you. I hope this won't be the last time," she said and extended her hand.

As Dillon took hold of her hand, she drew him closer and kissed him on the cheek, lingering a second or two longer than necessary. "Thank you again. I hope to hear from you," she said, then turned and strutted out of the room.

Dillon noticed two men at another table watching her exit. He sat down and watched her through the window as she climbed the stairs. He paid the bill, finished his coffee, and walked back to his car. There was a parking ticket on the window.

TWENTY-THREE

illon was back in the office forty minutes later and headed up to Special Branch. Suel was on the phone, and as Dillon walked past his desk, Suel snapped his fingers. Dillon turned as Suel held up a finger, signaling he'd be finished in a moment.

"Yes. Yes. Well, thank you for your time. Should anything come to mind, please call," Suel said and hung up. He glanced at Dillon, shook his head, and said, "Please tell me you came up with something."

"Afraid not. Amelia Maher basically said Donnelly was smart but kept making bad choices, and she would tell him not to contact her. Told him more than once. From the picture she painted, he was your poster child for a loser continuing to screw up, always getting caught, and never learning from his mistakes."

"So how does he go from that to murdering two people? Which causes someone to feel it was necessary to eliminate him?" Suel asked.

"Think about it. He goes down to Cork to prove how good he is. The thing is wrong right from the start, and whoever set it up eliminates Donnelly. I'm wondering if he was chosen with that end in mind. They planned to kill him right from the start. What they didn't plan on is the fact that it wasn't Punchy Sheehan who Donnelly shot."

"Beyond incredible," Suel said and shook his head. "I worked my way through the list of names you gave me. Everyone I talked to said Donnelly's murder wasn't surprising. The guy was a first-class screwup."

"Pretty much what Amelia Maher told me. At least I got to sit across the table from a nice-looking woman. She said she got so fed up with Donnelly that she told him on more than one occasion to stop calling her."

"But he kept calling?" Suel asked.

"Apparently. What she told me dovetails with what you just said. The guy was smart but basically just kept screwing up. He hung out with bad people and continued to make bad decisions. Not exactly a recipe for success." Dillon's phone suddenly signaled a text message.

He pulled out his cellphone. The text message, was from Hugh Healy in the medical examiner's office, read 'Call me when you've got a moment. Hugh'

"Maybe this is something. Let me make a call," Dillon said. He walked over to his desk. He ignored the dirty plate and two tea mugs that had been left there, sat down, and phoned Healy.

Healy answered on the second ring. "Dillon, that was fast. I just texted you."

"We're grasping at straws over here, Hugh. What do you have?"

"A couple of things. First, Mick Flanagan down in Bandon was kind enough to email those files on the Sheehan murders to us. There's a definite match between the rounds recovered from the Sheehan's and the rounds we removed from your man, Donnelly. The next thing is we did a work-up on Donnelly's blood. His alcohol level registered at 2.0."

"So he was basically shit-faced?"

"Mmm, yeah, you could say that. But more importantly, we've found traces of cocaine in his system. Quite possible he had been drugged or used drugs, in this case, cocaine, which would help explain the position he was found in. Namely, sitting in bed wearing a pair of boxers," Healy said.

"So you're saying someone drugged him so they could shoot him?"

"I'm saying he was drunk and drugged, possibly drugged himself, knowing exactly what he was doing. But at the same time, making it possible for someone simply to walk up to him and pull the trigger. His reaction time may have been virtually nonexistent. Think of it this way. Someone comes over, talks him into partying, and has him climb in bed. He's far enough out of it that he can't put up a fight and boom."

"Did you find anything suggesting he was gay? All our information points to him being a ladies' man or at least attempting to be one."

"He was definitely shot with the same weapon that was used down in Bandon. Maybe some woman set him up. Or, someone had a woman show up, party with him, and then let the killer in. Or maybe, he was so far gone the woman simply left, and the killer found him in some kind of comatose state. Either way, the rounds are identical to the ones from Bandon."

"Identical rounds. Well, the plot thickens. I appreciate the information, Hugh."

"Not a problem. I'll draft this report and send a copy your way."

"Much appreciated," Dillon said and disconnected. He walked back to Suel's desk and gave him the update.

"The same weapon as Bandon would suggest he wasn't alone down there, and whoever he was with is the person who killed him. I'm thinking this is beginning to sound like a setup," Dillon said.

"A setup?"

"Someone gets Donnelly involved. Donnelly thinks it's a move up the ladder. He's contacted when he returns to Dublin, probably looking for praise and a payment, but instead, whoever it is blows his brains out. He might have been killed because it wasn't Punchy. But what if the plan was to kill him all along?"

Suel shook his head. "And we still have no idea who this person is."

Dillon went back to his desk. Against his better judgment, he phoned Quinn O'Neal in the Tech Lab.

"Yeah," was how O'Neal answered.

"Hi, Quinn. Jack Dillon up in Special Branch. Hope your day is going well."

"It's been pure shite and just got shittier," O'Neal responded.

Dillon took a deep breath and bit his tongue for a second or two. "I was wondering if you've had a chance to check that cellphone for fingerprints."

"Yeah, I thought I sent you an email."

"I haven't seen one," Dillon said and quickly brought up his email account on his desktop computer. There wasn't anything from O'Neal.

"Well, no matter," O'Neal said. "I came up with a great big nothing. No unusual prints other than your man Donnelly."

"You're sure?" Dillon asked. "We're really grasping at straws up here."

"Nothing I can do about that. Other than Donnelly, I couldn't detect anyone else who had handled that phone. Sorry," he said, sounding anything but sorry.

"Damn it. Well, okay. Thanks for checking, Quinn. Better luck next time, I guess."

Click. O'Neal had hung up.

TWENTY-FOUR

Dillon pulled Amelia Maher's business card from his pocket and looked at it for a moment. Just her name and a phone number. It was too soon to call her, so he placed the card in his desk drawer. Suel was back on the phone. Dillon sent him a text message, giving him the update from Quinn O'Neal. Five minutes later, Suel walked over to Dillon's desk, shaking his head.

"I'm guessing you're coming up just as empty-handed as I am," Dillon said.

"Someone, somewhere, has to know something," Suel said, shaking his head.

"Well, if you come up with a name, let me know. I'll be happy to talk with them. We got a dead guy who could never do anything right. Suddenly, he's involved in the biggest event of his worthless life, and he doesn't tell anyone? That doesn't make any sense."

"Unless someone scared the living hell out of the knacker, and he kept his mouth shut for a change."

"Yeah, possibly. Based on what we know of him, that would be completely out of character. He'd normally be out buying drinks for anyone who'd listen and then bragging how he'd finally made the big time."

"I agree, except that he didn't do that. Could we be looking at the wrong level? Who would benefit from Punchy Sheehan getting killed? What if we start at the top and work our way down to whoever was crazy enough to bring Keegan Donnelly on board in the first place?" Suel said.

"I'm with you for most of that, but I think it makes sense that Donnelly was brought on board right from the start with the intention of killing him once the job was done. The fact it was some poor soul with the same name as Punchy just sped up the final act, namely killing Keegan Donnelly."

"Are you thinking it was the Doyle's up in Limerick?" Suel asked.

"It's possible, but the problem I see with them is why take the chance of using Keegan Donnelly and having him screw it up? They've got a number of cold-blooded killers on their payroll. Why take the chance of the hit being screwed up? I'm thinking the Linnehan's. They're living over in Spain. They set Donnelly up to pull the trigger. He does just that and is probably unaware that he killed the wrong guy. Actually, the wrong couple."

"So you're thinking what? We start looking into the Linnehan people still in the country?"

Dillon thought for a moment and nodded. "Yeah, well, unless you can think of a better idea. Right now, I can't come up with anything else. We've got three bodies, virtually no clues, and—"

"Suel, Dillon, a moment of your time, please," DCI McCabe said from the door of his office and then stepped back inside.

"Christ on a cross," Suel said under his breath. "Just when you think it can't possibly get any worse."

Dillon pushed back his chair and headed for McCabe's office. Suel followed at a distance.

"Take a seat, gentlemen," McCabe said without looking up. He was seated at his desk, signing a document. Once he finished, he closed the file and placed it on a stack off to the side. "So," he said and flashed a half-second smile. "The Donnelly murder and, by extension, the Bandon killings. Where do we stand?"

"In all honesty, sir, we're in the dark," Suel replied.

"Tell me," McCabe said.

Suel and Dillon went on for the next five minutes. McCabe listened patiently, nodding occasionally. Dillon mentioned his recent meeting with Amelia Maher. When they stopped, McCabe waited a few seconds, which seemed like an hour to Dillon, and then said, "I think your suspicions of someone connected to the Linnehan's is the better option. I can't see the Doyle's, with the people they have at their disposal, contacting this Donnelly character. Go with that and see what you can turn up. Anything else?"

Dillon and Suel looked at one another, shook their heads, and hurried out of McCabe's office. "Let me make a couple of phone calls," Suel said and hurried to his desk. Dillon collected the tea mugs and the dirty plate from his desk and took them into the break room. Suel was standing and pulling on his jacket a half-minute later when Dillon returned.

"You get something?"

"Calling in a favor. You want to join me?"

Five minutes later, Suel pulled out of the parking lot and headed toward the city center.

"Where, exactly, are we going?"

"A lad owes me a favor. He runs a club down in Temple Bar. He bought the club from the Linnehan's, at least that's what he tells everyone. Truth is, they still own the place, and they pay him, provided he continues to make money for them."

"A bar, in Temple Bar. What's the name of it? I've probably been there at one time or another."

Suel shot Dillon a look and shook his head.

"What? I've probably been there. As a matter of fact, I've probably been there with you."

"It's not a bar. It's a club called The Fantasy House. Your man's name is Cullen Fink."

"The Fantasy House? A club? You mean like a private club? The place sounds like a strip club."

"Lap dancing, actually," Suel said. "There's a fee to get in. Not to worry, we won't be paying."

"How'd you meet this guy?"

"He was targeted by the Liffey Lads gang."

"Never heard of them," Dillon said.

"They were before your arrival. Raised a lot of hell for about three years. Ended up basically being eliminated by the Linnehan's. At that time, there was a pub where the club is located. It more or less served as headquarters for the Liffey Lads. Anyway, the nice way to put it is that Cullen Fink eliminated the lads' use of the pub. The Linnehan's took control of the place and put Fink in charge. He's done well. We've exchanged information over the years. How would I describe him? I guess he serves as a good, private source of information."

"And the place is called The Fantasy House?"

"Yeah, you pay an entrance fee. The drinks are way overpriced and weak."

"It's a strip club?"

"No, I just told you, lap dancing is their thing. I forget what they charge, something like a hundred euros for ten minutes."

"Who can afford that?"

"You be surprised. A lot of Americans, for starters."

Suel drove along the Liffey for fifteen minutes. Traffic was just beginning to pick up with the beginning of rush hour. He drove across the O'Connell Street Bridge and took a right at the far end of the bridge, turning onto the Aston Quay, which turned into the Wellington Quay. About a quarter-mile past the Ha'penny Bridge, he pulled to the curb. The area was clearly marked as no parking allowed.

"You're not worried about getting your tire clamped?" Dillon asked.

"They'd run the license and see it's me," Suel said and climbed out of the car. Dillon shrugged and stepped out onto the sidewalk. "They're in on Temple Bar," Suel said. They walked to the corner, then took a left on Fownes Street Lower and walked a hundred yards to Temple Bar and took a right. Other than a McDonald's, the structures were at least a hundred years old. The Fantasy House was a two-story brick building attached on either side by other century-old structures.

The white entrance had an ornamental stone pillar on either side with gold leaves around the top—purple lights shown from inside the door. A red neon sign that read 'CLOSED' blinked off and on above the door.

"They're closed today?" Dillon asked.

"No, just at the moment. They're open seven days a week from half-past eight in the evening until three in the morning."

"What?"

"Dillon, it's the business. Hang on, let me call your man. Are you armed?"

"No. Should I be?"

"No. Leastwise, not here. They'll pat us down before they let us in." Suel said and pushed a speed-dial button on his cellphone. A moment later, he said, "Yeah, Cullen. It's Paddy. I'm out front with a friend. Okay. Thanks," Suel said and disconnected.

Dillon watched as tourists passed by for the next few minutes before he heard the locks snap on the door. He turned to see two very large, very muscular men, six to eight inches taller than himself, open the door and wave them inside. Once they were inside, one of the men locked the door behind them.

"If you'd step over here, please? We just need to pat you down," the other man said. He had a shaved head and a black goatee pointed at the bottom. His biceps looked almost the size of Dillon's thighs. As he patted Suel down, the giant who had opened the door and then locked it stood behind Dillon, just close enough so Dillon could feel his breath on the back of his neck.

Once the shaved head finished patting down Suel, he waved Dillon forward. Dillon stepped in front of him and extended his arms to either side. The man's hands looked about the size of ten-pound hams, and although fairly gentle, Dillon had the sense his fists would be like two granite boulders.

"Okay, if you'd follow me, please," the giant said as he turned and walked into a large room illuminated with purple lights. His thug partner brought up the rear. A granite-topped bar off to the right ran the length of the room. A stage in the shape of the number eight had two brass poles centered and attached to the ceiling. The edge of the stage was illuminated by soft purple lights. Tables, each with two chairs, filled the room.

They followed the giant to a door in the far wall and then took a staircase up to the second floor. Another bar, this time with four round stages each featuring a brass pole, a mirror on the ceiling, and again illuminated by purple lights. More tables for two filled the room. They followed through a door marked private and entered a hallway with normal lighting. Dillon blinked a couple of times as his eyes adjusted to the brighter light. They walked down the hall to a heavy steel door. The giant knocked on the door then opened it and stepped inside. Dillon and Suel followed. Dillon noted the steel door looked at least two inches thick.

TWENTY-FIVE

The man behind the desk was fat and bald. As he slid off the desk chair, he appeared to be just an inch or two over five feet tall." Paddy, long time no see. Come in, come in. What can I get you lads from the bar?"

"Nothing for us, Cullen, we're still working," Suel said.

"You sure? We've got some great whiskeys. Just the thing for this time of day. I promise not to tell," he said and grinned, revealing a space between his two front teeth.

"Thanks, but we better not," Suel said.

"Suit yourself. Come on, sit down, sit down. Daren, Bobby, you can wait outside. I'll call yous if I need anything. I'm not gonna need anything, am I, Paddy?" Fink said and laughed as the two giants stepped out of the office, closing the steel door behind them.

"Cullen, I'd like you to meet my friend, Jack Dillon. We work together," Suel said.

Fink nodded and gave Dillon the once over as he stepped forward. "Nice to meet yas, Jack. Any friend of Paddy's is a friend of mine."

"Very nice to meet you, Cullen."

"You an American?" Fink asked when he heard Dillon's accent.

"Yeah, I'm attached to An Garda Síochána," Dillon said as he shook Fink's hand.

"You might have read about him, Cullen. That little bit of trouble out at the airport a few years back," Suel said.

"The airport? Wait, you mean that shooting? The Russians?" Fink asked, turning his hand into the shape of a gun and pointing it at Suel. He pretended to shoot a half-dozen times.

"Yeah, ancient history now," Dillon said.

"That was some damn good work on your part. Quite the job. You shoot two of them?"

"Four, actually. Mind if we sit and chat?" Dillon asked, nodding toward a leather couch and two red upholstered chairs, hoping to change the subject from the event at the Dublin airport.

"Oh, yeah, where are my manners? Come on, sit down. Sit down. You sure I can't get you something, Paddy?"

"Thanks, Cullen, but we're just fine," Suel said as they all sat down. Suel and Dillon settled onto the leather couch. Fink sat in one of the red upholstered chairs. As he settled in, his feet dangled an inch or two off the floor.

Suel leaned forward with his arms resting on his knees. "We've been working a case, Cullen, and we're coming up empty-handed. Wondered if you may have heard anything."

"Is this that woman they found in the Grand Canal? Because if it is, Paddy, I can't help you. Don't know a damn thing about it."

"No, it's not that one. This happened, or at least started, down in Cork, outside of Bandon, in a half-parish called Desertserges. An American couple, last name Sheehan, your man's first name was Dennis, and we're pretty sure he was mistaken for Punchy Sheehan."

"County Cork? I wouldn't know anything about that. I got all I can do just keeping track of what's going on in here," Fink said and chuckled.

"Yeah, I'm sure you do," Suel said. "Thing is, we're pretty sure the shooter was a Dub by the name of Keegan Donnelly." Fink gave a slight, almost imperceptible nod. "Then maybe thirty-six hours after the shooting outside of Bandon, someone killed Donnelly in his bed. Shot him twice."

"Mmm, read about that in the papers," Fink said. "Tragic, very tragic. And you tied him to that shooting down in Cork? The two Americans?"

Suel nodded but didn't say anything.

"Sad state of affairs, two Americans killed. I suppose that's gonna foul up our tourist numbers. Not like there aren't other places for them to go and spend their money. Damn it."

"You hearing anything on the street about this? Anything on this Keegan Donnelly?" Suel asked.

Fink appeared to be thinking. No one said anything for a long moment. Finally, Fink said, "I'm not sure I got the names right, but you might want to talk to a guy named Tommy Thompson and another tramp named Brennan something. I'm blanking on that gobshite's last name."

Dillon was tempted to say O'Rourke, but Suel gave him a subtle hand movement, indicating not to say anything, so he sat there quietly and waited.

Fink cleared his throat a couple of times and then said, "I don't know if they were involved. I might have heard something like they were talking about that incident, the one down in Cork. Everything seemed to go awfully quiet once your man Donnelly was killed. You know how it goes, one day everyone's talking about it, and the next thing, no one knows shite. There is one thing, though. This Donnelly, he has a reputation of going through a lot of women. Pick 'em up and dump 'em a week or two later. I'm trying to think if any of our girls might have been with him for a bit. I can maybe check, you know, quiet like, if you want."

"Yeah, we'd appreciate that, Cullen. Whatever you learn would help."

"The name Amelia Maher ring a bell with you?" Dillon asked.

"No. No, never heard of her," Fink said, almost too fast. Dillon made a mental note.

"Anything I can do for you?" Suel said.

"Maybe the usual," Fink said and gave a quick glance at Dillon.

"He's good, Cullen. You expecting a visit?"

"Not that I'm aware of, but let's just say, I don't need one. We're running it clean here. What the girls do on their own time, who they go home with, that's got nothing to do with me or the club. That's strictly their own personal decision."

Suel nodded and said, "I'll double-check just to make sure. Appreciate your help, Cullen. You hear anything, please give me a call."

"You know I will, Paddy," Fink said. He slid forward on the upholstered chair until his feet touched the floor, and he pushed himself up. He walked toward the steel door as Dillon and Suel stood. Dillon gave a quick look around the room and followed Suel out of the office as Fink held the door open. "Always a pleasure, Paddy," Fink said. He looked at the two giants standing in the hall and said, "Show them out, lads. Sure I can't offer you a drink on the way out?"

"Thanks, Cullen, but we've still got a lot of work to do. You take care."

"I always do. Nice to meet you, Jack. Stop in sometime, on the house. Just ask for me," Fink said.

"Thank you, Cullen. I just may take you up on that."

"See that you do," Fink said as he closed the steel door. They followed the giants through the purple bar rooms, past the brass poles, and back out into the sunshine

TWENTY-SIX

Dillon said once they'd turned back onto Fownes Street Lower and were walking toward the car, Dillon said, "Your man Fink seems to be a bit of a character."

"Yeah, he is, but he's also been helpful from time to time. I'll check to see if anyone is planning to pay him a visit."

"Has he gotten nailed for running prostitutes?"

Suel shook his head. "No, that's not worth spending the time. They're more worried about women from Eastern Europe or Russia overstaying their visits. For a while, someone was running drugs out of there, but I don't think that's a problem anymore."

"They get fined?" Dillon asked.

Suel flashed a quick smile and said, "The place is a goldmine for Fink and the Linnehan's. Let's just say Cullen dealt with the problem."

Dillon thought for a moment and said, "Interesting he mentioned Tommy Thompson and Brennan O'Rourke. I wonder if it might be worth paying them another visit. Based on what Fink alluded to, they may know a little more than they let on."

"That's what I was thinking. How 'bout we catch them in the morning. By the time we find them tonight, they're both liable to be three sheets to the wind and completely worthless."

Dillon nodded and said, "Let's meet at Thompson's place in Cabra early tomorrow, maybe seven-ish?"

Suel nodded. "Yeah, we can…Oh, bloody hell. What the feck is this bit of nonsense?" he exclaimed as they came around the corner and stepped onto Wellington Quay. The car was just fifteen feet in front of them with what looked like a parking ticket stuck beneath the windshield wiper.

"You're lucky they didn't clamp you," Dillon said.

Suel tore the ticket out from beneath the wiper. "Bloody fecking hell. When I find out who did…Oh, for the love of, will you look at this? God love Tony," he said as he handed the ticket to Dillon.

Dillon looked at the ticket. A handwritten note said, 'Paddy, you owe me a couple of pints! Tony.'

"Lucky you," Dillon said.

"You kidding? It probably would have been cheaper to pay the ticket. Your man drinks like a fish."

Twenty minutes later, Suel dropped Dillon off in front of the station. Dillon checked the time on his cellphone, just after 5:00. He debated going up to Special Branch and then quickly decided against it. He climbed into his car and headed home. Along the way, he stopped at The Grapevine, a wine store, and bought two bottles of wine, a red and a white.

Lucifer met him at the door. He dashed outside and assumed the position just in front of Dillon's car. Dillon stepped inside and walked to the kitchen. Amazingly, everything looked to be in place. No wastebasket overturned, no papers or food scraps scattered around the kitchen. No deposit from Lucifer under the dining table. Dillon reached into the cookie jar that held the biscuits and grabbed one. He opened the front door and called Lucifer. When the dog turned around, he tossed the biscuit to him. Lucifer caught it in midair and inhaled the thing in two quick bites. Dillon left the door open and walked back into the kitchen.

He placed the bottle of white wine in the refrigerator and pulled out a plate covered with plastic wrap. At first, he thought it was a pork steak on the plate, but closer examination suggested a skinless chicken breast. He tore off the plastic wrap, took the bottle of Bar-B-Que sauce from the shelf on the refrigerator door, and slathered it over the chicken.

Lucifer wandered into the kitchen a moment later. Dillon tossed him another biscuit and carried the plate with the chicken to the sitting room. He turned on the TV and, against his better judgment, clicked the remote to bring up the news channel.

After dinner, he grabbed the leash and took Lucifer for a long walk. They looped around Albert Park three times, roughly three and a half miles. Once they finished the third lap, they settled onto a bench and watched a hurling match for a good half-hour before heading home.

Dillon debated having a glass of red wine, decided against it, and read a book of no redeeming social value for the better part of two hours before he turned off the lights, checked the locks on the doors, and headed up to bed.

His alarm woke him at 5:30 the following morning. He scrambled a couple of eggs, had two cups of coffee, coaxed Lucifer outside with a biscuit, and headed toward Cabra and Tommy Thompson's house on Killala Road.

It wasn't quite 6:45 when he pulled to the curb in front of Thompson's house. At no surprise, the place looked exactly the same, peeling brown paint on the trim, the rusted front gate. The weeds and what little grass there was appeared to be longer than the last time Dillon was there, which meant Thompson hadn't bothered to lift a hand.

At a little before 7:00, Suel pulled up, parked behind Dillon, and climbed out of his car. "All set for an exciting interview with your man Thompson?" Suel asked as Dillon opened his driver's door.

"I can hardly wait," Dillon joked and motioned with his hand. "Lead the way, DI Suel."

Suel glanced up and down the street, not so much as a bird flying. He studied the faded beige two-story, attached stucco structure for a moment. A piece of cardboard still covered the missing glass pane in the front window. Suel went to push open the rusted front gate and suddenly stopped. "What the hell?" he said as he slowly pushed the gate open.

"What is it?" Dillon asked, then saw the blood on the sidewalk leading up to the front door. There was a pool, easily the size of a dinner plate. The weeds next to the sidewalk were bent over from weight being placed on them, probably someone's body, maybe Thompson's. More blood covered the weeds. Suel stepped into the front garden, studied the blood on the sidewalk and weeds, and followed the blood trail up toward the front door.

More blood was on the front stoop and smeared across the front door. Remnants of blood coated the brass doorknob. Suel reached into his pocket and pulled out a latex glove. He slipped his right hand in the glove and then tried the doorknob. It was locked.

Dillon reached over and held his finger against the doorbell. They could hear it buzzing inside. He kept his finger against the doorbell for a good ten seconds and then began pushing it a number of times.

Suel pulled out his phone and punched a speed dial number. "DI Paddy Suel on Killala Road in Cabra, requesting backup. We suspect a shooting. Blood leading to the front door. Repeat, requesting backup." He gave the house number and disconnected. "I think we better go in. If your man is in there, he's in a desperate state."

Dillon took a half-step back then kicked the door hard, landing his foot just next to the doorknob. The door flew open, banging against the interior wall and knocking a picture frame to the floor.

Thompson was four feet inside the entry, lying face down in a pool of blood. Suel hurried over, knelt down, and placed his hand on Thompson's neck, checking for a pulse. He moved his hand slightly two different times, then looked up at Dillon and shook his head. "Nothing. He's gone," Suel said.

"We'd best wait for them outside," Dillon said.

Suel nodded, stood, and headed toward Dillon.

"Stop, Paddy, you're tracking," Dillon said.

Suel halted and looked behind him. Sure enough, he'd left two bloody footprints on the worn entryway floor. "Oh, for the love of…" Suel slipped both shoes off and followed Dillon outside in his stocking feet. They sat on the three-foot garden wall and waited for backup. Suel placed another call requesting a medical examiner and a forensics team. Dillon placed a call to DCI McCabe. He left a message explaining the situation, letting him know no officer was injured. He asked McCabe to send two officers to check on Brennan O'Rourke and ended with a promise to call back when he had more information.

It wasn't more than seven or eight minutes before they heard the distant sound of a siren, followed by two more, maybe a half-minute later. The first car pulled up, and an officer with sergeant stripes on his shirt climbed out from behind the wheel.

"What took you so long, Devan?" Suel said and chuckled.

"If I'd known it was the likes of you, Paddy, I would have stopped for breakfast. What do you have?"

"A body in the front entry. No pulse. We haven't checked the rest of the house. Two bloody footprints in the front entry belong to me. You can see the blood on the sidewalk behind us leading up to the front door."

Two more squad cars pulled up, and the officers hurried out. Devan, the first arrival, signaled with his hands to slow down, and then waved everyone over around Dillon and Suel. Suel gave a short update and explained that he'd already requested forensics and the medical examiner.

One of the officers opened the trunk of his squad car and pulled out a roll of blue plastic tape with white letters that said, 'An Garda Síochána Do Not Cross' in both English and Irish. He and another officer tied it to an overgrown bush in the corner of the front garden and ran it along the front garden wall. They tied it to the rusted frame at the entrance gate. Dillon and Suel moved off the wall, and the officers ran another length of tape across the other half of the wall.

TWENTY-SEVEN

Suel said, "As long as we're here, maybe start knocking on doors and see if anyone has any information." The three uniformed officers looked at one another, two set off across the street in opposite directions while the third headed down the left side next to Thompson's place to interview neighbors.

"Why don't you stay here while I knock on some doors?" Dillon said.

"Not a problem. Don't stray too far. I'll send you a text message as soon as forensics arrives. I'd like to get inside and have a look around," Suel said.

Dillon headed in the opposite direction of the three officers. He knocked on the door of the unit attached to Thompson's place. A woman smoking a cigarette eventually answered the door. She was barefoot and wearing a gray bathrobe. "What's he done this time?" she said, staring at the three squad cars in front of Thompson's place. She took a long drag off her cigarette, pointed her head toward the ceiling, and exhaled.

'Charming,' Dillon thought. "Wondering if you heard anything last night."

"Heard anything? Yeah, the girls had the TV on downstairs until at least 11:00, when I finally fell asleep. The dog was barking to go outside at around 2:30. My husband snored until 6:30, when he left for work. Yeah, I heard plenty."

"Anything from Mr. Thompson's next door?"

"Mr. Thompson? I've heard that bollox called a lot of things, but never Mr. Let me ask you again. What's he done this time?"

"We believe someone killed him."

She stuck the cigarette in her mouth and slowly clapped her hands. "Thank. You. Jesus," she said, clapping once with each word. "Our prayers have finally been answered. Good riddance."

Dillon waited a moment and then asked, "So how long have you lived here?"

"We moved in seven years ago," she said and took a long drag from her cigarette. "Thompson moved in maybe eighteen months ago. He's been a pain in the hole ever since."

"How? I mean, was he loud? Did he have a lot of parties? Leave trash in the garden?"

"All that and more. One time he had a woman screaming at him and leaning on the car horn at two in the morning. He'd have his knacker buddies over drinking up a storm, shouting all kinds of shite. They weren't exactly the kind of folks you'd want to complain to if you catch my drift."

"I get it," Dillon said. "You ever get any names?"

"Names? Of that lot? No way. We just made sure the doors were locked, and we got a dog. Not that he did anything, other than he does his business in the house almost every day."

"Anything else you can tell me?" Dillon asked.

"Only that you've made my day with the news. I'm gonna call my husband at his job site and let him know. We're sure as hell gonna party tonight, probably invite the neighbors," she said and took a final drag from her cigarette. She reached past Dillon and flicked the cigarette butt into her front garden. As she did so, Dillon couldn't help but glance at her exposed cleavage as her bathrobe opened, revealing a tattoo of red roses.

"Okay, well, umm, please feel free to call us should you think of any information that might help in our investigation."

"I'd like to shake the hand of whoever did us this favor," she said, shutting the door.

Dillon closed the gate behind him and walked to the next unit. The front garden looked well-tended. He walked up to the door, pressed the doorbell, and heard it chiming inside. A moment later, the door opened, and a gray-haired man Dillon guessed was maybe in his mid-seventies answered the door. The man had neatly trimmed hair, a mustache, and bright blue eyes. He wore a pair of cream-colored shorts and a light-blue golf shirt. "Yes?" he said.

"My name is Jack Dillon with An Garda Síochána," Dillon said. "We're checking on a possible disturbance last night and wondered if you may have heard any-thing."

"An Garda Síochána? You sound American," the man said.

"I am. I'm assigned to Special Branch. We're in the headquarters building over in Phoenix Park."

"Mmm, and why are you assigned over here?"

"Just helping out. Did you hear anything last night?"

The man shook his head. "Can't say that I did. I watched the evening news and went to bed. Same as every other night. You get to be my age, if nothing's hap-pening in the bedroom, you might as well go to sleep."

"Emmett?" a female voice called, and a woman stepped into the entryway. She was blonde and appeared to be in reasonable shape. Dillon guessed her age as late sixties, maybe seventy. "What's this about?" she asked as she stepped alongside her husband.

"Jack Dillon with An Garda Síochána, ma'am. Won-dering if you heard any disturbance last night."

"He's American," the husband said.

"Disturbance? Why? What's happened?"

"An incident at the Thompson residence," Dillon said.

"Thompson, that worthless bastard—"

"Emmett, please. Let's just answer the officer's question," she said.

"An incident at that Thompson hellhole?" the hus-band said, shaking his head. "Good lord, that's damn near an everyday occurrence. I've lost count of how many times we've called the Gardai, but nothing ever seems to change. Finally, you're here asking questions. Wouldn't you know it's after the first quiet night we've had in weeks? Honest to God. I think—"

"That's just about enough, Emmett. I think it might be time to tend to the roses in the back, dear. I'll answer any questions the officer may have."

"That worthless bastard Thompson should have been locked up a long time ago. If you ask me, I think—"

"Emmett, the roses, thank you."

Emmett shot Dillon a look, then walked toward the back of the house, mumbling.

His wife flashed a smile and held out her hand. "I'm Marilyn Kennedy, and you said your name was John?"

"Jack, actually. Jack Dillon, ma'am," Dillon said and briefly shook her hand.

"I'm afraid you'll have to excuse my husband. Actually, I agree with him wholeheartedly. If this was thirty years ago, there never would have been the likes of that Thompson character in the neighborhood. If there was, Emmett would have marched down the block and given him a talking to. Thompson's behavior is not on. What's he done this time, gotten some poor girl in trouble?"

"No ma'am, it would appear he's been shot, murdered actually."

"Oh! I suppose I should say that's too bad, but actually, I don't think you'll find any of the neighbors shedding a tear. His home is in constant need of attention. The parties, not to mention the awful group of ne'er do wells coming and going at all times. Dreadful, absolutely dreadful. Now you tell me he's been murdered. Well, all I can say is, that's not a surprise and good riddance."

"What can you tell me about the individuals coming and going?"

"Unfortunately, not much, other than they were dreadful. The sort of knackers you knew just from their appearance that no good would come with any interaction. The men were hoodlums, and the women, the few that were there, were, well, forgive me, but best left unsaid."

"Are you aware of any names, or maybe a license number? Something you recall that might—"

"No, in all honesty, we simply kept our distance. The entire neighborhood did. We just locked our doors and hoped they didn't try to break in. I wish I could help you, but honestly, due to the behavior of that lot, we and all our friends became prisoners in our own homes. I'm not sorry to see your man Thompson go. There'll probably be a celebration in someone's garden once the word gets out."

"Well, thank you for your time, Mrs. Kennedy. Should anything come to mind, please don't hesitate to contact us."

"Thank you, Officer Dillon, a pleasure meeting you. You've made our day."

Dillon knocked on two more doors and got pretty much the same response. Everyone was glad to hear Thompson was permanently out of the picture. They'd all kept their distance and had nothing to share other than he was a horrible neighbor. As he headed to the next home, Dillon's cellphone signaled a text message from Suel. 'Forensics is here. We've access to the house.'

TWENTY-EIGHT

Dillon walked back to Thompson's house just as two men in hazmat suits were opening rear doors on the white van labeled 'AN GARDA SIOCHANA FORENSICS' in blue letters. They pulled out two large black cases and headed into Thompson's house.

"Any idea how long it's going to take them?" Dillon asked Suel.

Suel shook his head. "At least a few hours," he said as he handed Dillon a pair of latex gloves. "They said we can have a look around upstairs. Just mind the stair rail on the way up."

"We looking for anything in particular?"

"Yeah, a video of your man shooting the Sheehan's down in Cork and a signed note telling us who shot Thompson."

"I'll be sure to keep my eyes peeled," Dillon said as he slipped on the gloves.

They headed into the house, making a wide path around the pool of blood on the sidewalk and the blood trail leading up to the front door. Dillon went up to the second floor while Suel explained to the Forensic team that they had kicked the door in and that the two bloody footprints were his.

Dillon stopped at the top of the staircase and looked around. The layout was standard for Dublin housing built back in the 1950s. A hallway with two small bedrooms and a bathroom overlooked the staircase.

The window at the top of the stairs had a yellowed shade covering it. He remembered the woman with the red roses tattoo telling him Thompson had moved in eighteen months ago. From the dust on the windowsill and along the top of the yellowed shade, Dillon guessed Thompson pulled the shade his first night in the place and never touched it again.

He stepped into the room at the top of the stairs, a master bedroom, such as it was. Clothes were strewn across the worn wooden floor. The double bed featured worn, soiled sheets and two sweat-stained pillows. The sheets looked like they hadn't been changed during the eighteen months Thompson had been there.

A small bedside table with a lamp was next to the bed. Three partially crushed beer cans lay on the table. The cans were blue, and Dillon recognized the Dutch Gold logo, one of the cheapest brands available. He opened the single drawer on the table. A half-filled bottle of lubricant, a vibrator, and five loose pills were in the drawer. Dillon didn't recognize the pills. They could have been aspirin, a legal prescription, or some mind-altering drug. He had no idea. His cellphone suddenly rang, DCI McCabe.

"Marshal Dillon," was how he answered.

"Dillon, got your message. A team is en route to check on this O'Rourke individual. What's your status there?"

Dillon told him Forensics was downstairs, and he and Suel were just beginning to go through Thompson's bedroom. He mentioned the responses he received from Thompson's neighbors.

"No surprise there. Keep me posted," McCabe said and disconnected.

As Dillon walked to the far side of the double bed, he had to turn sideways. As he made his way along the foot of the bed, his back brushed against the wall. He stood in front of a chest of five drawers. When he pulled the top drawer open, the chest wiggled slightly from side to side. The top drawer was filled with odds and ends, three cords for recharging a computer or possibly a phone, two XXX videotapes, which made him wonder who in today's world still watched a videotape? There were three shotgun shells casings, a half-dozen English coins, a costume jewelry necklace, but nothing of interest. The second drawer contained boxer shorts and four pairs of socks. The third drawer was stuffed with t-shirts, as was the fourth drawer. The bottom drawer held three pairs of jeans, a pair of brown slacks, and a swimsuit.

Dillon moved back around the bed and headed for the wardrobe against the wall just as Suel entered the room.

"Anything of interest?" Suel asked.

"There's a vibrator in that drawer beneath the lamp and a couple of videotapes in the dresser."

"Yeah, no thanks."

Dillon opened the double doors on the wardrobe. Two Dublin jerseys, a jacket, three wrinkled, long sleeve shirts, and a black negligee were on hangers. Four pairs of shoes along with a pair of sandals rested on the bottom. There was a drawer along the bottom, and Dillon pulled it out. One more XXX videotape and a brown paper bag.

He lifted the bag. It was heavy, and he said, "Hey, I think I've got something here." He set the bag on the floor, and opened it to find a pistol and a magazine with rounds in it. "A gun," he said to Suel.

"Let me take a look," Suel said kneeling down next to Dillon.

"Looks like a Walther P99 with a ten-round magazine," Dillon said and handed the bag to Suel.

Suel shook his head, mumbled, "Americans," and opened the bag. "It's an automatic."

"Actually, a semi-automatic. German Army, I think, beginning in the mid-90s, forty caliber. It's still in use by the Germans as far as I know. Pass it on to the guys downstairs. Pretty safe guess it wasn't used to shoot Thompson last night, but with some tests, it might turn up in some previous situation."

"Yes, sir, on it," Suel said and gave Dillon a fake salute. "I wonder how he looked in this negligee," Suel quipped, nodding at the see-through black garment dangling on the hanger.

"Makes you wonder, did he have a regular or was it for just in case the opportunity presented itself?"

Dillon pulled the negligee out of the wardrobe. As he did so, he caught a slight scent of perfume. "Whoever she was, she had a nice perfume."

"Give me that before you decide to try it on," Suel said. "Mmm, you're right, that is a nice perfume. Someone wore it recently, I'd guess. Maybe they can check it for DNA. Anything else in here?"

"Not that I can see. More than a little messy," Dillon said, looking around at the bed and the clothes scattered across the floor. "Why don't you run those things down to the forensic guys, and I'll head into the other room."

Suel stepped into the second bedroom a few minutes later. "Medical examiners are downstairs. What the hell is this place?"

The second bedroom was filled with boxes stacked on top of one another, a set of four chairs, a couple of suitcases, and just junk.

Dillon shook his head. "It looks like all the things you'd move, and then as you're unpacking, you wonder why in hell you bothered to bring them in the first place. Might as well grab a box and start going through it."

"We ought to empty these boxes out the window and set the pile on fire," Suel said as he grabbed a box. He opened it, groaned, and dumped the contents onto the floor. Three metal bowls, a half-dozen spoons, and a set of beaters for a kitchen mixer. "I have a hard time think-ing this worthless feck had the ability to cook anything."

It took the better part of two hours, but they eventu-ally made their way through all the boxes and three piles of what appeared to be more dirty laundry. Just as they were finishing up, a voice from downstairs called, "Dil-lon, Suel, we're done here. It's safe to come down, now."

"Hang on a minute, Artie," Suel called. "Come on, let's see if they found anything," and he and Dillon headed downstairs. Thompson's body was in a black body bag strapped onto a gurney.

As Dillon and Suel came down the stairs, Suel asked, "You learn anything?"

Artie Reilly shook his head. "Not really. Your man was shot at close range, residue and powder burns on his shirt. He fell to the ground out there in the front garden and whoever did this apparently kicked him in the head a couple of times. We don't know this, but I would say he was probably left for dead, most likely unconscious as the killer left. Thompson eventually came to, made his way inside the house, and dropped dead. Based on the amount of blood lost, I think we'll find the bullet clipped an artery. Umm, no exit wound, so a small-caliber weapon was used."

"You see the results of the Keegan Donnelly murder and those two Americans down in Cork?" Suel asked.

"Only the reports and the computer comparisons of the rounds. We'll run a comparison with this case. My sense is there's at least a fifty-fifty chance it was the same weapon. Too soon to tell. We should have some-thing for you after our examination, maybe around mid-day tomorrow."

"Thanks, Artie, give a yell when you've got some-thing," Suel told him.

"Don't I always?" Artie said and then stepped to the foot of the gurney and gave his partner a nod. They wheeled the gurney out the door and down the sidewalk.

"You lads find anymore negligees?" one of the guys on the forensic team called from the kitchen.

"We did, Mick, but I couldn't squeeze into it, so I left it upstairs," Suel joked and headed for the kitchen.

Dillon followed Suel. Both men on the forensic team were leaning against the kitchen counter, drinking from cans of lemonade. There were a half-dozen plastic evi-dence bags on the Formica counter containing a couple of glasses, some silverware, and a plate.

"There's one more can in the refrigerator," Mick, the older of the two, said as Dillon and Suel stepped into the kitchen. "Find anything else?"

Dillon shook his head. "A room full of worthless items stuffed in boxes. If I had to guess, I'd say he moved the stuff in here and then never used any of it."

"No surprise there. We'll go over what we've gath-ered, but it's looking pretty sparse. Probably our best chance is the pistol and that sweet-smelling negligee."

"Which has about a zero percent chance of helping," Suel said. "Who in their right mind would shoot this numbskull, place the weapon in a paper bag and leave it in the wardrobe?"

"Not to mention I heard Artie tell yous your man was shot with a small-caliber weapon, and I'm guessing the one in the paper bag is probably a nine millimeter, being German and all."

"Forty Caliber," Dillon said.

Mick looked over at Dillon. "Any word from the neighbors?"

"I talked with four of them," Dillon said. "I think they're planning on celebrating tonight. No one was too fond of Thompson. Two of them said they were glad to see him go. It sounds like he was the local pain in the ass, and they're more than happy to be rid of him."

Mick shook his head. "Amazing how some of these knackers are just slime."

"Add him to a very long list," Suel said. "We should check on the lads canvassing the neighbors. I'm sure they've gotten an earful."

TWENTY-NINE

Two of the officers were out in front of Thompson's house talking with a neighbor. As Dillon and Suel approached, the neighbor nodded, smiled, and quickly went on his way.

"Learn anything?" Suel asked.

Both men shook their heads, and one said, "Only that your man Thompson was a right pain in the bum for everyone on the lane. Didn't hear one good thing about him. Most of the people I talked to were happy he was dead."

The other officer said, "I was talking to a woman when she got a phone call. Apparently, the neighbors are getting together tonight and raising a glass in someone's back garden to say good riddance to your man Thompson."

"I wonder if that was the Kennedys who phoned. I talked to them, and the old man said he was going to invite the neighbors over for a glass," Dillon said.

"This Thompson must have been a real piece of work," one of the officers said.

Dillon's phone rang, DCI McCabe. "Yes, sir," Dillon answered and gave Suel a nod. He stepped off to the side. The two uniformed officers instinctively knew to remain quiet. "Yes. Well, let's hope so. Yes, we can. Will do, sir. On our way," Dillon said and disconnected.

"Now what?" Suel said.

"Maybe nothing. McCabe sent a squad over to O'Rourke's place, and they didn't get an answer. He wants us to go over there and check it out."

"Bloody Hell," Suel said. "I've a pound that says he was on the piss last night, and he's probably still passed out in bed."

"In today's world, that would be a euro you've got, mate," one of the uniformed officers said, and everyone laughed.

"All right, lads, best stay here for a bit. If your third man arrives, send him back to the station. Appreciate your help," Suel said.

"You want to follow me?" Dillon asked.

"I think I can find my way to the Ballymun apartments," Suel said.

"Suit yourself. I'll see you there."

"Take your time. I'm going to touch base with the lads inside. Let them know we're off to make a wake-up call on another eejit."

"Thanks for your help, fellas," Dillon said and headed over to his car. It was a fifteen-minute drive to the Ballymun apartments. Dillon almost had to pass his house on the way, and for a second, he thought about checking in on Lucifer and then immediately thought that would be a bad idea. He pulled in across the street from the Ballymun apartments and waited. Suel arrived ten minutes later.

They crossed the street and headed into the building. Unfortunately, this time there wasn't a group of young women focused on their cellphones. Dillon punched in the three-digit code for O'Rourke's unit, and they listened to it ring a dozen times. Next, he punched in the number for management. After five rings, a voice answered, "Yes?"

"An Garda Síochána," Dillon said. "We're in the front lobby. We need access to the building and access to unit 317 belonging to Brennan O'Rourke."

"What's this about ?" the man said.

"It's about you having a passkey and providing access to the unit. This is an emergency, so unless you want to be liable for damage or possibly a death, I suggest you get here pretty damn fast."

There was a pause and then, "Okay, okay, I'm on my way. Be there in a minute."

"He was busy having a tea?" Suel asked.

"Who knows. Sorry if I sounded pissed off. I don't get it. We keep ending up with bodies, and we're still no further ahead."

"It's a strange one. I'll grant you that," Suel said.

It wasn't two minutes before a heavyset man appeared on the other side of the security door. He wore a blue denim shirt with 'MANAGER Ballymun Apartments' embroidered in dark blue above his left breast. He was red-faced and breathing heavily.

"I'll need to see some ID," he said through the glass door.

Both Dillon and Suel pulled out their IDs and held them up. The man glanced at them and quickly opened the door. "Sorry, gents, but it's the rules. We've all sorts coming through, trying to get in, and raising hell."

"No problem," Dillon said. "We're here on a care call regarding Brennan O'Rourke. He's in unit 317."

The man nodded and said, "Follow me. The elevators are just over here. I've a passkey if yous need to get in."

"Appreciate your help. Sorry to interrupt your day," Dillon said just as the elevator doors opened.

"Not a bother," the man said as they stepped onto the elevator. He pushed the button for the third floor. "I was just having a tea, anyway."

Dillon shot a look at Suel, who was grinning. They stepped out of the elevator and walked down the hall to 317. Dillon knocked on the door, waited a few seconds, and then knocked louder.

"Maybe I should use the key," the manager said.

"I think that would be a good idea," Dillon replied.

The guy slipped the key into the lock, turned it, opened the door, and stepped aside so Dillon and Suel could enter.

"Mr. O'Rourke? Brennan?" Dillon called but didn't get an answer. The last time they were here, they only stepped inside a few feet. This time they entered the main room, which was relatively small.

A kitchen sink and a two-burner electric stove were off to one side with two artificial wood cabinets on either side of the stove. The sink held a couple of plates, a tea mug, and a whiskey glass. A worn couch faced a small flatscreen sitting on a card table. Dillon walked down a very short hallway into a bedroom.

At no surprise, the bed was unmade. Dirty clothes were scattered on the floor. The bathroom door was open, and O'Rourke wasn't there. The place was clearly empty.

"Looks like he made it to the hospital in time," Suel said, turning to the manager. "Your man thought he was having a heart attack, and we just wanted to be sure he wasn't up here in cardiac arrest."

"Hopefully, that's where he is, the hospital," the manager said.

"Listen, we don't want to take up any more of your day. Can't thank you enough for letting us in. Any questions, give us a call," Suel said and handed the man his An Garda Síochána business card.

"We'll just leave him a note, and we can let ourselves out," Dillon said as he walked the manager to the door.

The guy had a look on his face suggesting he was about to say something but then maybe thought better of that idea. "Happy to be of service. Name's Devlin if you need to get in touch," he said and left. Suel waited until they heard the elevator bell before he closed the door. "Let's do a quick check around here."

They proceeded to quickly go through the kitchen drawers, both closets, and the bedroom dresser drawers. They looked under the double bed, lifted both cushions on the worn couch, and searched the cabinet beneath the bathroom sink. After fifteen minutes, they came up empty-handed and left.

"That was another waste of time," Suel said as they rode the elevator down to the main floor.

"Maybe O'Rourke is out for a run, or maybe he has a job," Dillon joked.

"Yeah, why didn't I remember? He's the president of a bank. How could I forget? A job? For God's sake, Dillon. Let's head back to Special Branch so we can once again give DCI McCabe the good news that we came up empty-handed."

"No time like the present," Dillon said as they stepped out of the building and headed to their cars.

THIRTY

Once back in Special Branch, they both took a deep breath and knocked on the doorframe to McCabe's office.

"Come in, gentlemen, and take a seat," McCabe said without looking up from the file on his desk. He read for another minute or two, which seemed like an hour to Dillon. Finally, he closed the file and looked up. "So, what did we learn?"

Suel looked like he was about to say something, but Dillon waved a hand just below the edge of McCabe's desk, cutting him off.

"Unfortunately, sir, we've drawn another blank. Two blanks, actually. Unless forensics or the medical examiners come up with a link to someone regarding the Thompson murder, our list of suspects amounts to virtually every one of the man's neighbors. As a matter of fact, they're getting together this evening to celebrate Thompson's untimely death. Seems he wasn't too popular in the neighborhood."

Suel cleared his throat and said, "As for Brennan O'Rourke, we were actually in his apartment. No sign of O'Rourke or any violence, and after a quick look around, with the manager present, we left. I would say our next effort would be to attempt to find the location of his cellphone."

McCabe gave a long, slow exhale, looked at Dillon and Suel, and said, "Then best get on it. Keep me posted, gentlemen. I've a bad feeling about this. We've four bodies, no answers, and no suspects. This simply won't do. Find something. We need to wrap this up. That's all. Now get to it."

Dillon and Suel quickly rose to their feet and hurried out of the office. "For a moment there, I thought we might be skinned and hung out to dry," Suel said.

Dillon shook his head and said, "I don't think that's too far down the road. Let me call Emily down in tech and see if she can track O'Rourke's cellphone."

"I'll say a prayer and keep my fingers crossed," Suel said.

Dillon brought up the eFile Emily had sent him with the list of contacts from Keegan Donnelly's phone. He punched in the three-digit extension for Emily. She answered after quite a few rings.

"Emily, tech," she said.

"Hi Emily, Jack Dillon. How are things going?"

"I'm up to my proverbials. What do you need?" she asked.

"I need you to run a trace on a cellphone number for me."

"Give me the number."

"It's Brennan O'Rourke. He's linked to Keegan Donnelly, and we can't locate him. We think he—"

"Didn't I just see something come through from forensics related to the Donnelly investigation?"

"You may have. Would the name Tommy Thompson ring a bell?"

"Yeah, that's it. Quinn's working on a stack of things. This is related to that murder?"

"It may be," Dillon said. "Something, somewhere, has to break loose. We keep coming up with bodies and no answers."

It sounded as if Emily gave a sigh and said, "Well, give me that number, and I'll see what I can do. Just like before, no promises. If the phone is turned off or your man tossed it in the Liffey, there's nothing I can do."

"Yeah, I know that. Look, I feel like we're still grasping at straws, so give it your best shot, and what happens, happens," Dillon said and then read off O'Rourke's cellphone number to her.

"On it," she said and hung up.

"Any luck?" Suel called from his desk ten minutes later.

"We should know in the next hour or so. She's running the number now. She sounded busy, so I hope she can—" Dillon's desk phone rang, cutting him off. He stared at the phone for two more rings and then picked it up. "Jack Dillon."

"Dillon, it's Emily. I've got a location on the O'Rourke phone and—"

"Already? Oh, that's great."

"Well, maybe. Your man appears to be in a parking ramp, the one on Prince Street."

"Prince Street?" Dillon said.

"Oh, sorry. Yeah, it's just off O'Connell Street. It dead-ends roughly at the backside of Arnott's. The ramp is labeled as Arnott's Parking Ramp. He may have left the phone in his car. The problem is, I can't determine what level in the parking ramp the phone is on."

"But it's in the parking ramp?"

"Yes, Arnott's parking ramp, just at the end of Prince Street."

"Thanks, Emily, we're on it," Dillon said and hung up.

Suel was on his feet, heading toward Dillon's desk.

"We may have caught a break," Dillon said. He unlocked a bottom desk drawer, pulled out a pistol in a Stow-N-Go holster. He slid the holster inside the waist of his pants and attached the nylon clip to his belt.

"That's probably a good idea," Suel said and hurried back to his desk. He pulled a leather shoulder holster from his desk, strapped it on, and then slipped on a nylon windbreaker.

"You know where Prince Street is behind Arnott's department store?" Dillon asked as they hurried toward the elevator.

"That parking ramp? Yeah, right before you get to the GPO. I'll drive."

"Emily said it looks like O'Rourke may have left the cellphone in his car, but she can't determine what level it's on."

"When we get close, call her, and have her trace your phone, she can follow us through the parking ramp," Suel said.

"Good idea," Dillon said as they stepped off the elevator and hurried toward the door. They picked up the pace walking, but as soon as they stepped outside the headquarters building, they began to run toward Suel's car.

"Think we need to call for backup?" Dillon asked as he slid into the passenger seat.

"Let's see what we have once we get there," and Suel started the car. He raced down the lane, screeched to a stop as they came to the sidewalk, and then sped off after a quick glance up the street. They wove in and out of traffic along the Liffey, ran through two separate red lights, and arrived at O'Connell Street in near-record time.

Dillon pulled out his cellphone and called Emily. Fortunately, she answered after a couple of rings. "Emily, it's Dillon. Can you bring my cellphone up and track us as we enter the parking ramp? We'll be there in just a couple of minutes."

"I should be able to. Give me your number and—"

"You don't have it?"

"It's on my cell, Dillon. If you want this done, just give me the damn number."

"Oh, yeah, sure, of course," Dillon said and gave her his number.

Suel leaned on the horn and inched through pedestrian traffic and at least three different people giving him the finger. Only taxis and busses were allowed on this section of O'Connell Street, and two taxis honked as Suel pulled onto the street. The historic GPO and Prince Street were just a block ahead. Suel leaned on the horn again as he made a left-hand turn just before the GPO. He honked at a couple of pedestrians, and they jumped back onto the sidewalk as Suel sped down the lane. Arnott's parking ramp was at the end of the lane, just past a half-dozen motorcycles parked at the curb.

The parking ramp was a four-story brick structure blocking any further progress at the end of the short lane. A blue sign labeled 'PARKING' in white letters marked the entrance.

"Okay, I've got you about to enter the parking ramp," Emily said to Dillon.

"Feck all," Suel shouted and pulled out his wallet. He grabbed a credit card and inserted it into the meter.

"You're stopped at the entrance?" Emily asked.

"The meter is deciding if Suel's credit card is worth the risk," Dillon said just as the gate arm rose and Suel pulled ahead.

"I've got you moving," Emily said.

"Let me know when we're close to O'Rourke's phone," Dillon replied.

Cars were parked in tight spaces perpendicular to the narrow center lane Suel drove through. The first level was completely full, and he turned onto the rise that brought them to the next level. More of the same, all the spaces were full. Arrows painted on the floor indicated the one-way direction. A narrow, green-painted path directed people toward the stairwell and an elevator. A blue sign next to the door to the stairwell and elevator labeled the level '2B.'

"Anything?" Dillon asked and turned on the speaker on his cellphone.

"No, keep going," Emily said.

They drove up to the next level, 3A, and another level, 3B, after that. They passed at least a half-dozen empty parking spaces. "You still with me, Emily?"

"Yeah, I'm not seeing anything. Go to the next level, I guess."

Suel drove up to the next level, 4A. The level appeared to be only half-full. "What the hell? Did she lose us?" Suel asked.

"Tell Mr. Crabby I can hear him," Emily said. "Wait, Dillon, you should be near that phone. I've got both phones indicated on the screen. Are you in a center lane?"

"Yes," Dillon said. He signaled Suel to stop with a wave of his hand.

"It looks like that phone will be on your righthand side toward the end."

"You hear that?" Dillon asked.

Suel nodded and pulled his pistol from the shoulder harness.

"I'm getting out," Dillon said as he opened the door. He set his phone on the passenger seat, quietly closed the car door, and drew his pistol from his waistband. He crouched alongside Suel's car, rested his pistol on the hood, and waved Suel forward.

Suel began to move forward at a snail's pace. Dillon moved with him, focusing on two cars, one red, the other black. The black car was backed into the parking space at the far end. As they drew closer, two empty spaces appeared between the vehicles. Both vehicles appeared to be empty. They continued moving forward. Dillon focused from one car to the other but never picked up any movement. From a distance, he could see beneath the vehicles and didn't see anything that resembled the feet of someone hiding.

Suel suddenly waved at Dillon and sped ahead. He screeched to a stop, blocking in the black vehicle.

Dillon ran forward, holding his weapon with his arms extended. The red car, an Opel Astra, appeared empty and had an infant car seat in the rear seat.

The black car at first looked empty, but then Dillon focused on what looked like a blue blanket in the front passenger seat.

Suel was out of the car, aiming his pistol at the vehicle. He mumbled something, but Dillon was so focused on the front passenger seat he didn't understand what Suel said.

"Bloody hell, Dillon. A Volkswagen Jetta. A black Volkswagen Jetta."

It suddenly dawned on Dillon, the same type of vehicle on the CCTV tape of Keegan Donnelly refueling down in Cork.

"Cover me," Dillon said as he stepped forward. He reached over and knocked on the passenger window. He didn't expect a response. What at first appeared to be a blue blanket was actually the back of a long-sleeve blue jersey. The person in the driver's seat was leaning over into the passenger seat.

THIRTY-ONE

Dillon stepped over to the driver's side. The door was unlocked. He opened the door, reached in, took a handful of the curly black hair, and pulled the body back to the upright position behind the steering wheel. Brennan O'Rourke's deep blue eyes gave off a glassy stare, no doubt due to the bullet hole just above his left eye.

"Oh, for God's sake. For the love of…Is this shite ever going to end?" Suel said.

Dillon opened the passenger door on Suel's car and picked up his phone. "Emily, you still there?"

"Oh, thank God. What's happening? Are you all right?"

"Yeah, we're fine. Unfortunately, Brennan O'Rourke appears to have met an untimely fate."

"You found him? He has his phone? What's he doing there?"

"What's he doing? He's dead. Shot in the head." After a long moment, Dillon said, "Emily, are you there?"

"Yeah. Yes, umm, I'm here. Oh, I'm sorry, Dillon."

"Not to worry. We're okay. Thank you for directing us to him. We'll deal with this. I'm going to ring off.

We'll have to get the forensics team and the medical examiners here. Take a deep breath, Emily. You sure
you're okay?"

He actually heard her exhale, and then she said,
"Yeah, I think so. I just didn't expect this."

"Well, you're not alone. Neither did we. Thanks for
your help. Without you, there's no telling how long he
would have remained here. You did a good job, a great
job. Thanks, Emily."

"I suppose I'd better let you go," she said.

"Yeah, we're going to be here for a while. I'll touch
base with you later today. Thanks again. We wouldn't
have found him if it wasn't for you."

"Umm, okay," she said and quickly disconnected.

Suel was on his phone, so Dillon walked around the
Jetta, looking for anything that seemed out of place. God
forbid he'd find a shell casing or someone's wallet. He
didn't see anything.

"How's she doing?" Suel asked as he disconnected.

"Emily? I'd say she's a little shell-shocked," Dillon
said. "You call this in?"

"Yeah, about all we can do now is wait."

"It looks like more of the same. Small caliber, no exit
wound. Residue on O'Rourke's face and jersey. I'm
guessing whoever shot him was in the passenger seat and
pulled him down so he wouldn't be seen as they got out
of the car."

"You want to stay up here while I drive down to the entrance? It's going to be at least twenty minutes, maybe longer," Suel said.

"Yeah, I'll keep the crowds away up here," Dillon said and looked around at the empty parking area. Other than the few cars, there weren't any people, Suel and Dillon being the only exceptions.

Suel climbed into his car, gave a quick wave, and headed for the exit ramp.

Dillon had been waiting nearly half an hour when the green light flashed above the elevator door, and a woman stepped out with a shopping bag labeled 'Arnott's.' Based on the direction she started, Dillon figured she was headed for the red Opel Astra. She didn't notice Dillon until she was halfway to her car. She slowed her walk, clutched the shopping bag a little tighter, and gave a quick glance around.

"Excuse me, ma'am. I'm with An Garda Síochána," He smiled and called, as he pulled out the badge from his left front pocket. "Is that your car?" he asked, nodding at the red Opel Astra.

"Yes," she said, drawing out the word as if to say, 'what's this about?'

"Have you been parked here long?"

"I've only been on a short shopping trip. Maybe just an hour or so. Why? What seems to be the problem?" she asked, apparently getting her courage back.

"No problem with you or your car. Do you recall, was this other car parked here when you arrived?" Dillon asked and nodded at the Volkswagen Jetta.

The woman seemed to glance past Dillon. Unfortunately, she focused on Brennan O'Rourke leaning back in the driver's seat with his glassy stare and the bullet hole just above his left eye. She screamed, dropped her shopping bag, and took three or four steps backward.

'*Shit*,' Dillon thought. "It's okay, ma'am. It's okay," Dillon said as he slowly approached.

"Oh, that's terrible, terrible. Oh my God. Did he fall and hit his head?"

Her hands were up against her mouth, and Dillon placed his hands on her elbows and slowly turned her to the side so she wasn't facing O'Rourke in the Jetta.

"Did you call an ambulance?" she asked and gave a quick glance over toward O'Rourke.

"Help is on the way," Dillon said. It took a good five minutes before he got her somewhat calmed down. She couldn't recall if the Jetta had been parked there when she pulled in. Dillon got her name, address, and phone number and then helped her into her car. He stood between her car and the Jetta, hoping to block her view. She started the Opel Astra and gave a final glance toward O'Rourke. Dillon was still blocking her line of sight. He smiled and gave a little wave as she pulled out of the parking place and drove toward the exit.

Ten minutes later, Suel's car appeared with the same two forensic guys that had gone through Tommy Thomson's house earlier that morning. Suel pulled in three spots away from the Jetta, and all three climbed out of his car. The forensic guys were dressed in their hazmat suits.

"The forensics van was too big to make it in the entrance," Suel explained as he pressed a button on his key fob, and the trunk clicked open. He raised the lid and pulled out two large black cases. Dillon recognized the cases as holding the forensic evidence collection kits.

The younger member of the forensic team opened the rear door of the car and pulled out four metal stands that he quickly positioned around the Jetta. Suel reached into the trunk and pulled out a roll of blue and white tape with the words, 'An Garda Síochána Do Not Cross' in both English and Irish. He handed the tape to the younger member of the forensic team. He walked over, tied an end to one of the metal stands, and proceeded to tape off the area.

"What did you learn while I was gone?" Suel asked.

"The woman who was parked next to O'Rourke's car couldn't remember if it was parked there when she pulled in."

Suel stopped for a moment, looked at Dillon, and said, "Really?"

"Afraid so. She was in a bit of a shock. She saw O'Rourke sitting there behind the wheel and, well, just kind of lost it. I got her calmed down, got her name, address, and phone number. I'm thinking O'Rourke has been here for a while."

"You're right on that point, Dillon," one of the forensic guys called over. "Paddy, the blood's dried. Your man's lips are blue. I'm going to guess last night, early this morning. Once the medical examiners get here, they'll give you a tighter timeframe."

"I don't suppose you found a note with the killer's name on it," Suel said.

"Afraid not. You want to call McCabe, or should I?" Dillon asked.

"Be my guest," Suel said.

Dillon pulled out his phone and hit the speed dial for McCabe. Fortunately, he was dumped into voicemail. "Yes, sir. Marshall Dillon, calling in. We've found the body of Brennan O'Rourke in a black Volkswagen Jetta in the Arnott's parking ramp just off Prince Street. Forensics team is here just beginning to examine the scene. We expect the medical examiners to arrive at any moment. DI Suel and I will remain here until the scene has been cleared."

"Lucky you," Suel said.

Dillon heard the bell ring, announcing the elevator arriving. He glanced over just as the green light above the door flashed on. The door opened, and Hugh Healy angled the gurney out of the elevator. Dillon recognized Artie Reilly from the Thompson scene that morning. A black body bag was strapped to the gurney. Once they rolled the gurney out of the elevator, Healy stepped back in and grabbed two black cases containing the medical examiner's kits, placed them on the gurney, and wheeled it over toward the scene.

"How's it going, Hugh?" Dillon asked.

"Be a lot better if we weren't getting all these calls from you lot. Where's our latest victim?"

Dillon pointed to the Jetta behind the 'Do Not Cross' tape.

"Mmm, surprise, surprise."

"All right, anything you can tell us?" Reilly asked.

"Only that he's dead. He's tied in some way, shape, or form to Keegan Donnelly and Tommy Thompson, so be on the lookout for any similarities," Dillon said.

"All right, let's get started," Artie Reilly said. "Any contact?"

Dillon shook his head and said, "Man's name is Brennan O'Rourke. When we arrived, O'Rourke was leaning forward across the passenger seat. I think he was purposely positioned so no one would see him. I opened the driver's door, grabbed him by the back of his hair, and set him upright. At the time, we didn't know if he was alive or dead."

"Did you search him?"

"Once we could see his condition, particularly the bullet hole, we just let him be. He wasn't going any-where," Dillon joked.

Healy flashed a quick smile.

Artie Reilly stared at Dillon for a moment then turned and opened one of the cases resting on the gurney. "This shouldn't take too long, lads."

"Let's check the area," Suel said. "Looking for a shell casing. I'm guessing they've CCTV taping who comes and goes at the entrance. We'll want to get those tapes. I'll look around if you want to go down and check with security. I've alerted them to the situation. They've blocked off this level from customers."

THIRTY-TWO

Dillon took the elevator down to the first level and walked over to the parking ramp exit. A heavyset, dark-haired woman was seated in the cashier station behind a thick glass panel. She set the chocolate doughnut she'd been eating on the counter, licked her fingers, and watched as Dillon approached.

He raised his ID to her and said, "Hi, I'm with the team up on level 4A. Is there someone I can talk with to obtain a copy of your CCTV tapes from yesterday?"

The woman shook her head. "Sorry, but there aren't any. The system has been down for three or four weeks."

"Down? You don't have any recordings of vehicles entering or exiting?"

"No, I just told you, the system has been down for three or four weeks."

"Is there someone I can check with?" Dillon asked, hoping, maybe, on the off-chance there was a backup system.

She pulled open a drawer, grabbed a business card, and slid it through the slot. "Here you go, not that it'll do you any good. I'd be surprised if they even answer the phone."

Dillon took the card. He was tempted to make a comment about the chocolate doughnut but decided it would be better not to. Instead, he smiled and said, "Thanks for your help. Have a nice rest of the day."

He walked back to the elevator and headed up to level 4A.

As he stepped off the elevator, Suel caught sight of him and watched as he approached. "Well, that went so quickly it has all the ear markings of a complete cluster-feck."

"That about sums it up," Dillon said. "Apparently, the system has been down for three or four weeks, and there are no CCTV tapes to review."

"Oh, for the love of—Are you kidding? This can't continue. There must be some form of backup. One dead end after another? This is insane," Suel said.

"The cashier gave me the card of someone to call," Dillon said and held up the card.

Suel snatched the card from his hand and said, "Give me that damn thing. I'll call this plonker." He held the card out to read. "Elliott Kane, okay. Let's just see what Mr. Kane has to say for himself." Suel began tapping in the phone number on his cell phone.

Dillon's phone suddenly rang. He pulled it from his pocket and glanced at the screen. The words 'Unknown Number' appeared. His usual action was to let it fall into voicemail, and if it was someone who really wanted to talk, they'd leave a message. For some reason, he chose to answer.

"Marshal Dillon," he said.

"Oh, Jack, I wasn't sure I'd be able to reach you. This is Amelia Maher. I hope I'm not interrupting."

"Actually, Amelia, your call is the first good thing that's happened today."

She chuckled and said, "Well, thank you. But that sounds like things are not going all that well. I'll be quick. I, umm, just wondered if you would be interested in meeting for a glass of wine later this evening? Strictly social, time and place your choice."

Dillon thought for the briefest of moments, something positive, enjoyable, and not related to four unsolved, dead-end cases would be just the thing he needed. Unfortunately, the way things were going, the chance was slim to none that he'd be able to meet up. "I would love to get together. The problem is I'm not sure I can get away."

"How about this? I'm just about to make white chicken chili. One of my favorite dishes. Why don't you plan to come over whenever you can make it? Don't set a time. Just give me a call, and you can have a quick dinner and get back to work if you have to, no pressure."

"Oh, that's very kind of you, but I might be working late. Well, and then once I'm out of here, I've got to get home and deal with Lucifer, and I—"

"Lucifer?" she said.

"Yeah, my dog. It's a long story. Suffice to say, we tolerate one another."

"Sounds interesting. Maybe I could learn something from him. Tell you what, why don't you give me a call once you've seen to Lucifer's needs. I'll have dinner for two waiting. Don't you go out and get anything. I've got everything we'll need, including the wine."

"Oh, that sounds like a lot of work, Amelia. I think—"

"Don't think. Just say yes, and then call me when you're able to come over. No pressure. Deal?"

"Okay, you win. I'm looking forward to it. Thank you," Dillon said.

"See you tonight, at whatever time works for you," she said and disconnected.

"I can't believe the ineptness around here," Suel said as he shoved his cellphone back into his pocket. "You were right. They've no CCTV tapes, no backup system. Isn't that just grand? Honest to God, I just want—What in the hell are you grinning about?"

"Nothing," Dillon said. "I just thought it might be better if we took a little more positive attitude."

"A positive attitude? Dillon, in case you've forgotten, we've three, no wait, make that four unsolved cases. All related in some way, shape, or form that we can't quite figure out. McCabe is liable to have us out on the street directing traffic if we don't come up with something and fast. Meanwhile, all of a sudden, you're walking around smiling and carrying on about a positive attitude. For fecks sake!"

"Paddy, there's not much we can do except keep trying, and sooner or later, something is bound to break
loose. Until then, ranting and raving doesn't seem to be
helping. Might I suggest we take a deep breath and focus
on something upbeat?"

Suel closed his eyes, took a deep breath, and slowly
exhaled. He repeated the process and then did it one
more time. He opened his eyes, smiled, and said, "That's
one of the more stupid things you've said. Artie, you
have anything yet?" he shouted over at the medical examiners.

THIRTY-THREE

The medical examiners and the forensics team eventually finished. Brennan O'Rourke's body was on its way to the Dublin City Morgue over on Griffith Avenue. The autopsy was scheduled for tomorrow morning. The Dublin City tow truck had cleared the entrance to the parking ramp with a good two inches to spare and was currently in the process of hooking up the Volkswagen Jetta and hauling it over to forensics, where they would do a more involved examination, looking for fingerprints and possible DNA samples. Obviously, O'Rourke had been in the vehicle, but now the question was, was this the same Volkswagen Jetta that Keegan Donnelly was refueling at the Esso on the Run station in Silver Springs just outside of Cobh the night of the Sheehan murders. Both Dillon and Suel suspected that it was the same vehicle, which brought up more questions, not the least of which was, how was O'Rourke tied to the Sheehan murders?

Dillon and Suel didn't make it back to Special Branch until after 6:00 that evening. At least they wouldn't have to explain the most recent set of circumstances to DCI McCabe until tomorrow morning, or so they thought.

Dillon punched in the security code on the keypad, the door buzzed, and they entered Special Branch. There were only two officers in the office, both at their desks and on the phone. Dillon was in the process of wondering what kind of wine he should buy to go with Amelia's chicken dish. Suel was headed to his desk to check messages before he hurried out of the office.

The lights were off in McCabe's office. Dillon and Suel both felt a wave of relief until McCabe suddenly stepped out, pulled the door closed behind him, and inserted his key in the lock. There was no point in attempting to hide under a desk. McCabe was between them and the break room, so hiding there wasn't an option either.

Dillon took a deep breath and called, "Good evening, sir. Can we have a half-minute of your time before you head out?"

McCabe looked over his shoulder and smiled. "I've all the time in the world, gentlemen. Please, come join me and bring me up to date." He unlocked the door, stepped inside, and turned on the lights.

"Mother of Jaysus," Suel groaned under his breath as they headed toward McCabe's office.

"Please, take a seat, gentlemen, take a seat. I was hoping we might meet up. Long day?"

"Very," Suel said as they sat down.

"So?" McCabe asked once they were seated.

Dillon waited a moment for Suel to begin. He finally glanced over at Suel, who, with a nod of his head, suggested the privilege of beginning belonged to Dillon. "Yet more questions and not many answers," Dillon said. "Brennan O'Rourke was found dead in a black Volkswagen Jetta that was parked in Arnott's parking ramp just at the end of Prince Street. The medical examiners estimated his time of death between midnight and 12:30 a.m. this morning."

"One round to the head," Suel said. "Close range, small caliber. We suspect the round will match those from the Sheehan murders, the Keegan Donnelly murder, and Tommy Thompson's murder."

"The Volkswagen Jetta has been towed to forensics. They'll be conducting a thorough examination tomorrow morning. The odds are it's the same vehicle Keegan Donnelly was refueling on the CCTV tapes the night of the Sheehan murders."

"Was there a previous link to this O'Rourke and Donnelly?" McCabe asked.

Dillon shook his head. "Only social. Nothing that seemed to tie them to the Sheehan murders. Obviously, that's changed now. O'Rourke insisted he hadn't seen Donnelly in weeks. We have evidence of a phone call where they were planning to get together, but that meeting never happened, at least according to O'Rourke."

"We're still pretty much in the dark," Suel said. "At this stage, it doesn't seem to make much sense that Donnelly concocted the murder of the Sheehan's on his own.

That said, I can't really see O'Rourke or Thompson being the brains of this operation."

Dillon jumped in. "It seems logical that someone higher up got Donnelly involved initially. He, Donnelly, may have asked for some help from Thompson and O'Rourke. But whoever the brains of this so-called operation was, Thompson's and O'Rourke's involvement, I think, may have come as a surprise."

McCabe nodded. "And yet they're all dead."

"I think their involvement may be just as big a surprise to whoever is behind these killings as it is to us," Dillon said. "While the scenes don't appear to leave much as far as evidence, the timing is strange. That, and the fact that none of the victims appear to have tried to flee the scene. They appear to have been surprised or caught off-guard. None of them were armed. None of them appear to have tried to flee. Thompson and O'Rourke had at least twenty-four hours to disappear after Donnelly's murder. Thus far, we've not found anything that suggests they were about to leave. No sense of a struggle or attempted escape at the murder scenes. They seem to have been caught completely off-guard. It would appear whoever killed them had their trust and was not viewed as a problem."

McCabe shook his head. "Any idea who is the brains behind this debacle?"

"We've found nothing that points to anyone. No names have surfaced," Suel said.

"We were thinking possibly a connection with the Linnehan's, but that's tenuous at best," Dillon added.

"What about a Russian connection?" McCabe asked.

"Nothing thus far," Suel said.

McCabe shook his head. "All right. Keep at it. Something, somewhere, is bound to turn up. Anything else?"

Both Dillon and Suel shook their heads.

"I suggest you lads head home, take a deep breath, and get back at it in the morning," McCabe said.

Dillon and Suel nearly jumped to their feet. "Yes, sir. We'll be on it. Something's bound to break," they said in unison and hurried out the door.

"Good night, gentlemen," McCabe said a couple of minutes later as he passed them on his way out of Special Branch.

They waited a minute or two after McCabe left the office before Dillon leaned back in his desk chair and asked, "What do you think?"

"I'm thinking it would be a good idea if we both kept our fingers crossed in the hope forensics and or the medical examiners come up with something that will lead us in the right direction. I also intend to follow McCabe's advice and head out of here in a couple of minutes. You have time for a pint?" Suel asked.

"I would love to, but I better get home and attend to whatever mess Lucifer has left for me. I'm looking forward to a quiet night eating some leftover dinner in front of the TV."

Suel smiled and said, "Actually, that doesn't sound all that bad. I'm sending a text to your man Healy in the medical examiners asking for a time on O'Rourke's autopsy tomorrow. One of us should be there. Unless you have some secret desire to go, I'd be happy to attend."

"Be my guest. I'll tie myself to this desk and go back over our files. There has to be something we've missed," Dillon said.

"One can only hope."

Suel said good night and left a few minutes later. Dillon waited another five minutes and then hurried out to his car. No sooner had he stepped out into the parking lot than a voice from behind him called, "Dillon, a quick question." He turned to see McCabe exiting the building.

"Yes, sir."

"You mentioned this woman, Amelia?"

"Yes, sir. Amelia Maher. I met her for lunch. She seemed nice, almost too nice. Answered all my questions as best she could. Basically, she had been friends, maybe even more, with Donnelly and eventually just got fed up with the bad choices the man continued to make. She viewed his death as unfortunate but not surprising. That said, I don't know. There just seems to be something not adding up."

"How so?"

"I can't describe it, just a sense, maybe."

"Trust your sense, Dillon," McCabe said and walked off toward his car.

Dillon drove to the Grape Vine, the wine store near his home, and picked up two chilled bottles of a Sauvignon Blanc. He pulled into the parking area in front of his house and hopped out of his car. Lucifer met him at the front door.

He let the dog out and stepped inside to grab the leash. Amazingly, the kitchen wastebasket was still standing, but then he'd emptied it that morning, so there was nothing to entice Lucifer's misbehavior. He pulled the front door closed behind him, attached the leash to Lucifer's collar, and they headed out on a walk. Forty-five minutes later, they settled onto a bench in Albert Park after walking around the park three times. In the distance, a Gaelic football match was underway, and they sat and watched for a good fifteen minutes before heading home.

Once inside, Lucifer curled up on his cushion in front of the TV. Dillon grabbed a biscuit from the jar on the kitchen counter, turned on the TV, and took a quick shower. He shaved, pulled on some casual clothes, and headed out the door. As he climbed into his car, it suddenly dawned on him he didn't know where Amelia lived. He pulled out his phone and called her.

"Can you still make it tonight?" was how she answered.

"I can if you tell me where you live. I just realized I don't know."

She laughed and said, "I'm in Sandycove. The address is number one Sandycove Road. I'm the corner unit behind a green hedge. Feel free to park out front or open the gate and drive in. There's plenty of room."

"I'm heading out now, so I'll see you in maybe forty minutes if traffic allows."

"Take your time. We're on your schedule," she said.

THIRTY-FOUR

Sandycove was a nice trendy area on the south side of Dublin, on the shore of Dublin Bay. It was nearly forty minutes from Dillon's place up on the north side. He drove through the city center and across the Liffey River. He passed through Ballsbridge, Merrion, Monkstown, and Dun Laoghaire sections of Dublin. The homes in Sandycove were older, exquisite, and priced way out of Dillon's range. His GPS took him right to the door of number one Sandycove Road. An elegant two-story stucco structure Dillon guessed was probably built over one hundred years ago. A double wrought iron gate led into the parking area in front of the home.

Dillon pulled partway onto the sidewalk and parked. He grabbed the bag with the two bottles of formerly chilled Sauvignon Blanc wine and stepped through the front gate. The gravel parking area in front of the house was large enough for three or four cars. Currently, a dark-blue Mercedes Roadster was parked next to the steps leading up to the front door. Based on the license plate, the Roadster was just a year old. Dillon made his way up the steps.

He could hear the doorbell chime inside. A moment later, Amelia pulled back the lace curtain on the front door, grinned, waved, and opened the door. She gave him a peck on the cheek and said, "Come in. You made good time. Any problem finding the place?"

"No, amazingly, I never got lost."

"Well, I suspect you know your way around the city rather well. Oh, you didn't have to do this," she said as he handed her the bag with the wine bottles.

"It's the least I can do. So kind of you to invite me. The bottles used to be chilled."

"I'll put them in the refrigerator. Come in, come in."

The entry had a white marble floor and a gilt-framed antique oil painting of Benbulben mountain out in Sligo hanging on the wall above the staircase." Lovely home," Dillon remarked as he stepped inside.

"Thank you. I don't mind saying it's been a lot of work, updating. When I first moved in, I didn't think anything had been done in at least sixty years. Come on back to the kitchen," she said. Dillon caught the hint of perfume that reminded him of something he couldn't place. He dutifully followed, admiring Amelia's tight black slacks and the white blouse as she led the way.

She walked through what could only be described as a formal dining room. There was a marble fireplace and elegant paneling on the walls. A table that seated eight sat on an oriental rug. An antique oil painting of the Cliffs of Moher hung above the fireplace mantel. She pushed open a swinging door, and they entered a bright white kitchen. "Grab a stool and sit down. How about some hors d'oeuvres and a glass of wine? We can both begin to relax. Thanks again for coming over."

"Thank you for the invitation. This is just what the doctor ordered."

"Crazy day at work?" Amelia asked as she filled two wine glasses from a crystal carafe.

"They're all crazy," Dillon said.

She pushed a glass of white wine across the granite counter then raised her glass. As they clinked glasses, she said, "Here's to a degree of sanity." Dillon took a healthy sip and felt the stress begin to release. She slid a plate of crackers and cheese between them. "Dinner's ready whenever you want, but no rush."

"Thank you. You have a gorgeous home. You mentioned you've had a lot of work done."

"You wouldn't believe it. Tons of money on things you can't see. Updating the plumbing and electricity. Roof repair, not fun when it's a slate roof. I had to have a number of walls replastered. There was only one bathroom in the house, and that was from the 1920s. For the longest time, it seemed to be just one thing after another, all necessary, all expensive. I just had the kitchen redone, and I'm still trying to remember where I've put things." She laughed.

They chatted on through two more glasses of wine. Amelia seemed to search a couple of drawers before she found her silverware. They ate dinner in the kitchen, a white chicken chili from a pot on the stove. They drank more wine and laughed at each other's comments. After the meal, Amelia refilled their wine glasses yet again and took Dillon on a tour of the house. She opened one of the wine bottles Dillon brought and never let his glass be less than half-full.

Eventually, they settled into a study on the second floor. The walls were lined by bookcases filled with leather-bound books. They sat on a couch in front of the fireplace, facing each other. A quilt hung over the back of the couch. Dillon sat with his legs stretched out, sipping yet another glass of wine, trying to remember when he last felt this relaxed.

Amelia sat with her legs tucked beneath her, smiling and going on about the various projects she'd done in the home. At one point, she said, "You still seem a little tense."

"Tense? Actually, it's been weeks since I've felt this relaxed. I can't tell you how wonderful this has been. Really, this has been a marvelous evening."

"If you've been that tense. I know what could really help."

"Oh?"

"Yeah, here," she said as she took Dillon's wine glass and placed it on the table behind the couch. "Turn around and let me give you a little back rub."

"Oh, you don't have to—"

"It will really help. You're more stressed than you realize. Come on, turn around. I can tell you really need this."

Dillon turned around, and she slowly, methodically began to massage his shoulders and neck. "Oh my God. You are really knotted up. We're going to take care of that right now. Stretch out on the rug, and let me work on your shoulders and back."

"I'm okay. You've done more than enough and—"

"Yes, and I'm going to do this. Now come on, stretch out on the rug."

Dillon stretched out on the oriental rug in front of the fireplace. She straddled him and began to massage his shoulders and back. It felt wonderful, and she seemed to work at it for the longest time.

When Dillon woke up, she was next to him on the oriental rug. The room was dark, with the exception of the glowing embers in the fireplace. They were both naked, and the quilt from the back of the couch was covering them. He thought for the briefest of moments about quietly getting up, then quickly erased that thought and drifted back to sleep.

At some point, he was vaguely aware of Amelia moving. The next thing he knew, she was gently shaking his shoulder. "Dillon, Jack, Jack, it's time to wake up. Jack?"

Dillon's eyes slowly opened. There was a stabbing pain in the back of his skull, and his first thought was, *'I will never, ever, drink another glass of white wine in this life.'*

"Here, I made some coffee for you," Amelia said and handed the mug to him.

He took a sip. It didn't seem to help.

"If you want to shower and get dressed, I'll get breakfast going for you."

"Oh, umm, I should probably head home. What time is it?"

"It's early, not quite six. Grab a quick shower. The bathroom is just off the bedroom through that door. By the time you're dressed, I'll have breakfast ready for you. You'll feel a lot better. Oh, and thank you for last night," she said and kissed him on the lips. As she stepped out of the room, he made note of the red silk robe that left nothing to the imagination.

He took another sip of coffee and rose to his feet. The wine glasses and two empty bottles from the previous evening were gone. He gathered his clothes and went through the door she'd indicated, stepping into a large bedroom with a king-sized four-poster bed and a white duvet. The bathroom door was on the far side of the bed, and the light was on.

Dillon turned on the shower and stepped in. He seemed to revive somewhat with the water running over him. He dried off, dressed, and carried his empty coffee mug down to the kitchen.

He was all ready to tell her he should head home, but then he opened the kitchen door and smelled the bacon. Amelia set a plate with scrambled eggs and bacon on the counter and pushed it toward him.

He settled in on the stool and placed the empty coffee mug on the counter. He noticed a plastic container with a barcode labeled 'White Chicken Chili' in the wastebasket. He was about to make a joke about it but thought better of it.

As Amelia grabbed the coffee pot and filled his mug, she set a bottle of aspirin next to his plate. He caught the scent of a wonderful perfume that rang a distant bell he couldn't quite place.

"Did you enjoy your evening?" she asked.

"I must have. I can't remember very much of it."

"Oh, funny." She laughed. "Just so you know, I took advantage of you."

"You won't hear a complaint from me," he said and shoveled in a forkful of eggs and bacon.

THIRTY-FIVE

He had lingered a little too long after breakfast and was now racing home to let Lucifer out. Despite his current hangover, from what he could remember, the previous night was the best in quite some time, and he apparently had no memory of the most important part.

He made it home in time to let Lucifer out before there was a mess. Dillon filled Lucifer's food and water dishes, coaxed him back inside with a biscuit, and hurried over to Special Branch, still wearing the same clothes from the night before.

Suel was already at his desk as Dillon walked past. "What's with the outfit? And do I detect perfume?" Suel asked.

"Just wanted to look my best for you," Dillon replied. "Anything on O'Rourke's autopsy?"

"Yeah, they're scheduled for 9:00. I figured if I got down there around 11:00, I might get the initial results. I checked with Brendan Davis in forensics. They're already going through the Jetta. You might think about stopping in later this morning and see what they've found."

Dillon hadn't planned on it. Suel's suggestion added some pressure, but it sounded like a good idea. "Yeah, I'll leave about the same time you do. In the meantime, I'll go through those files again. I'm going to start over at square one and see if there isn't something we've missed that will answer all our questions."

He went into the break room, grabbed a coffee and two more aspirin, and settled in at his desk. He began reviewing files hoping he would find some key point they had missed. Over the course of the next few hours, nothing presented itself. All of a sudden, Suel was standing at his desk, saying he was going to head over to the medical examiners to get the autopsy results on Brennan O'Rourke. Dillon closed the current file that had provided no help and followed Suel out the door. They parted ways on the first floor. Suel headed out to his car, and Dillon took the long hallway down to the forensics garage.

The Volkswagen Jetta was up on blocks when he walked in. All four tires and doors had been removed. Brennan Davis was wearing a blue hazmat suit along with a pair of goggles, latex gloves, and a mask. At the moment, he was applying clear tape to the dusted fingerprints on the Volkswagen's glovebox.

"Any luck?" Dillon asked.

"Maybe, we'll run these prints and see. We've collected some hair samples from the headrests. There were footprints on the windshield."

"Someone tried to kick in the windshield?"

"Not quite," Davis said and smiled. "My guess is there was a bit of coital interaction."

"What?"

"Let me put it in terms you'll understand, Dillon. Your man, or one of them, since there are at least two lads associated with this vehicle, had sex with a woman sitting in the passenger seat. Her feet ended up pressed against the inside of the windshield. Get it?"

"Oh, yeah, sure. Sorry, I was thinking of something else there."

"Yeah, sure you were. Oh, by the way, this vehicle is owned by a dental hygienist and was reported as stolen in Monkstown about three weeks ago."

Dillon had driven through Monkstown this morning on the way back from Amelia's, and his mind wandered into what little he remembered of their late night.

"What the hell are you smiling about?" Davis asked as he stood.

"Oh, just trying to guess which one got lucky, Keegan Donnelly or Brennan O'Rourke."

"Well, don't hold your breath. I've got the sense that whoever shot this O'Rourke lad took the time to try to clean up any trace they may have left behind."

"That would seem to match the other scenes," Dillon said.

"Yes, it does," Davis said. "The medical examiners are probably finishing up with their autopsy about now. My money's on the bullet matching the previous cases, including that American couple down in Cork. There is no sign of a struggle in the vehicle. One man was shot in bed. One was shot in his front garden. O'Rourke was shot in this car. No one seems to have put up a fight. This O'Rourke knew about Donnelly and Thompson being killed, yet he's apparently with the killer in the car at midnight, in an empty parking ramp, and for all intents and purposes, it doesn't appear he was the least bit concerned. I honestly don't get it."

"Hopefully, something will turn up with the fingerprints," Dillon said.

"We'll know soon enough. I'll give you a call one way or the other," Davis replied.

Dillon pulled out his wallet and opened it to grab a card with his cellphone number. Something wasn't right. The cards were at the opposite end of his wallet from where he always placed them.

As he handed a card to Davis, he said, "Call me on my cellphone just in case I'm out of the office."

He headed up to Special Branch. He kept thinking of Davis's comment about no one appearing concerned with the individual who killed them. Could the killer have appeared out of nowhere? But how do you appear out of nowhere when someone is in bed? How do you appear out of nowhere on the fourth level of a mostly empty parking ramp? It didn't make sense unless it was someone they were all familiar with, someone they all trusted.

He sat down at his desk and pulled out his wallet again. Nothing appeared to be missing, and yet, it was different. His US driver's license, plastic with a photo, was in the correct leather pocket, but it was backwards and in front of the Republic of Ireland ID, also plastic with his photo. He always kept the Irish ID in front. Strange. He checked the cash, two twenty euro notes, which matched his memory. Had he been in his wallet last night, getting or showing something to Amelia?

It was close to 2:00 when Suel finally arrived back at Special Branch. He headed straight to Dillon's desk and plopped down a multi-page report. "Here you go. At no surprise, the round they removed from O'Rourke matches the rounds from Tommy Thompson, Keegan Donnelly, and the American Sheehans. What did you find out at forensics?"

"A number of things." Dillon went on to bring Suel up to date on the forensic findings. "Someone had sex in the front seat of the Volkswagen. Whoever this killer is, they all seem to have been comfortable with him. No signs of a struggle or any attempt to resist. Forensics is analyzing hair and fingerprint samples from the car as we speak. My sense is when we hear from them, we'll be no further ahead."

Davis phoned Dillon an hour later. Unfortunately, the forensics results were just as he had feared. "Prints and hair samples from four individuals were recovered. Unfortunately, one was Keegan Donnelly, and another was Brennan O'Rourke. DNA on the headrest suggests a woman with auburn hair, but I've not found a match with our files. I'm currently running the information through the American FBI system and fully expect to come up empty-handed."

"Nothing on the woman in the passenger seat?" Dillon asked.

"That's the auburn-haired woman, and whoever she was, she's not in any files, at least thus far. I was able to confirm her interaction was with Donnelly. I sent someone to get a DNA test from the owner of the vehicle. I should have that within the hour. We'll run it and eliminate her. There's maybe a one percent chance she's the woman who interacted with Donnelly."

"So, in other words, you've come up empty-handed," Dillon said.

"Yeah, pretty much. I'll keep you posted, but don't hold your breath. Whoever was in the vehicle in the parking ramp with O'Rourke wiped it down with alcohol wipes. If they're that cautious, it's not a huge leap to suggest they may have even worn latex gloves. Hell, they could have been in a hazmat suit for all we know."

"Not what I would call encouraging. Let me know either way what you get from the FBI files," Dillon said. He thanked Davis and disconnected.

THIRTY-SIX

Just before 5:00 that evening, DCI McCabe stepped to the door of his office and said, "Dillon, Suel, McCarthy, and McDonald, a moment of your time, please."

Suel and McCarthy met at Dillon's desk. McCarthy set an empty tea mug on the desk, and they headed into McCabe's office. No one had any idea why they were called in.

"McDonald will be along shortly, sir. He's finishing up a phone call," McCarthy said.

McDonald hurried into the office a moment later. "Sorry, sir. On the line with forensics. Unfortunately, no news."

McCabe nodded and said, "Thus far, other than collecting more bodies, we've accomplished next to nothing. Based on the email I've just received, that may be about to change." He turned his computer screen in the general direction of the four men standing in front of his desk. Other than the Weston Airport letterhead, the copy on the screen was too small for any of them to read at a distance. Weston Airport was a small, private airport approximately eight miles outside of Dublin.

McCabe cleared his throat and said, "I received this copy of Weston's General Aviation Report. It would appear Dennis Punchy Sheehan is scheduled to arrive at Weston on a private plane from the UK tomorrow afternoon at approximately 4:00. Given the recent spate of…incidents, I think it might be to our advantage to meet Mr. Sheehan under the guise of offering protection and use that opportunity to obtain some answers to our questions. The four of you will be posing as maintenance workers, arriving in thirty-minute intervals over the course of two hours beginning at 7:00 tomorrow morning. We will be meeting in interview room three in thirty minutes with more specific instructions. Any questions?"

"How sure are you that Sheehan will arrive?" McDonald asked.

McCabe shook his head. "About as sure as we were the last time he was supposed to arrive and didn't. However, given the lack of any information whatsoever, it's my decision that we treat this as gospel until told otherwise. Please hold any other questions for thirty minutes, gentlemen. Thank you, that is all."

Dillon was back at his desk, on the phone, attempting to reach his neighbor, Tara. He hoped she might be home and able to take Lucifer for a walk. After a half-dozen rings, he hung up and, against his better judgment, was about to call his miserable next-door neighbor when his cellphone rang.

"Hi, Amelia," was how he answered.

"You seem to sound a lot better than you did this morning. Just wanted to check to see how you're holding up. Oh, and I wanted to apologize for deliberately over-serving you last night."

"Oh, thanks. That's very kind of you. To be honest, I have to assume full responsibility for drinking every last drop you placed in front of me. I could have said 'no, thank you' at any time but didn't."

"Fair enough." She laughed. "Say, short notice, but I'm up on the north side of town and wondered if you'd like to join me for dinner. You choose the place, and I'll pay."

"Oh, God, I'd love to, but something just came up, and we're about to head into a meeting. As a matter of fact, I'm trying to get in touch with a neighbor to let my dog out, but I'm not getting an answer. They must know it's me calling," he joked.

"Oh, well, can I help?"

"You don't have to do that. I'll call another neighbor and—"

"It's not a problem. If you wanted to leave a key at your front desk, I could swing by and pick it up. You said your dog's name is Satan?"

"Lucifer, actually," he said just as Suel walked past his desk, indicating the meeting was about to start in the break room. "Umm, tell you what, if you wouldn't mind. I just don't want to come home to a mess tonight, and he hasn't been out since this morning. There's a large flowerpot just outside the front door. A key is hidden a half-inch beneath the surface in the back of the pot."

"Not a problem. Would it be all right if I took him for a walk?"

"Oh, Amelia, he'd love it, but you don't have to do that." Dillon caught sight of McCabe stepping out of his office and heading for the break room.

"Actually, I'd enjoy it. I'll need to get your address," she said.

Dillon gave her the address, said a quick 'thank you,' and hurried to interview room three. Everyone was seated around the table. Suel nodded at an empty chair as he took a sip from a steaming cup of something.

As Dillon sat down, McCabe passed a stack of four handouts to McCarthy, who took one and passed the stack to McDonald. Once everyone had a copy, McCabe began. "This first page is an overview of the airport layout. The main building is two stories tall. It houses the control tower, offices, a restaurant, and a bar. The structure behind the main building consists of three hangers that serve the airport. Sheehan's plane will land and drive to the front of hanger number two. That's the middle hanger, and Sheehan will deplane at that point. There will be a vehicle waiting for him. We will have four two-man teams of Gardai in unmarked vehicles just outside the airport in the event we are unable to detain Mr. Sheehan when he steps off the airplane. Ideally, we will question him inside the hanger, record the interview, and send him on his way."

"He won't be arrested?" Suel asked.

"No, he won't, at least not at this time. Our purpose is merely to interview him. Five individuals have been murdered. Any assistance Sheehan can give in closing those cases will be the focus of our interview tomorrow."

"Would you consider bringing him back here?" McCarthy asked.

"My sense is he will not want to come. We will be asking him politely and accept whatever answer he provides. Our focus here is to determine who is responsible for these murders," McCabe said.

"When you arrive at the airport, you will park in the main parking lot. Need I say, do not park next to one another? From your vehicle, you will move to your assigned positions. Dillon, you'll be first to arrive. You will proceed to the main building, do a walk-through of the entire building, to include the control tower, and remain on site. You three are each assigned to a hanger. McCarthy, hanger number one. Suel, hanger number two. McDonald, hanger number three.

"Each hanger houses a number of small aircraft. You will perform a search of those aircraft every ninety minutes. Flights will not be scheduled to depart from the airport after 2:00 in the afternoon. As of thirty minutes ago, the Sheehan flight is the only arrival scheduled for the entire day. We will meet here, in Special Branch, at

5:00 a.m. tomorrow morning. We'll assign radios, weapons, and code words at that time. Any questions?"

"Food?" McDonald asked, and the other three smiled.

"Breakfast, lunch, and possibly dinner will be available from the restaurant. Pay for the meal and submit your receipts."

"Is there a menu we can look at?" McDonald asked, and even McCabe chuckled.

"Any other questions?" McCabe scanned the group. No one asked a question. "I'll see you here nice and early tomorrow morning at 5:00. Please study this airport layout. If there's nothing else, you are free to go. Have a safe and quiet evening," McCabe said.

Dillon folded the airport layout and placed it in a back pocket. He thought about calling Amelia then came up with a better idea.

"Are you thinking of stopping for a pint, Dillon?" Suel said.

"Thanks, but I'd better not. I've got to get home, take Lucifer for a walk, and with a 5:00 morning meet up here, I better play it low-key. I'll take a rain check. Maybe tomorrow evening?"

"Oddly, you seem to have come up with the better idea. I'll see the likes of you early tomorrow morning," Suel said.

Once Suel left the office, Dillon knocked on McCabe's doorframe. McCabe looked up from his desk. "Yes, Dillon, everything all right?"

"Yes, sir, at least I think so." He went on to explain his evening with Amelia Maher. He mentioned the fact that the eFile of her ID showed a blonde woman but that she now had auburn hair. "Then Davis in forensics phoned me and said they had an auburn hair sample recovered from the Jetta, but he was unable to match it to any of our files, so he was running the sample through the FBI."

"After your, umm, interlude last night, can you confirm that she was a blonde or a redhead?"

"I'm afraid not, sir."

"I see. Would you happen to have her address in Sandycove?"

"I remember it exactly, number one Sandycove Road. A very luxurious house."

McCabe wrote it down and said, "I wouldn't worry. I'll have this checked out. That said, allow me to caution you regarding any personal interaction, of any sort, with a potential witness. I'll let it go this once, but it is the first and last time. Do I make myself clear?"

"Yes, sir, very," Dillon said, deciding there was no point in mentioning Amelia taking Lucifer for a walk.

Once in his car, he phoned Il Corvo, a restaurant on Drumcondra Road, and ordered two take-out meals. By the time he drove over to the restaurant, the meals were ready for pick-up. It was a five-minute drive to his house from the restaurant. He drove past Albert Park but never saw Amelia, or Lucifer for that matter. They weren't on St. Pappins Road when he turned off Ballymun, but

Amelia's dark-blue Mercedes Roadster was parked halfway up on the sidewalk in front of Dillon's house.

He pulled into the front garden parking space and hurried inside. "Amelia, Lucifer," he called and got no response. He set the meals on the kitchen counter and hurried outside with a plastic bag. He cleaned up Lucifer's deposits from the last four or five days, tossed them in the trash, and hurried back inside. He literally ran up the stairs, changed the clothes he'd worn last night and all day today, tossed them onto the closet floor, applied some deodorant, and hurried back downstairs.

He'd just finished pulling the white Styrofoam food containers out of the plastic bag and setting two wine glasses on the counter when he heard the front door open. Amelia called, "Dillon? Jack? Are you home?"

"Back here in the kitchen," Dillon responded and hurried toward the front door.

THIRTY-SEVEN

Amelia wore a casual short black skirt, a sleeveless top, and pink running shoes. She had just unclipped the leash from Lucifer's collar. She stood, smiled, and gave Dillon a peck on the cheek that lasted a second or two longer than expected. "Mmm, so, how's your sanity?"

"It's still there, or at least a semblance of it."

"Had a delightful walk. He's such a wonderful dog."

"Lucifer? Really?"

"He was great. We did three times around the park and then sat for a few minutes and watched a football match, two girls teams."

"Probably the nearby schools."

"Well, it was really fun. What a lovely park and almost right outside your door. You're very fortunate."

"Yeah, I'm pretty lucky. Can I interest you in some dinner?" Dillon said just as his stomach growled.

"I think I'd better say yes," Amelia said and followed Dillon into the kitchen.

He nodded toward the biscuit jar and said, "Grab a biscuit and toss it to Lucifer. It'll make you his lifetime friend."

Amelia tossed a biscuit to Lucifer. He caught it in mid-air and disappeared into the entryway. "You have a nice place. Have you lived here long?"

"I've been here almost four years. Nice of you to say so. Of course, it doesn't begin to compare to your mansion."

"Hopefully not your last visit. Next time, let's promise each other we won't sleep on the floor. Not that I didn't enjoy myself."

"Glass of wine?" Dillon asked, changing the subject.

"Yes, I'd love one."

He poured two glasses of wine, handed one to Amelia, and raised his glass in a toast. "Here's to you."

"And to you," she said as they clinked glasses.

Dillon took a small sip, promising himself he wouldn't repeat his intoxication from the previous night. He took two plates from the cupboard, silverware, and paper napkins from the drawer and pushed them across the counter.

"What did you get for dinner?"

"A chicken and mushroom dish."

"Tagliatelle con Pollo e Funghi?" Amelia asked.

"If you say so. You're familiar with the restaurant?"

"Actually, no, but I speak a little Italian. I have this ability to pick up languages, and I've been to Italy a couple of times. It's a standard and very popular dish. Which I happen to love."

"Well, eat up," Dillon said and handed her a Styrofoam tray.

"Oh, fancy," Amelia said and laughed as she transfered the food to her plate.

They chatted about Lucifer, Sandycove, and things in general. Dillon barely touched his glass of wine, although he refilled Amelia's. When they were finished with dinner, he topped off Amelia's wine glass, and took two Magnum double caramel ice cream bars from the freezer, and handed one to Amelia.

"Oh, are you kidding? God, I haven't had one of these since I don't know when. I absolutely love them. Thank you," she said as she tore off the wrapper and took a bite. "Mmm-mmm."

"It meets with your approval?"

"Mmm-hmm." She nodded and took another bite.

Dillon moved their plates to another counter, and they sat and chatted for a few more minutes. As Amelia finished her ice cream bar, Dillon asked, "Would you like another?"

"Oh, I'd love one, but I'd better not."

"You sure? I've got a box and—"

"Oh, thanks, but I'd go through the entire box and then hate myself in the morning."

"Okay. Say, I've got a very early start tomorrow morning, so please don't take it personally, but you probably shouldn't stay tonight."

"Oh, that's okay. Just as long as it doesn't become an everyday occurrence."

"Just a very early meeting tomorrow."

"Everything okay?"

"Yeah, guests from out of the country. It happens occasionally."

"Say, I should visit the loo. Is it upstairs?"

"Yes, it is."

"Thank you again for the wonderful dinner."

"Thanks for being here and for your help with Lucifer."

"My pleasure," she said. She slid off her stool, blew Dillon a kiss, and headed upstairs to the bathroom.

Dillon loaded the dishwasher. He debated refilling his wine glass and decided against it. He tossed the Styrofoam boxes in the trash, ran the bag out to the bin in the back garden, and busied himself in the kitchen. He turned on the wall-mounted TV and clicked onto Sky News. He watched a report on the fishing industry, an increase in airline costs, and an update on Ireland's rugby team. It suddenly dawned on him that Amelia was still upstairs.

He walked around the kitchen counter and noticed her pink running shoes beneath the stool she'd been sitting on. He stepped out of the kitchen, ready to call upstairs to make sure she was okay, when he spotted her sleeveless top lying on the floor at the foot of the stairs. Her skirt was on the third step. Her bra was draped on the banister halfway up the staircase, and just at the top of the stairs was a red thong.

He climbed the stairs, collecting the items as he went. The bathroom door was open, and the light was off. He pushed the partially opened bedroom door and peeked inside. The duvet on his bed was pulled back, and naked Amelia was crawling onto the bed, smiling.

"Well, it certainly took you long enough. I thought it might be a good idea if we burned off the calories from that delicious ice cream bar. What do you think?"

It was just a few minutes before midnight when Dillon stood in the open front door and watched as Amelia walked to her Mercedes Roadster parked half-way up on the sidewalk. She opened the driver's door, called "Thank you," waved, and climbed into the car. A moment later, she drove around the corner and disappeared.

Dillon glanced up and down the lane just to be sure DCI McCabe wasn't parked somewhere keeping tabs on him. So much for the warning regarding any personal interaction with a potential witness. He closed and locked the front door, got the coffee ready for tomorrow morning, and headed up to bed. He set his alarm for 4:00 in the morning, smiled at the wonderful perfume scent on the pillows and was sound asleep in thirty seconds.

THIRTY-EIGHT

Dillon jumped out of bed when his alarm sounded, turned it off, and hurried into the bathroom. After a quick shower, he wandered back into the bedroom and opened his closet door. His clothes from the day before were on the floor of the closet but not as he'd left them. And then there was the matter of the folded airport layout from DCI McCabe. Dillon was positive the three-page document had been in his left rear pocket. Now, it was in the right rear pocket.

He didn't think he'd placed it right rear pocket, but that left only one other option. Amelia had read it. Why? Was she looking for something or just curious? Had she planned to hide in the closet? More importantly, what now? Did he tell DCI McCabe and deal with the consequences, which would probably be a dishonorable dismissal and a return to the US? Or was he simply stressed and driving himself crazy?

He dressed, gently woke Lucifer, and coaxed him downstairs with the suggestion of a biscuit. He let Lucifer out and filled a travel mug with coffee. He brought Lucifer back into the house and headed to Special Branch. Apparently, he was the first one there since no one else was in the office. He turned on the lights and went to his desk.

McCabe arrived a few minutes later. He smiled, said, "Good Morning," and headed into his office. Dillon debated telling him about Amelia. In the end, he did nothing.

Suel and the other members of the team arrived over the next twenty minutes. They met in interview room three. This morning, two additional officers, in uniform, joined them. Dillon recognized both officers from the armory. What looked like four large computer bags were stacked on the table.

McCabe gave a nod to the Armory officers. Each grabbed two bags and placed one in front of the four men.

"If we could begin please, gentlemen," McCabe said. "Along with your side arms, each of these bags contains a Heckler & Koch MP7. We're not sure what, if anything, you'll be facing. In any event, we want you prepared."

The two officers reviewed the safety procedures and the loading and unloading of the weapons. McCabe went on to review everything they'd covered the night before. He had a copy of the three-page airport layout up on the flat screen and reviewed the layout of the airport and when and where people would be stationed. Earphones and radios were distributed and checked. Everyone pulled on a safety vest, and suddenly it was time for Dillon to leave for Weston Airport. As he drove, he hoped he hadn't appeared nervous, but inside he felt like he was being torn apart.

Why did Amelia look at the airport layout? What if one of them was injured and she was involved? Should he speak up? If he did speak up, the event might well be canceled. Dillon's career with An Garda Síochána and as a US Marshal would probably be over. He'd be lucky if he didn't end up in jail. What was the life expectancy of a US Marshal sentenced to prison?

In no time at all, he was taking Junction 5 off the M4 onto Cellbridge Road. A few minutes later, he drove past the Lucan Golf Club and turned into Weston Airport. It was just as he remembered except that, at this hour, instead of six or eight cars in the parking lot, there was only one. Dillon parked a half-dozen spaces from the other car, grabbed his bag with the MP7 along with an empty thermos to make him look like an employee, and strolled toward the entrance to the main building.

The two-story building was an off-white, almost beige stucco. A set of double doors were centered in front. Above the doors in blue letters were the words '**Weston** Est. 1931 **Airport**.' Dillon opened one of the doors and stepped inside. He walked up two flights of stairs and down a hallway to the entrance to the control tower.

Naturally, the door was locked. He pressed the button on the intercom mounted on the wall.

"Yes?" a voice answered a moment later.

"Marshal Jack Dillon with An Garda Síochána," Dillon said.

"Oh yeah, come on up," the voice said. A moment later the door buzzed, and Dillon pulled it open. He climbed two more sets of stairs and walked into an octagonal room with windows looking out in all directions. A number of computer screens and keyboards were positioned around the room.

"Hi, you're Dillon? I'm Tommy Reid," a man said and extended his hand. Dillon pegged him at maybe fifty. As they shook, Reid said, "We heard you lads were coming in today. I thought there was going to be more than just you."

"They're tied up at the moment, but we'll all be here by 8:30. Anyone else around?"

Reid shook his head. "No, as a matter of fact, I'm about ninety minutes ahead of my normal time. We had to reschedule three separate flights today, basically shut everything down for the day. Your man is coming in later this afternoon?"

"Yes, he is."

"What is he, some important politician? An American? Someone with the EU?"

"Not quite sure. We just want to make sure everything goes well. I noticed a number of offices on the second floor. Are there many people working down there?"

Reid shook his head. "No. Four of the offices are for airport staff, our accountant, a manager, and two other folks. Four people total, but they've got the day off. Two of the rooms are waiting rooms for people coming and going. The room at the end of the hall is for someone if they want to catch a short nap. They'll all be empty today."

"And the bar and restaurant?"

"On a good day, they may serve a dozen people between noon and 2:00. It'll be much quieter today, just because we had to reschedule the flights." He opened a drawer beneath one of the computers and pulled out a key. "This will give you access to the room at the end of the hall. You can store your gear in there and wander around. I'll be up here all day and can buzz you in. If I don't respond, it means I'm dealing with someone on the radio. It's unlikely that will happen, but you never know."

"Thank you," Dillon said as he took the key. "I'll store my bag in there. As long as I'm down there, do you need anything? A coffee, a soda, or maybe a pastry?"

"Oh, thanks, but nothing's open down there until 11:00. That's why I bring my thermos. I see you're prepared."

Dillon held up his empty thermos and nodded. "Well, nice to meet you, Tommy. If you'll excuse me, I better make myself familiar with the building. I'll see you in a bit."

As he left, Dillon looked out of the control tower across the airfield. There were two parallel runways on the far side. The three hangers were actually housed in one long structure behind the building he was in and facing the runways. On the opposite side, actually behind the main building and the hangers, were ten smaller buildings spread out along a road. Behind those buildings was the Liffey River. The area was basically flat, and standing in the control tower, Dillon would be able to see anyone approaching, whether on foot or in a vehicle.

He went down the stairs, walked to the end of the hall on the second floor, and unlocked the door. Two not-so-new couches were positioned against the walls. A ratty pillow sat on one end of both couches. Dillon glanced out the window at the parking lot. He watched as a red car pulled in and parked in the row behind his car and a half-dozen spaces away. A moment later, McCarthy climbed out of the car. The headlights on his car flashed as he clicked the fob lock and headed around the main building toward hanger number one. Dillon pulled his cellphone out and checked the time, 7:22. He pulled the MP7 from the computer bag, adjusted the shoulder strap, and placed a small set of binoculars around his neck.

He walked through the main building three times before he went back up to the control tower. He stood in the tower, leaning against the counter, actually enjoying the view. Suel's car was now parked in a far corner of the parking lot. Just after 10:00, Dillon watched a yellow car park in front of a building along the road behind the airport. A gray-haired woman climbed out of the car and entered the building.

Tommy Reid was monitoring flights on a computer, none of which were bound for Weston Airport.

Dillon walked through the building two more times. Other than a woman working in the restaurant kitchen, no one else entered. He ordered two grilled cheese sandwiches and two coffees for lunch, paid, and took them back up to the control tower.

"Hope you don't mind, but I took the liberty of ordering you a sandwich for lunch and a coffee," Dillon said and set a paper bag next to Reid.

"Oh, that's really nice of you. You didn't have to do that but much appreciated," Reid said.

If the morning was uneventful, the afternoon was downright boring. Dillon was walking through the building every thirty-five minutes. He could check the entire place in less than ten minutes from the time he left the control tower until he returned. Absolutely nothing was happening. Just after 2:00, a maintenance man Reid identified parked in the parking lot and made his way to hanger number two, where Suel was stationed.

Suel verified his ID, and a while after that, the man raised the large door to the hanger and wheeled out a set of steps he positioned off to the side.

At 3:40, Reid was on the radio with the flight coming in from the UK. Dillon passed the word to the Special Branch team via their radio.

THIRTY-NINE

ot too long after that Reid said, "There's your flight now, visual sighting." Based on the digital clock on his computer, the time was 4:01. "They'll be touching down in just a moment."

Dillon passed the word on to the Special Branch team and watched as the black dot in the distance began to acquire wings and wheels. He slowly turned around in the control tower, looking through his binoculars across the airfield, beyond the hangers, across the road to the small commercial buildings, and out toward the parking lot.

The four unmarked cars had suddenly appeared and blocked the entrance and exit to the airport as planned. Two of the men were talking to the driver of what looked like a black limo, no doubt the driver to pick up Punchy Sheehan. One of the men nodded and signaled for the cars to let It enter.

Dillon watched as the plane, actually a small silver jet with a long nose and an Irish flag painted on its tail, touched down on the runway and gradually slowed to almost a crawl. At the end of the runway, it turned and headed for the hangers. The man who had wheeled the stairs out now wore ear protection and held two flashlights with orange cones on the end. He directed the jet alongside hanger two. When the engines were shut off, he wheeled the stairs up to the door and locked them in place.

A man in a Gardai uniform stepped out of the jet, gave a look around, and hurried down the stairs. Once on the ground, he looked around again, lifted his wrist, and seemed to speak into it. That would be standard security, but Dillon wondered who he was speaking to. They were supposedly the only people at the airport besides Reid, the woman in the restaurant, and the man who had rolled the stairs in place, who was now on his knees wedging blocks in front and behind the wheels of the jet.

"Everything seem okay to you?" Dillon asked Reid.

"Yeah, looks fine. Nothing out of the ordinary."

"Hanger two. Hanger two," Dillon said into his radio.

"Two," Suel said.

"Your man at the base of the stairs. He's talking into a wrist phone. Who is he calling? We're the only people here."

"I recognize him. He's one of us. Oh, here comes Punchy now," Suel said.

Dillon looked out of the control tower. The figure in the jet's door was definitely fat and about the same height as Punchy Sheehan. He wore a black fedora, which, if memory served, Punchy always wore. Dillon focused his binoculars and was sure of one thing, the guy standing in the doorway of the jet wasn't Punchy Sheehan.

"That is not Punchy Sheehan. I repeat, that—"

"At ease, Dillon," McCabe interrupted.

The individual lingered for a long moment at the top of the staircase and then began to walk slowly down the steps. On his third step, he suddenly seemed to jerk, fell backward, and tumbled down two more steps.

"What the hell?" Reid shouted.

"Shots fired. Shots fired," someone shouted on the radio. The man in the Gardai uniform crouched down behind the staircase. Suel suddenly appeared, racing out of hanger two. He jumped up the first two steps, grabbed the man, now upside down by the shoulders, and pulled him down the steps.

The officer crouched behind the staircase was glancing toward the hangers. The maintenance man was lying down behind a set of rear wheels and pointing across the road beyond the hangers.

Dillon spun around with his binoculars and scanned the commercial buildings across the road from the airport. On the fourth or fifth building, he caught the flash of something or someone on the roof.

"Across the road, the building with the red sign and the yellow car. I think there's someone on the roof," Dillon shouted into the radio just as a figure dressed in what appeared to be camouflage fatigues and a black cap dashed across the roof of the building. "Shooter on the roof. Building with the red sign and the yellow car.

Shooter on the roof in camouflage fatigues and a black cap. He's just entered the building."

The four vehicles blocking the front entrance to the airport suddenly reversed and raced toward the building with the yellow car.

Dillon scanned the building through his binoculars but couldn't detect any movement. Three of the vehicles raced into the parking lot. The fourth parked across the entrance to the lot, effectively blocking in anyone attempting to drive away.

"Form up in the airport parking lot, now," McCabe shouted into the radio. "On the double, form up." A moment later, McCabe appeared two stories below, hurrying toward a black four-door SUV in the parking lot.

"Reid, place a shots fired call and get an ambulance here," Dillon shouted as he ran out the door and down the stairs, taking them two at a time. McDonald was just ahead of Dillon as he ran out of the building and headed toward McCabe in the SUV. Both rear doors were open. McCarthy jumped in the front seat. McDonald went around to the far side of the car and was just pulling the door closed as Dillon hopped in on the other side.

As McCabe floored the SUV, Dillon's door slammed shut, just missing his right ankle. McCabe bounced over a curb, clipped a fence post, and sped onto the road. He raced into the parking area of the building next door to where Dillon spotted the figure in the camouflage fatigues. The SUV skidded to a stop along the side of the building, and everyone jumped out.

"Keep your distance. Keep your distance," McCabe shouted over his shoulder, leading the way. They stopped at the corner of the building, and McCabe cautiously peered around. There was a small parking lot with a loading dock and, beyond that, a narrow, weed-covered bit of land maybe thirty feet wide that led to the Liffey River just in front of them.

"You two," McCabe said to McDonald and McCarthy, "the loading dock. Dillon, down toward the Liffey with me."

Just as McDonald and McCarthy took off, Dillon heard what sounded like a lawnmower starting up. *'What the hell,'* he thought just as a small aluminum boat with an outboard motor suddenly appeared, racing across the Liffey. A figure in camouflage fatigues and a black balaclava glanced back toward them.

"What in God's name?" McCabe said, just as the figure raised a weapon and fired a burst. Everyone dove onto the asphalt. A window next to the loading dock shattered. Another burst bounced off a green steel dumpster.

Dillon rolled to his left, away from McCabe, shouldered his MP7, and fired a burst at the boat. The figure jerked for a moment, or maybe not. He couldn't be sure.

"Don't fire, Dillon. Don't fire. There are people on the far shore," McCabe shouted.

Dillon lined up his sight, took careful aim, saw two people on bicycles following a path along the far shore, and knew McCabe was correct. It was too dangerous.

McCabe was on the radio half-screaming at someone. All they could do was watch as the boat ran aground on the far shore. The camouflaged figure jumped out and charged toward a car parking on the side of the road. A woman hurried out of the car with her hands raised. The camouflaged figure jumped into the vehicle and five seconds later disappeared from sight.

The four teams from the building next door joined them a minute or two later. McCabe was still shouting into the radio, giving a vague description of the vehicle across the river. Dillon explained what had happened, and they hurried back to the building where the shooter had fired from the roof. They went through the building, essentially clearing it, although all but one of the offices were locked.

In the unlocked office, they found the older woman Dillon had watched climb out of the yellow car six hours earlier. She was taped to a chair with what appeared to be packaging tape. Three or four layers were wound over her mouth and around her head.

Dillon left the building and walked back across the road toward the hangers. The jet was still parked in front of hanger two. A yellow Irish ambulance was parked next to the jet. 'EMERGENCY AMBULANCE' in green letters was on the side of the vehicle, with green squares marking an emergency vehicle running along the lower third of the vehicle.

The rear doors were open, and the figure of the Punchy Sheehan look-alike was seated on the rear of the ambulance with a pillow next to him and his shirt off. He was talking to Suel at the moment. The left side of his face was swollen and in the process of turning black and blue from tumbling down the steps. There was a square of gauze taped over his left shoulder, and he was smoking a cigarette.

"You're not Punchy Sheehan," Dillon said.

"Oh, about time," Suel said. "This is the American I was telling you about, Marty. Dillon, meet Marty Donovan. He's out of the Kevin Street station."

"You were shot?"

"Nice to meet yas, Dillon. Yeah," Donovan said and nodded toward his left shoulder. "Hurts like a bitch, but that's all. Thank God for the protective vest. Nothing like walking out of the jet with a bullseye on my chest. You get that bastard?"

"Afraid not. He had a little boat he took across the Liffey. Too many people on the far side to take a shot. Bastard jumped out of the boat, dragged some woman out of her car at gunpoint, and drove off. McCabe was on the radio calling it in. Unfortunately, everyone is over here on this side. Was Punchy even on the jet?"

"Yeah, the medics are checking him out now. McCabe is going to be having a little 'Come to Jesus' meeting with him in a bit, not that it will do any good," Suel said.

Donovan shook his head. "What a bollox. I had to fly over with him from London. Very impressed with himself, and for the life of me, I can't figure out why."

"What are they going to do with him?" Dillon asked.

"They're not going to arrest him if that's what you're wondering. He was begging to fly back to London. They had to drag him off the jet. He wanted to stay in there. With any luck, he'll come to the conclusion that the Emerald Isle is not for the likes of his fat arse," Suel said.

FORTY

It was almost midnight by the time an exhausted Dillon made it home. He let Lucifer out into the front garden and decided he would deal with the kitchen mess the dog had made in the morning. He was beyond tired after going at it for twenty hours and was asleep in less than a minute. It was a fitful sleep. Unpleasant dreams about Amelia left him unrested when his alarm went off the following morning.

He let Lucifer out into the front garden, cleaned up the kitchen, placed the trash in the bin, and scrambled some eggs for breakfast. He filled Lucifer's food and water dishes, enticed him inside with a biscuit, and then climbed in his car.

Instead of driving to Special Branch, he drove through the city center and across the Liffey River. He passed through Ballsbridge, Merrion, Monkstown, and Dun Laoghaire, headed to number one Sandycove Road and Amelia Maher. Her dark-blue Mercedes Roadster was parked up close to the front door. He pulled across the entrance to her home and parked, blocking any possible attempt to drive away.

He walked across the gravel parking area and paused for a moment at the front door, not sure what he should do. He finally pushed the doorbell, heard it chime inside, and waited. He rang the doorbell again and got no response. After the fifth time ringing the doorbell, he finally gave up and wandered around to the rear of the house.

He looked in the kitchen window. The lights were off. Nothing seemed out of place. He tried the door, but it was locked. He walked back to the front of the house and tried the door. It was locked.

He climbed in his car and drove to Phoenix Park and headquarters. The lights were off in McCabe's office. Suel was at his desk, sipping a tea and regaling two people with a joke.

"Well, look what the cat dragged in," Suel said. Thirty seconds later, he was at Dillon's desk. "How are you doing?"

"Tired. Slept like shit," Dillon said.

Suel looked around and said, "Let's grab a coffee in the break room. We can talk in there."

Dillon followed him into the break room, poured a coffee from what appeared to be a freshly made pot, and took a sip. It was just as bad as he expected.

"We're all on desk duty for the next seventy-two hours. McCabe is at the hospital."

"What happened?"

"When your man fired at you lot and he went down, he thought he sprained his wrist. Turned out it was broken. He's in surgery as we speak. Not sure if he'll be in later today. I kind of doubt it."

"Any news on the shooter?"

Suel shook his head. "No, nothing. If there's any good news, it's that your man Punchy Sheehan chartered a plane to the US the moment he landed back at Heathrow. I doubt we'll be seeing the likes of him anytime soon."

"And Marty Donovan?"

"He'll be relaxing for the next few days. He's fine, but he looks like shite after banging his head on those stairs."

"He's lucky he's able to tell the story. Two inches to the right and he would have been dead," Dillon said.

"Can you believe it? They had a pillow stuffed over his protective vest to make him look fat."

Dillon shook his head and took another sip of coffee. It was just as bad as the first sip.

"You going to link up with that woman you saw?"

"No, I don't feel like it. There's something there that just doesn't seem right, and I don't need the hassle," Dillon said, hoping if he downplayed Amelia, Suel would let it go.

"Yeah, well, we've both been there before," Suel said. "Anyway, that's all I know. I'd guess we've both earned a couple of light days."

"Say, I didn't mention it, but a hell of a good job getting Marty Donovan off those steps. He was a prime target at that point."

"I'd say he used up a lot of his luck yesterday," Suel said and chuckled. "I'm thinking a relaxing lunch, maybe at the Autobahn, and we make ourselves scarce for the afternoon. Oh, yeah, and forensics grabbed that boat your man took across the Liffey. Surprise, surprise, it was stolen. I don't know if they'll find anything, but at least they've got it."

"Crazy day," Dillon said and shook his head.

Back at his desk, he couldn't get Amelia out of his head and the fact that she had looked at the three-page airport layout. He went online and looked up the property records on Amelia's house, number one Sandycove Road. Amazingly, it had been purchased by an organization named Cullen, Inc. Dillon thought about the name for a moment before it dawned on him. Cullen, as in Cullen Fink? Suel's informant and the operator of The Fantasy House. When Dillon asked him if he'd ever heard of Amelia Maher, he'd denied it but almost too fast.

"Hey, Paddy," Dillon called Suel and waved him over.

Suel came over and asked, "What you got?"

"I got a problem, and I think you can help. Let me just show you this, and let's step outside." He indicated the page on his computer screen.

"What the hell is Cullen, Inc.?" Suel asked.

"Some organization that apparently purchased this mansion in Sandycove."

"I'm not following," Suel said.

"Come on with me," Dillon said and headed out of the office. Neither one of them said anything until they were out of the building.

"You going to fill me in?"

"I'm gonna do more than that. I think I've got a real problem. Hop in my car," Dillon said.

He drove them out of the parking lot and headed toward the city center. "Where in the hell are we going?"

"Sandycove," Dillon said, and as they drove, he filled Suel in on his dealings with Amelia Maher.

"I've never heard of her," Suel said.

"Right now, I'm not even sure that's her real name."

"And you took her to bed?"

"More like she got me drunk and took me to bed, except we ended up on the floor. I mentioned her name to your pal Cullen Fink, and he said he'd never heard of her, but he said it so fast it just made me think he might be bullshitting. Anyway, she was at my place two nights ago and—"

"This is after McCabe warned you?"

"Yeah, and believe me, I'm kicking myself. The thing is, I'm pretty sure she saw that three-page airport layout McCabe put together."

"You ask her what she was doing?"

"I didn't find it until yesterday morning. She left around midnight the night before. I had no idea she saw it. When I woke up, I found the airport layout in a different pocket of my jeans."

"Jesus Christ."

"Yeah, I know. Believe me, I know. I'm wondering if Cullen, Inc. is somehow related to The Fantasy House, and maybe your man Fink set her up there? She comes on to me. I was thinking with the wrong head. Did she tell someone about Punchy Sheehan flying into Weston Airport?"

"Did she know about O'Rourke, Thompson, and Donnelly?" Suel asked.

"I honestly don't know. I checked her place out earlier this morning before I came in. Her car was there, but it seemed like no one was home. She never answered the door. No lights were on in the place. Now there's a possibility Cullen Fink may have bought the place some years back. You said he was lined up with the Linnehan's."

"I think you need to take a couple of deep breaths and calm down. You're driving yourself crazy," Suel said.

They didn't talk for almost fifteen minutes until Dillon pulled in front of the mansion on Sandycove Road. He parked in the same place he had earlier, blocking the exit from the parking area. The dark-blue Mercedes Roadster hadn't been moved.

"That's her car?" Suel asked.

"It's what she's been driving."

"Did you check it out?"

Dillon shook his head no.

"Oh, for feck's sake," Suel said and pulled out his cell phone. He pushed a speed dial number and a moment later said, "Yeah, Colleen, Paddy Suel. I need you to run a plate for me. Yeah, thanks," he read the license plate number. "Yeah, I'll hang on." A moment later, he said, "Are you sure? I've got it on a blue Mercedes, a Roadster actually. When was that? Okay, thank you," he said and disconnected.

"That didn't sound good," Dillon said.

"That license plate is listed to a 2020 Audi up in Malahide."

"A 2020 Audi?"

"In Malahide, which is a pretty sure indicator that the Roadster is hot, as well. Let's check the place out," Suel said and climbed out of the car.

Dillon led the way across the gravel parking area to the front door. He rang the doorbell a couple of times and got the same result, no Amelia. He led them around to the back of the house. The door was still locked. Suel pulled a small brown leather case from his pocket, gave a quick look around, and then inserted a couple of picks into the door lock. Dillon heard the lock click less than a minute later.

Suel shook his head and said, "Lock is original to the house. Spend all sorts of money bringing everything up to date, and you don't change the locks, Jaysus."

He opened the door, and they waited to see if an alarm went off. Fortunately, it didn't. "Nice digs," Suel said, stepping inside. They both pulled on a pair of latex gloves.

Dillon stepped over to the refrigerator and opened the door. "Oh shit," he said and stepped aside so Suel could see the small plastic bottle of Evian water and two slices of pizza in a plastic bag. Other than that, the refrigerator was completely empty.

Suel began opening cupboards. One was filled with a set of four plates, dishes, cups, and saucers. Three were basically empty except for salt and pepper and a stack of sugar envelopes, the kind you'd see in a restaurant.

"Looks like she must have dined out quite a bit," Suel said.

Dillon headed out of the kitchen through the formal dining room and up the stairs to the library, where he had ended up on the floor. The quilt they'd been under was neatly folded and hanging over the back of the couch. He noticed that the ashes had been removed from the fireplace. He walked into the bedroom. The king-sized bed was stripped, exposing a bare mattress.

Suel began opening drawers on the two antique dressers in the bedroom. They were empty. Dillon opened the doors on the Armoire opposite the bed. With the exception of a dozen metal hangers, it was empty.

"I think we've established she didn't live here," Suel said.

"Oh, shit," Dillon said and shook his head.

FORTY-ONE

As they went out the kitchen door and walked around to the front of the house. Suel asked, "You got her phone number?"

"Yeah, I don't think she'll answer, but it's worth a try. If I get dumped into voicemail, I'll ask her out to dinner."

"Good idea."

Dillon pulled out his cellphone as they came around the side of the house and hit the call button on Amelia's number. He put the phone on speaker, and a moment later, they heard the phone ringing. A ringing sound also seemed to be coming from inside the Mercedes Roadster. After five rings, Dillon was dumped into voicemail.

"Sorry, can't take your call just now. Leave a message, and I'll get back to you just as soon as I can."

"Hi, Amelia, Jack Dillon. Hey, my turn to ask you out to dinner. I've got some time over the next few days. Please give me a call. Would love to see you. Thanks, Bye-bye," he said and disconnected.

"So her phone is in this damn Mercedes," Dillon said. "You know, I'm thinking we're at the point where we should get a warrant for the house and the car. Let's have forensics go over this, maybe find out who, exactly, she is."

"Let me make the call on the warrant," Suel said. "It might be wise to avoid McCabe. I'll place that call now, and then I think it may be time to pay a little visit to Cullen Fink."

Suel spoke with a woman in the An Garda Síochána legal department, explaining how the vehicle had illegal license plates, and they had strong evidence that the individual who had been in the house was there illegally and quite possibly related to five murders. He had the feeling it was going to be an uphill battle until he mentioned the five murders and the victims, Dennis and Maureen Sheehan, Keegan Donnelly, Tommy Thompson, and Brennan O'Rourke by name. She said she would have the warrants for the car and the house signed by 4:00 that afternoon if he wanted to pick them up at the office.

While Suel was on the phone with the legal department, Dillon glanced through the windshield and wrote down the VIN number on the Mercedes.

Suel said, "Thank you," and disconnected from his conversation with the legal department. Next, he called Cullen Fink and ended up leaving a message. "Strange," he said. "Fink isn't in the office. He's always in his office."

"You think he's just not taking your call?"

"That isn't at all like him, but I suppose it's possible. Let's make it our next stop."

Twenty minutes later and a quarter-mile past the Ha'penny Bridge, Dillon pulled to the curb in the no parking zone Suel had parked in the last time they visited The Fantasy House.

"You got a couple of business cards?" Dillon asked.

"Yeah. Why?"

"Leave them on the dashboard just in case your pal comes by and wants to leave a ticket."

Suel pulled out three cards and placed them on the dashboard. They locked their pistols in the trunk of the car and headed down Fownes Street Lower, then turned onto Temple Bar. As soon as they were in front of The Fantasy House, Suel pulled out his phone and called Cullen Fink again. He spoke into the phone slowly. "Hello Cullen, it's DI Suel. It is important and urgent that I speak with you. If I don't hear from you, I'm going to have to go through channels to get inside the club. Neither one of us wants that, so please call me back in the next five minutes. I'm outside the front door right now," he said and disconnected.

"You think he heard you?" Dillon asked.

"I don't know. If he's not in the office, someone is probably in there covering for him. Hopefully, they heard my message."

Suel checked the time on his cellphone about every thirty seconds over the next few minutes. He was about to come up with another plan when the same two muscular giants who'd patted them down last time suddenly appeared. Just like before, they let Dillon and Suel inside the club and patted them down. As Suel was being patted down, he gave Dillon a look suggesting it was a good idea they'd locked their weapons in the trunk of Dillon's car.

They were led through the purple bar room, up to the second floor, and through that bar as well. They walked through the entrance marked 'PRIVATE,' down the hall, and stopped in front of the steel door. The larger of the two knocked on the door and then opened it just like before, only this time when the door opened, a woman was seated behind the desk, and Cullen Fink was nowhere to be seen. Suel and Dillon stepped into the office.

"Darren, Bobby, this should only take a minute if you wouldn't mind waiting in the hall," the woman said. Once the door closed, she looked at Suel and said, "How may I help you?"

"We need to see Cullen Fink," Suel said.

"Interesting. So do we. Unfortunately, he disappeared forty-eight hours ago, and we have no idea where he is," she said and flashed a quick smile meant to be anything but charming.

"What do you mean he disappeared?"

"Just that. He didn't show up for work. As far as I know, that was the first time it's ever happened. We've tried to contact him. I've sent people to his home. We don't know where he is. When I heard your message, I was hoping you might have some information. It would appear you do not."

"Shit," Suel said, not quite under his breath.

"I share your sentiment. Now, if there's nothing else, I have a mountain of things to catch up on. I really should get back to work."

"What do you know about a woman named Amelia Maher?" Dillon asked.

The woman got a funny look on her face and shook her head. "Absolutely nothing. Was she one of our performers? I suppose I could check if you'd like."

"If you would please," Dillon said.

She turned her chair toward the keyboard and began typing. She brought up a file on the screen and said, "Yes, okay, here we go. You said her name was Amelia?"

"Yes," Dillon said.

She typed it in and said, "Spell the last name for me."

Dillon did, and the woman shook her head. "This list goes back five years. That's one year longer than legally necessary. There is no record of anyone with that name on our database. Anything else?"

"Would you happen to have a card?" Suel asked.

She flashed the quick smile again and pulled two business cards from a drawer. "One for each of you."

Suel glanced at the card and said, "Thank you for your time, Miss Linnehan."

"Sorry I couldn't be of more help. If you'd let yourselves out," she said and nodded toward the door.

Suel looked like he was about to say something then just turned and opened the door. They followed the two muscle-bound thugs back down to the front door and stepped out onto the street.

"Damn it, I'd say that puts an end to my source, at least for the time being," Suel said.

"Moira Linnehan, you know anything about her?"

"No, but my guess is Fink's disappearance is not temporary. Let's head back to Special Branch," Suel said. "It would be nice to get forensics lined up to go through that home in Sandycove."

"And that Mercedes," Dillon said. "Which reminds me," he pulled out his cellphone and called McDonald. "Yeah, Johnny, it's Dillon. Hey, can you run a check on a VIN number for me? Great, you got a clean space on the wall to write this down? Okay, here's the number. Yeah, thanks, much appreciated," he said and disconnected.

It was closer to five that evening before Suel got the warrant to search number one Sandycove Road. Forensics couldn't begin until the following morning, so they arranged to have an officer park in front of the home overnight, just in case Amelia Maher returned or someone else attempted to enter.

FORTY-TWO

Dillon and Suel met just before 8:00 the following morning at the Sandycove residence. A squad car was parked, blocking the entrance to the parking area. The officer, dressed in a blue uniform and hat, was wearing a florescent green vest. He was leaning against the squad car and watched as Suel parked behind Dillon, and they both got out of their vehicles. They shook hands, introduced themselves, and thanked the officer for watching the place.

"Any activity?" Dillon asked.

The officer shook his head and said, "No. Very quiet, which was just what I hoped for."

"We've forensics coming in shortly. They'll be towing the Mercedes and spending some time in the house. Are you aware of any activity here?" Dillon asked.

The officer shook his head. "No. I've been past the place probably a thousand times on patrol, but it's basically a quiet area. Anything happening is more likely going to be down near the beach, and even then, it's more a case of someone locking their keys in the car or a car that won't start. It's quiet out this way, and we like that."

"Can't say as I blame you," Suel said.

The officer moved the squad car.

Dillon opened the gates, and they both drove in and parked twenty feet away from the Mercedes Roadster. Suel took out his brown leather case with the lock picking implements and unlocked the front door. Fifty minutes later, the forensics team arrived in their white van labeled Technical Bureau in English and Irish. Directly behind the van was a Gardai flatbed tow truck.

Brendan Davis climbed out of the forensic vehicle, gave a wave to Suel and Dillon, and walked toward them. Niall Reid appeared at the rear of the vehicle and began unloading two black cases that held their testing kits. "I should have known it would be the likes of the two of yas. What do we have?" Davis asked as he approached.

"You tell us," Dillon said and went on to explain the suspicions they had regarding Amelia Maher and that they suspected the house was purchased by Cullen Fink, who had now been missing for over forty-eight hours.

"And you're thinking this is somehow tied to the murders down in Cork and Keegan Donnelly and the other two lads up here?"

"It's still somewhat tentative, but it seems to be headed in that direction," Dillon said. "Amelia Maher presented herself as the owner of the home. Turns out she's not, and from what we can surmise, at best, she was here for a couple of nights, or a week, tops."

"Where is she now?" Davis asked.

"We don't know, unfortunately."

"The two of yous were at Weston Airport yesterday?" Davis asked.

They both nodded.

"We went over the boat last night. Got a couple of partials on the boat motor and a shell casing. Nothing definitive and no match in our files. The roof of the building where the shot was fired was clean."

"That figures," Suel said.

As they were talking, the tow truck had backed up to the Mercedes. The car was now attached to chains and was being slowly dragged up onto the flatbed. Ten minutes later, the Mercedes was secured. The driver gave Davis a wave and shouted, "Catch you later," as he pulled out of the parking area.

"We'd better get to work inside," Davis said.

Suel pulled out his cellphone and hit a speed dial number.

"Who you calling?" Dillon asked.

"Just checking to see if Fink answers his phone," Suel said and shook his head a moment later. "No, dumped me into voicemail. Damn it."

They cooled their heels for the next three hours, waiting outside and exchanging thoughts and ideas about the series of unsolved cases. It was just after the noon hour when Davis and Reid began hauling a handful of evidence bags out to the forensics van. Davis placed the bags he was carrying in the back of the vehicle and walked toward Dillon and Suel. Reid headed back into the house.

"Anything?" Dillon asked.

"Not really. Clearly the place has been thoroughly wiped down, a few hair fibers that may or may not be relevant. Merely a thought on my part, but the fact that it's been wiped down and damn near sterilized would seem to be similar to the previous sites we've examined. It will be interesting to see what we find in the Mercedes, but don't get your hopes up. I can tell you this much. We aren't dealing with an amateur."

"Well, keep us posted," Suel said.

"Niall is going to be working on what little we gathered inside. When we get back, I want to look at that Mercedes. Did either of you get a VIN number off the vehicle?"

Both Dillon and Suel rolled their eyes. "The license plates are registered to a 2020 Audi from Malahide. I had Johnny McDonald checking it out for me. He was going to leave a note on my desk, but I haven't been in the office yet. Let me call him now." Dillon placed a call to McDonald and got dropped into his voicemail. "Yeah, Johnny, you ever find anything out on that VIN number? I haven't made it into the office yet. Give me a call when you get this. Thanks."

Davis shot a quick look and said, "We find anything, you'll be the next to know. See you later, gents."

Dillon and Suel stepped back into the house and looked around. "You really think Fink owned this place?" Suel asked.

"You know him better than me. All I know is Amelia was lying when she said she owned it, and I bought it, hook, line, and sinker."

Suel chuckled. "Like you said before, you were thinking with the wrong head."

"She had my number right from the start and knew how to play me. I guess we should lock up and go back to the office."

"You go if you want. We're supposed to be on light duty, and I've already overstepped the bounds getting that warrant and forensics out here. I'll see you tomorrow. You should do the same."

"I'm having a tough time letting go of this thing."

"That's because of the woman. Take a deep breath and relax," Suel said.

"I'll think about it," Dillon said. He drove back to the office. When he pulled out his desk chair, there was a folded piece of paper. He opened it and read the note from McDonald.

"2020 Mercedes Roadster. Dark-Blue. Reported stolen from St. James Hospital parking lot twelve days ago. Owner is listed as Dr. Malcom O'Meara. Resides in Portmarnock."

'At no surprise,' Dillon thought. He spent the next two hours going through anything that might give him a handle on Amelia Maher and came up empty-handed. He looked up her business, Maher Marketing Group, and found absolutely nothing. The closest thing he could find was an organization out of Texas. He'd turned off his

computer and decided maybe Suel's advice wasn't all that bad. Go home, take Lucifer for a walk, get a takeout dinner from Eurospar, and just take a deep breath. He'd just locked his desk drawers when his phone rang. He stared at it for two more rings before he answered.

"Jack Dillon."

"Dillon, Brendan Davis, glad I got you. We just opened up the Mercedes. You might want to come down here. The medical examiners are on the way."

"Medical examiners? There was a body in the car?"

"Just get down here," Davis said and hung up.

Dillon hurried out of the office. He pressed the button for the elevator and then pressed it a half-dozen more times before the bell rang and the door opened. He stepped inside and pressed the button for the ground floor. He almost bowled a guy over as he charged out of the elevator. "Oh, sorry, excuse me," he called as he hurried down the long hallway towards the forensics garage.

When he walked into the garage, he spotted Davis immediately. He was wearing a hazmat suit and was surrounded by four other individuals, all in hazmat suits. Niall Reid was the only other person he recognized.

The Mercedes Roadster was in the garage with all four doors and the trunk open.

"What'd you find?" Dillon called to Davis.

"Come and see for yourself," Davis said and stepped over to the back of the car.

Dillon stood next to him and looked in the trunk. There was a large, heavy-duty white plastic bag in the trunk. There was no mistaking the fact that a body was in the bag. Next to the bag was a black balaclava and a small pistol. He recognized the pistol as a .380 auto. The same weapon suspected in virtually all the murders, the Sheehans, Keegan Donnelly, Tommy Thompson, and Brennan O'Rourke. Now there was another body.

Whoever it was, the form of the body appeared to be too fat and too short to be Amelia Maher. But then Dillon wondered if her body had maybe swollen and…

"You going to open the bag?" Dillon asked.

"Not until we have the medical examiners here."

One of the other guys in a hazmat suit set up a stand just off to the side and mounted a video camera on the stand. "If I could get you gentlemen to move over a bit. I want to aim this and have it ready for the medical lads."

"Sure thing," Davis said, and he and Dillon stepped back.

It was a good twenty minutes before the medical examiner's vehicle backed up in front of the garage. Hugh Healy and Artie Reilly climbed out of the cab and gave a wave to everyone. They opened the rear doors on the van and pulled out a gurney with a body bag strapped to it. Reilly stepped into a blue hazmat suit and headed toward the group. Healy placed two black cases with the medical examiners' kits on the gurney, then sat down in the rear of the van and pulled on a hazmat suit.

As Artie Reilly approached the group, he glanced over at the trunk of the Mercedes and joked, "Perfect, just before dinner time."

"How's it going, Artie?" Davis asked.

"You tell me. You in on this, Dillon?"

"Afraid so. It's most likely related to the three murders up here and the two Americans down in Cork. There's a .380 auto next to the plastic bag and a balaclava. That incident yesterday out at Weston Airport, the shooter who escaped across the Liffey was wearing a Balaclava. This vehicle was stolen twelve, well now thirteen, days ago and used by a woman who seems somehow to be related to a number of the incidents."

"Well, let's take a look, shall we? I see we're going to be filmed. Probably a good idea. Any thoughts on timeframe here?" Reilly asked and nodded toward the Mercedes. As he spoke, he pulled on a pair of latex gloves and a face mask just as Healy wheeled the gurney over next to the Mercedes.

The guy who set up the video camera adjusted it slightly as Reilly approached the trunk of the car. He opened up one of the black cases on the gurney and pulled out a surgical knife. He glanced at Dillon and Davis, then bent down and ran the blade along the length of the white plastic bag.

Dillion took a deep breath in anticipation of seeing Amelia Maher.

Reilly spread either side of the plastic bag, revealing the fat, bald body. Dillon let out a quiet sigh of relief as he recognized Cullen Fink sporting a bullet hole in the middle of his forehead.

"I recognize that guy. Who the hell is he?" Davis asked.

"Cullen Fink, he runs The Fantasy House or at least he did, and he supposedly owns that home out in Sandycove. He's been missing for over two days."

Two hours later, Fink was strapped to the gurney and on his way to the Dublin City Morgue. Davis and team were back to examining the Mercedes and, at no surprise, were coming up empty-handed.

Dillon phoned Suel, brought him up to date, and headed home. He took Lucifer for a long walk, thought off and on about Amelia Maher, and then went home and climbed into bed.

FORTY-THREE

Dillon was up the following morning by 7:00, ate a leisurely breakfast, and arrived at Special Branch just before 9:00. The lights in McCabe's office were off. Since Dillon was supposed to be on light duty for the next forty-eight hours, he placed a request for airport security footage. He was looking for Amelia Maher flying out of the country in the previous forty-eight hours. He was rewarded with seventy-two hours' worth of blurry footage from the three security stations in Dublin airport.

Suel arrived just before the noon hour, and on his way back from the break room, he stopped at Dillon's desk. "What are you looking at?" Dillon gave him the update, such as it was. "You think she left the country?"

"I think she's very smart, and she probably had a hand in if not pulled the trigger in all the murders, including Fink and the Sheehans. She's probably sunning on a beach somewhere in Spain or down in the Canary Islands. You up to anything?"

"I stopped in at The Fantasy House and brought your woman Moira Linnehan up to date on Cullen Fink."

"What did she say?"

"Well, let's just say she didn't seem surprised."

Dillon shook his head. He was on his fifth or sixth cup of lousy coffee, trying to stay awake while he reviewed the airport security tapes. His desk phone rang, and he answered, "Jack Dillon."

"Yeah, Dillon, Brendan Davis down in forensics."

"Brendan, please tell me you found a signed confession from someone."

"I only wish. I did find something interesting. You remember that balaclava that was in the trunk of the Mercedes?"

"Yeah, along with the .380 auto."

"Yeah, I'll get to the gun in a moment. But the balaclava, we did not find a trace of Cullen Fink on the thing. If it belonged to him, he never wore it."

"Oh, great. Was the thing just tossed in there to confuse us even more?"

"Well, hang on. It may have been tossed in there to confuse us, but what we found were three samples of hair, auburn hair, to be exact. All three samples contained the root sheath."

"Meaning what?"

"Meaning the Barr bodies in the root sample identify the sex of the individual as female."

"Auburn hair from a female. Are you sure?" Dillon asked.

"Oh, yeah. Male sex is identified by fluorescent Y bodies."

"Okay, interesting. And you said you had something on the gun?"

"Wait a minute, one more thing on the hair samples. The three in the balaclava match a sample we found in the shower drain at number one Sandycove Road."

There it was, the definite link to Amelia Maher. It had been her at Weston Airport. *'God,'* Dillon thought.

"Now, as far as the gun, that .380 auto…" Davis said, but Dillon only heard bits and pieces. "Once again, we're dealing with someone who was very careful and basically wiped the weapon clean. We did find a partial that matches a partial we found in the Sandycove residence, but beyond that, we're unable to identify the individual. We've run them through EU and American sites to no avail. Having said that, the rounds fired from that pistol match the rounds recovered from the murder victims. Therefore, the same weapon, that .380 auto, was used in all six murders."

"Well, that's more than we knew before," Dillon said. He thanked Davis and returned to reviewing airport security tapes, all the while thinking about auburn hair in the balaclava and the figure in the boat jerking when Dillon had fired. *'Was it Amelia? Did he hit her?'* He started in again on the airport tapes the following morning but never came up with an image that resembled Amelia.

DCI McCabe returned to his office with his arm in a sling and a black and blue hand extending out from a cast. Dillon and Suel brought him up to date on the cases, basically telling him the suspected killer, now known as Amelia Maher, was nowhere to be found.

"What about this Fink individual? He's associated with the Linnehan's, isn't he?" McCabe asked.

"Yes, he is, or was," Suel said.

"The autopsy on Fink has him dead before Weston Airport. The individual who went across the river was wearing a balaclava. The balaclava found in the trunk of the Mercedes with Fink's body contained three auburn hairs that belonged to a woman," Dillon said. "The three hairs matched one found in the shower drain in Sandycove."

"And do we know who the woman is?"

"Nothing definite," Suel said.

"We suspect Amelia Maher," Dillon said and held his breath.

McCabe seemed to think for a moment, shook his head and said, "Very well, any changes, please keep me posted."

As they headed out of McCabe's office, Dillon's heart was pounding, afraid McCabe might call him back. Fortunately, it didn't happen.

The string of murders stopped. As far as Dillon and Suel could tell, Punchy Sheehan remained back in Boston and apparently had no plans to return to Ireland, ever. Dillon's social life revolved around occasionally joining Suel for a pint or taking Lucifer for a walk, and that was just fine with him. However, he did find a new hiding place for his front door key.

EPILOGUE

It had been more than a month, and Dillon and Suel were on to new cases. Dillon arrived home from work, and Lucifer was waiting at the door. He let him out into the front garden. The mail had been dropped through the slot in the door, and a pile of five envelopes rested on the entry floor. Dillon picked them up and examined the envelopes as he walked into the kitchen. He tossed three of the envelopes into recycling without opening them. The fourth one was from his insurance company, and he set that on the kitchen counter.

The fifth envelope was plain white. His name and address were nicely written in blue ink. There was no return address. As he opened the envelope, a hint of a familiar perfume struck him. He pulled out the folded sheet of paper. Instead of a message, a happy face emoji was drawn on the paper. The hair on the happy face was red. He checked the stamp and the postmark, Spain. He thought for a brief moment, shrugged, and tossed the paper and the envelope into the trash.

THE END

Thank you for taking the time to read the Jack Dillon tale, <u>Mystery Woman</u>. If you enjoyed the read please take a moment and leave a review. It really helps. Thanks!

Don't miss the following sample of <u>Second Chance</u>, the sequel to <u>Mystery Woman</u> on the following page.

SECOND CHANCE

PROLOGUE

The man held the door to the Library open and said, "Glad you made it back to the Spanish sunshine, Amelia. He'll see you now. Let me warn you, he's not happy with the news, so best to mind yourself."

Amelia Maher walked in. Cormac Linnehan was seated in a wingback chair in front of the fireplace. He was sipping something from a crystal glass Amelia assumed held whiskey. He didn't look up as she approached but continued to stare at the empty fireplace. She stood next to the chair opposite him. Eventually, he looked up.

"Word has it, Punchy Sheehan isn't all that excited about conducting any further business in Ireland. I suppose I should tell you well done." He raised his glass toward her then drained it. "There's just one fecking problem," he said, raising his voice. His face suddenly flushed. He threw the crystal glass, and it shattered in the fireplace.

"What problem, sir? I couldn't kill Punchy since he wasn't there, but you seem to have the same result, he's not going to be doing business in Ireland. With the six bodies, I'd say the Doyle's have been put on notice to keep their fat asses in Limerick. I don't know what else I could have done."

Linnehan turned to look at her. His eyes bored holes, and after a long moment, she blinked and glanced at the floor. "All well and good, there's just one little problem. You let this wanker from the Special Branch get away. He knows it was you that did the killing. What in God's name were you thinking? Did you fancy the bastard? Was it the fact he was an American?"

She took a deep breath and spoke calmly. "It was the fact that, if I'd killed him, I never would have made it out of the country. If I'd killed him, An Garda Síochána would have traced the act to you in a heartbeat, and instead of sipping whiskey here in Costa del Sol, you'd be in hiding for the rest of your life because both the Garda and the Americans wouldn't give up until they got you. And once that was accomplished, they would go after your sons. Those are the facts, Cormac."

He seemed to think about that for a moment and acknowledged it by grudgingly saying, "Well, maybe. But we still need to eliminate him."

"I agree, but we have to wait, get some distance from this whole operation. Give it a couple of months. Let things cool down, and they'll move on. Given the work this Dillon in the Special Branch is involved in, I can set it up so there is no way in hell they'll think you were involved."

"Two months? That seems an awfully long time."

"I can rush back now, tonight if you want, and shoot the knacker. That will give you just enough time to pack a bag and stay on the run for the rest of your life. Do you really want to do that? Or, would it be a better move to enjoy the sun and some more whiskey for sixty days while I figure out how, exactly, we'll do this?"

"Sixty days, and then I want you to get that gorgeous bum of yours back into Dublin. You've a second chance to eliminate this bastard once and for all. What the hell did you say his name was?"

"Dillon. Jack Dillon."

ONE

CI McCabe, head of Special Branch, stepped out of his office and surveyed the room. "DI Rafferty and Marshal Dillon, a moment of your time, please," he said and disappeared back into his office.

Dillon waited for a half-second to make sure McCabe was out of sight before he shook his head. Three more reports yet to do, and apparently, he was getting called to another case.

"Let's go, old-timer. No sense in keeping the man waiting," Rafferty said and followed up with a laugh as he hurried past Dillon's desk.

"A little more respect, Kevin," Dillon replied and followed Rafferty into McCabe's office.

"Good morning, gentlemen. Take a seat," McCabe said without looking up from the pile of reports on his desk. He read for another half-minute, signed his name on the bottom sheet, and placed the file on a smaller stack just to his left.

"Gentlemen, apparently, there was a shooting out in Skerries. DI Suel is currently unavailable. Rafferty, you'll take his place."

"Yes, sir, it's only that I have a physical exam sched-uled in three hours, and I've had to cancel twice already."

"I'm aware of that, Rafferty. I've notified Suel. He'll join you in Skerries at some point. You've my permission to leave for your physical. That said, I want the two of you making an initial appearance together. Skerries Garda has requested our assistance. Thus far, we know it was a shooting last night. The victim was an American by the name of Dennis Hickey, age fifty-six, apparently from the city of Chicago. I'd like you to examine the scene of the shooting as well as his room, a rental at the Harbour Hotel. I've been told the gentleman's room is currently under lock and key."

"The shooting?" Dillon asked. "Was it an altercation? A robbery?"

"We've no indication it was either. The gentleman's wallet containing credit cards and two hundred euros along with his passport and cellphone were still in his possession. He ate a quiet dinner by himself at the Stoop Your Head pub. His body was discovered just off Harbour Road. There is a public toilet overlooking the sea, and he was fifteen feet from that structure."

Dillon knew the area. A friend, Sean, lived in Skerries, not along the harbor but near enough. He swam a mile or more year round in the Irish Sea a number of times a week with a local group called the Frosties. They swam not far from where the body was found.

"Has the American Embassy been contacted?" Dillon asked.

"I would presume so, but I don't know that for a fact. The sooner you get out there, the sooner a number of your questions will be answered."

"Point of contact?" Rafferty asked.

"Sergeant Declan Reilly with Skerries An Garda Síochána. Here's his number. Call him en route. Anything else?" McCabe asked as he handed a post-it-note to Rafferty.

Both men shook their heads as they stood. They waited for a half-second for any final direction. McCabe returned to the stack of files on his desk, and they hurried from his office.

"I'll drive," Rafferty said. "I have a department vehicle signed out, and if Suel plans to meet us out there, you can grab a ride back with him, well, unless you want to drive yourself."

"No, I'll ride with you and keep my eyes closed all the way back with Paddy behind the wheel."

"Good idea," Rafferty said and chuckled. It took them no more than five minutes to assemble what they needed, turn off computers, lock their desks, and head out the door.

"You expecting weather?" Rafferty asked as they headed out of the Headquarters building. He indicated the tan raincoat Dillon carried under his arm.

"Well, it's rained every day for the past five days, and listening to this morning's forecast, yeah, I'm expecting wet weather."

Rafferty glanced up at the clear sky and shook his head. "We're liable to get a sunburn."

"You keep thinking that way. I'll take the raincoat just to play it safe."

"Suit yourself," Rafferty said and clicked the fob in his hand. The lights blinked on a red Toyota Corolla Cross, an SUV. The color was officially described as Barcelona red metallic. The passenger door on the driver's side was dented.

"What did you run into?" Dillon asked.

"Fortunately, not me. I'm sure whoever had it at that point tried to return it without mentioning the damage."

"I wonder how that worked?" Dillon asked.

"How do you think?" Rafferty replied as he opened the driver's door.

The drive to Skerries was uneventful. Dillon phoned Sergeant Declan Reilly in Skerries, guesstimating their arrival time. Reilly said he'd meet them at the Garda station, which wasn't too far from the crime scene and the Harbor Hotel. Once they turned off the M1 and onto the R132, Dillon enjoyed the country view. It was a thirty-five-minute drive, and fortunately, Rafferty knew exactly where he was going. He parked on the street in front of the Garda station.

The station, a two-story white stucco structure at least a hundred years old, looked more like an elegant home. A sidewalk with red flowers blooming on either side led up to the door painted with shiny blue enamel. The three windows on the main floor each had twelve glass panes. The four windows on the second floor consisted of nine glass panes. All the window trim was painted white. Flower boxes hung below each window.

Dillon followed Rafferty as he opened the door. A wooden counter was positioned just inside. Two officers, a man and woman, sat behind the counter.

The woman flashed a smile and said, "Good morning. How may we help?"

"DI Rafferty and Marshal Dillon from Dublin Special Branch to see Sergeant Declan Reilly," Rafferty said.

"Oh, yes, he's been expecting you, dreadful incident last night. Absolutely dreadful," she said, shaking her head.

The man next to her pushed three keys on the phone and placed the receiver to his ear. A moment later, he said, "They're here." He nodded and hung up the phone. "Sergeant Reilly will be out in just a bit."

Dillon could hear what sounded like someone hurrying down a set of stairs, and a moment later, a dark-haired man with sergeant stripes on his shirt and a neon green high visibility vest entered the room. He immediately headed for Dillon with an outstretched hand and said, "Marshal Dillon? Declan Reilly."

Dillon shook hands and said, "Pleased to meet you, Sergeant. Sorry, it's under these circumstances."

"Kevin Rafferty," Rafferty said and extended his hand.

They shook hands, and Reilly said, "Appreciate you coming out, lads. Let's head out to the scene, and then we can go to your man's hotel room. A sad state of affairs. We've not had anything like this going on two years."

"Where's the body at this point?" Dillon asked.

"Dublin morgue, transported last night. You're American?"

"Yeah, I'm assigned to An Garda Síochána Special Branch in Dublin."

"Were you involved in those shootings out at Dublin Airport a couple of years back?"

"Yes, I was. We heard your shooting took place last night around the harbor. An American by the name of Dennis Hickey, from Chicago," Dillon said, changing the subject.

"Yes, near as we can figure, it was right around 11:00. No report of anyone hearing the shots, let alone seeing something. A man out walking his dog actually found the body. Phoned us right away."

"We'll want to talk to him," Dillon said.

"Figured that would be the case. He's retired and expecting your call. Why don't you follow me? It's not more than a minute or two drive," Reilly said, and they headed out the door.

Dillon noticed a bank of clouds beginning to form. He didn't say anything to Rafferty, but he was glad he brought his raincoat.

TWO

Reilly was right. It was just a two-minute drive. They followed the Garda squad car he was driving. The vehicle was white with a neon yellow stripe running from front to back on either side. Flashing lights, blue in this case, were attached to the top of the squad car. The word 'GARDA' was written in bold blue letters on all four sides of the car. In the two minutes it took to drive to the scene of the shooting, easily a half-dozen people walking along the sidewalks gave a friendly wave to Reilly.

"Your man must be popular," Rafferty said at one point as two women waved.

"Typical small town," Dillon said. "I always liked this place."

From Quay Street, they turned onto Harbour Road and drove past the Stoop Your Head and the Blue Bar pubs. A little further on, Reilly pulled to a stop. The public toilets were just to the left. Ahead and around the corner to the right was the Life Boat Cafe & Bar. Just before that, an area in front of the Skerries Sea Memorial was sectioned off by white tape with blue lettering reading

'AN GARDA SIOCHANA DO NOT CROSS!' The words were written in both English and Irish.

Other than two uniformed officers, no one else was around. This initially struck Dillon as strange until he realized there was absolutely nothing to see. Reilly waited as they climbed out of the car and then led them up to the taped-off area. If he didn't know better, Dillon would have thought they had the wrong area secured. There appeared to be no sign that anything resembling a crime, let alone a murder, had taken place.

"This is it?" Dillon asked.

"It is," Reilly said. "We suspect your man may have walked this way last night just to view the sea. We know he had dinner at 8:00 at the Stoop, a starter and a sandwich along with a pint of Guinness. No telling how long he was here or if he used the public toilet in the harbor. His wallet, passport, and phone were found on his person. The wallet still contained two hundred euros in cash, which would seem to suggest robbery was not the intent."

"You find a shell casing?"

Reilly shook his head. "No, unfortunately, and we searched the area. There were powder burns on his skull, suggesting the weapon was fired at a very close range. Based on the fact there was no exit wound, my guess is a small caliber weapon was used. I'm sure they'll be able to confirm that during the autopsy."

"Did he have a cellphone?"

"Yes, he did. We've got the wallet, passport, and cellphone in evidence bags for you. His hotel room is locked, and other than a quick glance, we haven't searched it. Thought, since you were on your way, we'd leave that to the likes of you."

"Any idea when the autopsy is scheduled?" Rafferty asked.

"I know they were backed up. There was a car-truck accident that killed three, and that's ahead of the Hickey autopsy. I'm guessing sometime tomorrow, but I haven't received confirmation as of yet. I'll let you's know as soon as I hear."

Dillon slipped on a pair of white latex gloves. "Mind if we check it out?" he asked as he lifted the blue and white tape and slipped beneath.

Reilly shrugged and shook his head.

Rafferty followed Dillon. They spread several feet apart and slowly headed toward the center, all the while scanning the ground. "There's the spot there," Dillon said. He stopped and pointed toward an area six feet in front of them. A small amount of blood, easy to miss, was splattered on the grass. Dillon pulled out his phone and photographed the area.

They spread a little further apart and approached the area. The small amount of blood on the grass was really the only indication something had happened. There was nothing suggesting a trail through the neatly trimmed grass. Dillon glanced at the sky. The blood would be easy to miss in the daylight, and with the bank of clouds moving in, any rain would completely obliterate the scene. He circled the blood on the grass, taking more pictures.

Looking around at the lack of clues, he was reminded of the murder scene in Desertserges down in County Cork almost two months ago. An American named Dennis Sheehan and his wife. Both shot with a small-caliber weapon.

"What do you think?" Rafferty asked, bringing Dillon back to the here and now.

"I think we should check that hotel room and then talk to the guy who was walking his dog," Dillon said. They stepped back beneath the security tape and followed Reilly back to the cars.

"Parking's tight at the hotel. It'd be best to leave your car here, and I'll give you's a lift. It'll be fine. The lads will watch it," Reilly said. The drive from the crime scene to the Harbor Hotel took about a minute. It took Reilly almost as long to back the car up and turn around as it did to drive to the hotel.

The Harbor Hotel was a two-story brick structure and, at no surprise, overlooked Skerries Harbor. At the moment, there were only three boats in the harbor, all three small, private, pleasure craft. The fishing boats were out doing just that, fishing.

Reilly pulled up onto the sidewalk and parked in front of the hotel. The clouds were now over the harbor, and rain was just beginning to mist. Dillon slipped his raincoat on and smiled at Rafferty. He pulled a cap from the pocket and placed it on his head.

"Ah, for the love of, don't even say it," Rafferty said.

The entrance to the hotel was through a set of double doors two feet from the sidewalk. They followed Reilly through the double doors into a dingy lobby that didn't appear to have been updated in the past eighty years. Off to the left was a small sitting area with a couch and two upholstered chairs. A striped cat rested on the back of one of the chairs. The cat ignored the three of them as they walked past and headed toward the reception counter.

Reilly tapped his finger twice on the bell resting on the counter. A moment later, a woman, mid-forties to fifty, opened a door and stepped behind the counter. She was wearing jeans and a T-shirt. Smiling, she said, "Hi, ya, Declan. Here to go through your man's room?"

"Yeah, Mary. Shouldn't take too long. It's still locked?" Reilly asked just as the cellphone in his pocket rang

"Just as you said. He was in 204. The girls are up cleaning on the floor, but they've been told to stay clear. Follow me. I'll lead you's up." She grabbed a key from a small rack behind the reception counter. The key was brass and attached to a green plastic keychain with the number 204 in white numerals. As she stepped around the counter, she gave a nod to Dillon and Rafferty and headed toward the staircase off to the right.

The staircase was about six feet wide, with a wooden stair rail on either side. Ten steps led to a landing, and six more steps led back from the landing to the hall on the second-floor. They stepped through a door into the center of the hallway. There were four rooms to the left and four rooms to the right, two on either side of the hall. They took a left, 204 was the closest room.

The woman inserted the key, and Dillon heard the lock click. She stepped back. Reilly opened the door. "It's all yours, gentlemen," Reilly said as he pulled his cellphone from his pocket and checked the screen. "I've to get back to the station. You okay without me?"

"Not a problem," Dillon said. He reached into his pocket, pulled out his white latex gloves, and slipped them on.

Rafferty did the same thing.

"I'll just be a phone call away. Call when you've finished, and we'll pay a visit to Ultan Healy. He's your man who discovered the body last night."

"I'll be in the office behind reception. Ring the bell if you's need anything," Mary said, and she and Reilly headed back down the stairs. "So, how's it going?" Mary asked Reilly as they headed down to the main floor. Dillon stepped into the room without hearing Reilly's answer.

THREE

Rafferty stepped into the hotel room, looked around, and said, "Jaysus. I hope your man didn't think he'd have someplace fancy."

There was a window that looked out on the harbor. Due to the slightly irregular glass surface, Dillon guessed the window was original to the structure. Heavy beige drapes were pulled back on either side of the window. It had begun to rain in earnest, and although the window was locked, the drapes were moving back and forth slightly due to an air draft.

The walls were papered with a gray floral design. The background had probably been an off-white color that had since yellowed with age and probably decades of nicotine. A four-inch section in an upper corner had curled away from the wall. The covers were pulled back on the double bed, and the pillow featured an indentation suggesting someone's head had rested there.

Dillon pressed his hand against the thin mattress and the even thinner pillow. Neither one felt as if they would have been very comfortable. A desk against the far wall had an open black suitcase with clothes still held in place by two black nylon straps. Next to the suitcase was a walnut box eight inches high with a brass plaque on top. The image of a pair of hands folded in prayer was engraved on the front of the box.

Rafferty walked over to the box, pulled the top off, and said, "What the hell is this? Cat Litter?"

Dillon stepped over, glanced in the box, and looked at the brass plaque on the lid. The plaque read, 'Maureen Hickey, June 12, 1967 - 14 February 2021.' "It's not a litter box, Kevin. It's a cremation box. Apparently, the remains of someone named Maureen Hickey. Possibly the victim's wife. It looks like she died on Valentine's day."

Rafferty took a step back and shook his head. "Why would he bring something like that?"

"Maybe she wanted to be buried here, or they had a trip planned, and she died before they went. Who knows?"

"That's really strange."

"Actually, it's pretty sad, not to mention the fact that now he's dead as well."

Dillon pulled out his phone and took a photo of the cremation box and then the suitcase. He unhooked the nylon straps holding the clothes in place. He took a photo, removed a pair of black trousers and a white shirt, and took another photo. He took six pictures in all. The suitcase contained nothing unusual, just clothes, along with a shaving razor, toothbrush, and deodorant.

He closed the lid on the suitcase and unzipped the two front pockets. The top pocket was the smaller of the two. He reached in and pulled out two boarding passes and a three-page travel itinerary from Delta Airline stapled together. The bottom pocket was larger and empty. One boarding pass was for a Chicago to Amsterdam flight two days ago. The second was for an Amsterdam to Dublin flight arriving yesterday morning. Dillon photographed the boarding passes and the flight itinerary. Hickey was scheduled to return to the US via Amsterdam to Chicago in three days.

The suitcase suddenly made sense. By the time Hickey would have cleared the airport and probably taxied to Skerries, it would have been late morning, maybe early afternoon. He checked into the hotel, probably slept a few hours, and grabbed dinner at the Stoop Your Head pub. After dinner, he walked over to the Skerries Sea Memorial to look out onto the sea or maybe view a ship passing, and he was shot. Why?

"Who in the hell would shoot this guy?" Dillon said just as someone knocked on the door. Dillon turned just as his Special Branch partner, Paddy Suel, stepped into the room.

"Don't you lot say a fecking word," Suel said.

Dillon had to bite his tongue to keep from grinning. Suel's left cheek was swollen. It had ballooned out looking like he'd stuffed half a chicken in his mouth. "So, your dentist finally had enough of you and hauled off and hit you."

"God save me. Fortunately, he'd put me out before he pulled the tooth."

"Does it hurt?" Rafferty asked.

"Not yet. They gave me a mess of pills. I'm supposed to take one every eight hours."

"You could probably sell those on the street and make some money," Dillon said.

"Don't even go there, Dillon."

"You good to give your man Dillon a ride back to the station when you're finished up here? I've got to get to a physical exam in forty-five minutes," Rafferty said.

"I suppose I don't really have a choice now, do I?"

"That's about right."

"Yeah, against my better judgment, I'll give him a lift. As long as he stays on his best behavior."

"Whatever that is. You parked out in front?" Rafferty asked.

"What of it?" Suel replied.

"Well, nothing, except it's raining cats and dogs now, and I've to walk back to where the car is parked. I was thinking I might borrow the Marshal's raincoat if you wouldn't mind."

"Oh, so all of a sudden, it turns out to be a good idea that I brought it?" Dillon said as he slowly pulled off his raincoat and handed it to Rafferty. "Only cause I'm a nice guy."

"Thanks, I'll leave it at your desk in Special Branch," Rafferty said and headed out the door.

"So, what do you have?" Suel asked.

"You sure you're okay for this?"

"Yeah, it looks a lot worse than it is. It's just a blessing to get what was left of the tooth out. I was eating
pasta, of all things, and suddenly, I was spitting out
pieces of a molar. Had to wait until late this morning to
get in to see your man. Just glad he knocked me out."

"Better you than me," Dillon said. He glanced out the
window and watched Rafferty in the rain hurrying back
along the Harbour Road toward the car. He was wearing
the raincoat and the cap Dillon had shoved in the pocket.
"Glad we looked at the scene of the murder before this
rain started. Not that there was anything to see."

"What'd it look like?"

"It looked like nothing happened. There was a little
bit of blood on the grass. That's gone by now. I took
some pictures. Nothing like footprints or even bent grass.
Nothing. The Skerries team went over the area looking
for a shell casing, never found one. Your man Reilly
said, based on the wound, it looked to be close up. Powder burns on the victim's scalp. No exit wound, so he
was thinking small caliber. The victim, an American
named Dennis Hickey, has already been transported to
the Dublin Morgue. Reilly didn't think the autopsy
would happen until tomorrow at the earliest."

Dillon went on to tell Suel about the cremation box
and the boarding passes. "The guy hadn't been in the
country more than fourteen hours, and he's shot. There
has to be some reason. I'm not seeing this as random.
Once we're finished here, we're to call Reilly. He'll take

us to your man who found the body last night. Apparently, someone was just out walking a dog. After we talk to him, I'll give a call to Eric Bergman at the American Embassy and touch base. Maybe he'll know something. Let me give Reilly a call now and tell him we're finished here."

Dillon pulled out his phone and called Reilly. He answered on the second ring. "Finished already?"

"Not an awful lot to see. Could you direct us to your man who found the body?"

"I'll do better than that. I'll take you and introduce you. He was a mate of me da's. Ultan Healy. I'll be there in a few minutes, just finishing up here. Oh, the autopsy on your man is scheduled for 2:00 tomorrow afternoon, Dublin Morgue."

"Got it, see you shortly. Say, Declan, if you could bring some evidence bags with you. There're a few things we'll be taking back."

"Not a problem," Reilly said and disconnected.

"He'll be here in ten minutes," Dillon said. He returned the clothes to the suitcase and zipped everything closed.

FOUR

It was closer to forty-five minutes before Reilly returned. They could hear him charging up the staircase. A moment later, he stepped into the room. "Sorry to keep you waiting, lads. You know how it is, the phone just keeps on ringing. Then I couldn't get Ultan to answer his damn phone. Drove over to his place, and the plonker didn't have his hearing aids in. God deliver me. Oh, the evidence bags," he said and handed a stack to Dillon. "And here is your man's wallet, passport, and phone. If you'd sign this form just to maintain the chain of evidence," he said as he handed Dillon three evidence bags, each with Hickey's wallet, passport and phone.

"Thanks," Dillon said and set the bags on the desk next to the suitcase. As he signed the chain of evidence, he said, "Declan, this is my partner in Special Branch, DI Paddy Suel. DI Rafferty has some medical appointment back in Dublin he had to get to. Paddy, Sergeant Declan Reilly, Skerries An Garda Síochána."

Reilly and Suel shook hands and immediately started exchanging names of mutual acquaintances on the force. Dillon placed the cremation bin, the boarding passes, and flight information in separate evidence bags. He placed an evidence tag around the handle of the suitcase. After another look around, they headed downstairs and out the door. Suel carried the evidence bags, including Hickey's wallet, passport, and phone. Dillon carried the suitcase. Fortunately, the rain had stopped. Dillon placed the suitcase in the boot of the car, and Suel placed the evidence bags next to it. They climbed in the car and waited while Reilly had a brief conversation with Mary from reception. When he'd finished, Reilly gave a wave and climbed into his car.

"You okay to drive?" Dillon asked.

"Not a bother. We get in an accident, I've got these pain pills, so I won't feel a thing," he said. He pulled off the sidewalk and followed Reilly in the squad car.

They drove all of two blocks. Reilly pulled onto the sidewalk, leaving barely enough room for someone to make their way between the two-story stone structure and his car.

Suel stopped and said, "You'd best get out here."

Dillon climbed out of the passenger seat. Suel pulled ahead and parked behind Reilly's squad car. Rather than navigate the narrow passage between the cars and the stone structure, they stepped into the street, walked past two doors and stopped at the third.

Reilly glanced at them and said, "Your man is Ultan Healy. Hopefully, he still has his hearing aids in." He pounded on the door three times, not a gentle knock. A moment later, the door opened, and an older white-haired man smiled. He couldn't have been more than five feet and an inch or two tall.

He looked at Reilly and said, "Well, Declan. Come in, come in. You're late, by the way. Shades of your father."

"I learned from the best, Ultan. Let me introduce you to two gentlemen from Special Branch in Dublin. They're assisting in our investigation. This is DI Paddy Suel and Marshal Jack Dillon. Gentlemen, may I present the man of the hour, Ultan Healy."

"The pleasure is all mine, lads. Please, please, come in." A small dog suddenly stepped out from behind Healy and sniffed Dillon.

"Don't mind Lady. She's just hoping you brought a treat. Grab a seat, sit down, lads, sit down," Healy said

They stepped into a compact sitting room. A black leather couch and two wingback chairs were centered around a stone fireplace. Turf was burning in the fireplace, and it gave a pleasant warmth to the darkened room. Healy settled into one of the wingback chairs and picked up a tea mug resting on a small table.

"Can I get you's a cuppa?"

"Thank you, but none for me," Dillon said.

"Just had a tooth pulled this morning, so I'd better say no. Thanks all the same," Suel said.

"So, Ultan," Reilly said, settling in next to Suel on the couch. "Would you mind going over what you told me this morning?"

"Not at all, not at all," Healy said. "So, I take Lady for a walk every night, usually around 9:00. I'd been out to me brother's yesterday afternoon for a load of turf, had a pint with him, loaded up the car, and then stacked it all in here," he said, pointing at the four-foot pile of turf next to the fireplace. From there, Healy went back three generations explaining the location of the family farm, the neighbors, and two neighbors killed back in 1916 in the Easter Rebellion. It was close to twenty minutes before he actually returned to the previous night.

"So, after hauling the turf, having a pint with me brother, stacking the turf in here, didn't I fall asleep right here in this chair. If it weren't for Lady, I'd probably still be asleep," he said and chuckled. "She barked and woke me a little after ten. Out we went on our walk, same route as every night." He went on to give specific directions on the route for five minutes.

"Now, we'd just passed the Life Boat Cafe, only two cars parked, which seemed a bit on the light side to my way of thinking, but who knows. So we come up to the Sea Memorial. Lady always likes to sniff around and do a bit of her business, don't you know. We're walking across the grass, and I see your man stretched out on the ground. My first thought is he's gazing at the stars, but then I realize he's face down, so that can't be right. I thought maybe he'd enjoyed himself a bit too much at the pubs, so I walk over and kick him, gentle like, on the sole of his shoe. No response. I kick him again, same thing. That's when I look at the back of his head, see a bit of blood and think, this ain't right. Lady and I hurry over to the Garda Station, tell your man at the desk. Who was that, Declan?"

"Officer Mullen, Eion Mullen."

"Yes, that's the lad. Now isn't he James and Eileen's oldest?"

"He is," Reilly said.

"Funny story about the parents. This is before they were married. They decide to take the train…" Another ten minutes went by before he was back to the body.

"So, I told officer Mullen what I'd found. He gets on the radio, and the next thing I know, there's been a murder in Skerries."

"Did you hear anything like a gunshot, a scream, maybe someone shouting?" Suel asked.

"No, not a thing, but then I'd taken the hearing aids out. I got them, oh, must be six or seven years ago. Still not quite used to them. I remember…"

Fortunately, the hearing aid story was only a minute or two. "You didn't see anyone around, maybe a car driving away?" Dillon asked.

Healy shook his head. "No sir, a quiet night all around. You see, Lady and I usually head out just before 9:00. Now I was hauling turf all afternoon and then had a pint with me brother…"

Dillon and Suel were headed out of town on the R132 toward the M1.

"Not a bad interview," Suel said.

"Yeah, it only took about ninety minutes, and I learned more about turf and your man's family farm than I ever thought possible."

"Has a time of death been established?" Suel asked.

"Between 10:00 and 11:00 yesterday evening."

"So Hickey flies in from the US. Chicago, as a matter of fact," Suel said.

"Chicago to Amsterdam, Amsterdam to Dublin," Dillon said.

"Yeah. He goes from Dublin airport to Skerries. Probably sleeps a few hours. Grabs dinner at the Stoop."

"A starter, a sandwich, and a pint of Guinness."

"He leaves the Stoop and is found just before 11:00. Reilly mentioned he still had his passport and wallet. Did they ever find a cellphone?"

"That was with him as well."

TO BE CONTINUED . . .

Thank you for checking out the sample of the next Jack Dillon Dublin Tale, <u>Second Chance</u>. Better grab a copy and see what happens . . .

Check out the list of books by Mike Faricy on the following page.

BOOKS BY MIKE FARICY
CRIME FICTION FIRSTS

A boxset of the first four books in four crime fiction series:

Russian Roulette; Dev Haskell series
Welcome; Jack Dillon Dublin Tales series
Corridor Man; Corridor Man series
Reduced Ransom! Hot Shot series

The following titles comprise the Dev Haskell series:

Russian Roulette: Case 1
Mr. Swirlee: Case 2
Bite Me: Case 3
Bombshell: Case 4
Tutti Frutti: Case 5
Last Shot: Case 6
Ting-A-Ling: Case 7
Crickett: Case 8
Bulldog: Case 9
Double Trouble: Case 10
Yellow Ribbon: Case 11
Dog Gone: Case 12
Scam Man: Case 13
Foiled: Case 14
What Happens in Vegas… Case 15
Art Hound: Case 16

The Office: Case 17
Star Struck: Case 18
International Incident: Case 19
Guest From Hell: Case 20
Art Attack: Case 21
Mystery Man: Case 22
Bow-Wow Rescue: Case 23
Cold Case: Case 24
Cash Up Front: Case 25
Dream House: Case 26
Alley Katz: Case 27
The Big Gamble: Case 28
Bad to the Bone: Case 29
Silencio!: Case 30
Surprise, Surprise: Case 31
Hit & Run: Case 32
Suspect Santa: Case 33
P.I. Apprentice: Case 34
Rebel Without a Clue: Case 35
Puppy Love: Case 36

The following titles are Dev Haskell novellas:
Dollhouse
The Dance
Pixie
Fore!
Twinkle Toes
(*a Dev Haskell short story*)

The following are Dev Haskell Boxsets:
Dev Haskell Boxset 1-3
Dev Haskell Boxset 4-6
Dev Haskell Boxset 7-9
Dev Haskell Boxset 10-12
Dev Haskell Boxset 13-15
Dev Haskell Boxset 16-18
Dev Haskell Boxset 19-21
Dev Haskell Boxset 22-24
Dev Haskell Boxset 25-27
Dev Haskell Boxset 28-30
Dev Haskell Boxset 1-7
Dev Haskell Boxset 8-14
Dev Haskell Boxset 15-19
Dev Haskell Boxset 20-24
Dev Haskell Boxset 25-29

The following titles comprise the Jack Dillon Dublin Tales series:
Welcome
Jack Dillon Dublin Tale 1
Sweet Dreams
Jack Dillon Dublin Tale 2
Mirror Mirror
Jack Dillon Dublin Tale 3
Silver Bullet
Jack Dillon Dublin Tale 4

Fair City Blues
Jack Dillon Dublin Tale 5
Spade Work
Jack Dillon Dublin Tale 6
Madeline Missing
Jack Dillon Dublin Tale 7
Mistaken Identity
Jack Dillon Dublin Tale 8
Picture Perfect
Jack Dillon Dublin Tale 9
Dublin Moon
Jack Dillon Dublin Tale 10
Mystery Woman
Jack Dillon Dublin Tale 11
Second Chance
Jack Dillon Dublin Tale 12
Payback Brother
Jack Dillon Dublin Tale 13
The Heist
Jack Dillon Dublin Tale 14
Jewels To Kill For
Jack Dillon Dublin Tale 15
Retirement Scheme
Jack Dillon Dublin Tale 16
The Collector
Jack Dillon Dublin Tale 17

Jack Dillon Dublin Tales Boxsets:
Jack Dillon Dublin Tales 1-3

Jack Dillon Dublin Tales 4-6
Jack Dillon Dublin Tales 1-5
Jack Dillon Dublin Tales 1-7
Jack Dillon Dublin Tales 6-10

The following titles comprise the Hotshot series;
Reduced Ransom! Second Edition
Finders Keepers! Second Edition
Bankers Hours Second Edition
Chow Down Second Edition
Moonlight Dance Academy Second Edition
Irish Dukes (Fight Card Series)
written under the pseudonym Jack Tunney

The following titles comprise the Corridor Man series:
Corridor Man
Corridor Man 2: Opportunity knocks
Corridor Man 3: The Dungeon
Corridor Man 4: Dead End
Corridor Man 5: Finger
Corridor Man 6: Exit Strategy
Corridor Man 7: Trunk Music
Corridor Man 8: Birthday Boy
Corridor Man 9: Boss Man
Corridor Man 10: Bye Bye Bobby

Corridor Man novellas:
Corridor Man: Valentine

Corridor Man: Auditor
Corridor Man: Howling
Corridor Man: Spa Day

The following are Corridor Man Boxsets:
Corridor Man Boxset 1-3
Corridor Man Boxset 1-5
Corridor Man Boxset 6-9

THANK YOU!

Contact the author:
- Email: mikefaricyauthor@gmail.com
- Twitter: @Mikefaricybooks
- Facebook: Mike Faricy Author
- Website: http://www.mikefaricybooks.com

Published by

MJF Publishing

www.ingramcontent.com/pod-product-compliance
Lightning Source LLC
Chambersburg PA
CBHW070340010826
48976CB00017B/351